Counting

Raindrops

Through a

Stained Glass

Window

CHERLYN MICHAELS

Counting Raindrops Through a Stained Glass Window

HYPERION

NEW YORK

Library of Congress Cataloging-in-Publication Data

Michaels, Cherlyn.
    Counting raindrops through a stained glass window / by
Cherlyn Michaels.—1st ed.
        p.   cm.
    ISBN 1-4013-0813-9
    1. African American women—Fiction.   2. Commitment
(Psychology)—Fiction.   I. Title.

PS3613.I344C68   2005
813'.6—dc22   2005040314

Hyperion books are available for special promotions and premiums. For details contact Michael Rentas, Assistant Director, Inventory Operations, Hyperion, 77 West 66th Street, 11th floor, New York, New York 10023, or call 212-456-0133.

FIRST EDITION

10 9 8 7 6 5 4 3 2 1

For my mother, Barbara—
you knew I was a writer before I did.

Acknowledgments

I am thankful and forever grateful to so many people who have offered nothing but love, encouragement, and support in the commencement of my writing career.

I would like to thank my mother, Barbara, who recognized and encouraged my writing ability at an early age. To my sister, Kimberly, thanks for your eager support and your help with me and Mom in selling and promoting my first book. I could not have done it alone. I appreciate your love and support. I also would like to thank my father, James, and my brothers, Gerald, Chris, and Tate.

Thanks to Tiffany Clark, Traci Buckner, and Summer McLin, for reading this book in the initial stages and providing me with my first honest feedback about my writing and the story. Your excitement deeply encouraged me and gave me the confidence to continue.

Much love for the support and encouragement of many of my friends: Tracy Williams, Medena (Knight), Angelia Anderson, Nolan Ferguson, Shawn Smith, Patricia Ramsey, Jesse

LeGrande, and Sherron Daughtery. Thanks to Jamel White for your awesome support.

To my fellow serious novelists Linda Dominique Grosvenor, Shelia Goss, Peggy Eldgridge-Love, and Carla Curtis, I offer warm thanks. Your sisterhood has been a blessing to me and I don't know what I would have done at times without each of you. You ladies are my joy. It is with great affection that I thank my fellow authors Alisha Yvonne, Eric Pete, and Franklin White for your love and your continued encouragement. Thanks to authors Nancey Flowers, Gloria Mallette, Eric Jerome Dickey, and Rosalyn McMillan for taking time to answer my questions and even offering additional advice in my early days of publication. Your words are gold to me and your advice is being heeded even now.

Special thanks to my agent, Jenoyne Adams. Jenoyne, you have an absolutely beautiful spirit. I've shared so much with you in my writing journey and feel like you are more than just an agent, you are my friend. Thanks for lending me your confidence when I was running low. Thanks to Jim Levine and the entire Levine Greenberg Literary Agency for your belief in me and my writing.

Thanks to Ellen Archer and everyone at Hyperion Books for your interest and excitement in my first book. Your energy takes mine even higher and adds fuel to my fire. Thanks to my editor, Leslie Wells, and copyeditor, Rita Madrigal. Your input was phenomenal and you made this new experience fun and engaging. I enjoy working with you both and I'm looking forward to doing this again!

Much love to Tee C. Royal and members of RAWSISTAZ book club, Heather Covington of Disilgold, LaShaunda Hoffman of SORMAG, Shunda Leigh of Booking Matters, Delores Thornton, and Angie Pickett-Henderson for your support and promotion of my novel. Whatever success that I have is due to each of you.

Major thanks to many bookstores and booksellers, including Ujamma Maktaba (St. Louis), Knowing Books & Café (St. Louis), Karibu Books (Baltimore), Nubian Books (Atlanta), Cushcity (Houston), and many, many more.

Special thanks also to Bill Beene, Shante Davis, and the *St. Louis American* for the exposure you provided and your support of my writing career and first novel.

Finally, I would like to thank my supportive sorors of Delta Sigma Theta Sorority, Inc., Faye Childs of Blackboard, and readers everywhere, old and new. I hope you enjoy reading my first novel as much as I enjoyed writing it.

Much love,
Cherlyn Michaels

Counting

Raindrops

Through a

Stained Glass

Window

Prologue

"IS THIS WHAT YOU want me to do?" I remember my father asking as he flung his right leg out of the second-story window of our two-family flat in St. Louis.

August's late-night breeze blew waves into his earth-brown polyester shirt. His narrow eyes were framed by three heavy creases in his forehead. Even from the far end of the makeshift bedroom that transitioned into the living room where he straddled the ledge, I could hear the quick, frantic heaving of his breath. His ashy hands clutched both sides of the white wooden ledge as chipped paint fell to the tattered carpet.

My father continued to hurl fever-pitched words at my mother, who calmly ironed the day's laundry and appeared to be completely unaffected by the unfolding drama. He seemed totally ignorant of my presence at her feet. Or perhaps he thought that a three-year-old brain had not yet developed the capacity for storing long-term memories, and that in a few seconds this scene would be permanently rubbed out of my mind.

"I'll jump if that's what you want me to do. Just say it. Just tell me to jump and I'll jump." Dad leaned his right shoulder outside of the window a little farther. He maintained a secure grip as he straddled the ledge and sustained his balance with his left hand.

I remember dropping the multicolored LEGO pieces that I'd been fiddling with for twenty minutes or so. It wasn't like I could build a masterpiece out of the yellow, red, and blue rectangles. Besides, I thought the little scene that Dad was creating was a lot more fascinating. At the time, I wanted to see him jump. I wanted to see him jump and then see the word "Splat!" in big fat black letters floating up to the window inside a balloon. I smiled at him in anticipation.

"Jesse, come on now," Mom said without looking up. She sighed heavily through her nose as she ironed a bedsheet. When Dad continued, the corners of her mouth curled as her jaws tightened. "Don't you see the baby right here? What you trying to do—traumatize the girl? If you keep on you're going to wake Babysista." Mom gestured with her head toward the open door of the second bedroom just inches behind us.

"Look, I'm telling you that I want to come back. What else do you want me to do? Tell me. What do you want me to do? I'm saying I want to be a father to my kids. To all *my* kids." His beady eyes fixed on Mom's large belly. "I'm trying to do what's right. What you want me to do? Kill myself? Huh?"

Dad's voice grew louder with each word. His breathing got heavier and faster. I saw veins bulge along the side of his neck, and his face dripped fury-laden sweat. Then that entertaining show became scary to me. Somehow, it didn't end as funny as it began.

I looked up at Mom.

She pressed down hard on the sheet, concentrating on one spot for several seconds as the iron emitted puffs of steam. Then she jerked the iron back and forth a couple of times before stopping on another area. Her stern eyes focused on the sheet as her hand choked the iron's handle.

"Tell me, Veda. What do you want? What you want me to do? Huh?" Dad repeated.

Mom had had enough of Dad's tirade. She slammed the iron down in its upright position. It fell over, iron-side down. She gripped it again, raised it to its upright position, and dared it with her eyes to fall again.

"*You* left, Jesse. You *left*. You left your kids. You left me. For five months! Now all of a sudden you're back? Suddenly you decide you want to come back and just like that I'm supposed to say okay?" She waved her hands and pointed her finger for emphasis. "No explanation, no reason from you, no nothing?" Mom's face crumpled. She gasped, threw her arms in the air, and shook her head from side to side.

"I made a mistake. I said I was sorry. If that's not good enough for you, then I'll jump. Just tell me that's what you want and I'll jump. I'll jump right now." Dad shifted and moved his rear toward the outside of the window ledge. He deftly leaned down and gripped the inside of the ledge tighter. His calculated balancing act was deserving of a Tony Award in this one-man off-Broadway play.

"Jesse, stop it!" Mom finally yelled. I think she started to believe that the fool might actually jump. "Jesse, Van's right here. What are you doing?"

Mom reached down and covered my face for a very brief moment. By that time, I was already clinging to the hem of her dress and tears were on the verge of spilling over the bottom rim of my eyelids. I didn't know what was going on, but I knew it wasn't a funny show anymore. Something had changed. I didn't understand what, but then things took a turn for the worse. I wrapped my arms around Mom's right leg and began to whine. It seemed appropriate. Maybe it would make Dad stop.

"Just tell me to do it and I will. Whatever you want, Veda. Just tell me. All you got to do is say it."

Dad had shifted more to the right and now gripped the bottom of the window ledge with his lower left leg and his left arm. He was confident that he had his balancing act under control.

"Come back in," Mom said. "Come back in and get out of the window." She pulled away from me and ran toward the window.

A smile developed behind his eyes. Satisfied with the reaction he'd garnered from her, he lifted his left arm to pull himself back inside. As he reached in, the disproportion of his weight across the ledge caused him to slip farther outside of the window. Dad's eyes widened; his mouth opened as if he was trying to call out but couldn't. His eyes now harbored panic. His left arm fell against the inside of the ledge and began to slip upward as the weight of his body pulled him down.

"Jesse!" Mom screamed. When Mom screamed, I screamed, and then, as if to fall in line with the women of the family, Babysista wailed from the bedroom behind me.

I cried out as Mom grabbed Dad's left hand. She couldn't hold it. His hand was slipping from hers. She kept repositioning her hands over his sweaty one, cupping it and trying to pull it close to her pregnant belly, but it kept slipping from her grasp.

"I love you, Jesse. I love you!" Mom yelled. She was crying and panting and struggling to pull him in.

Dad's mouth was open and silent. He shifted his leg back over the top of the ledge and searched for a groove in which to anchor the heel of his foot. His movements slowed as his eyes anxiously searched Mom's for a miracle.

"Baby, I do love you, baby. I love you, baby," she repeated as she repositioned her grip again and again. I wailed as I sat watching from beneath the ironing board. Babysista wailed, too.

Dad stopped moving. Warm air brushed past him, whisked inside the room, and dried my face. Mom moved her hand once more to get a better grip so she could pull him in. As she lifted her right hand, Dad's hand slipped out of her left. Then I didn't see any more parts of Dad at all.

Mom leaned out of the window, speechless. I stopped wailing. Babysista whimpered.

I followed Mom down the long flight of monster stairs that led to the front door. I was usually afraid of them because of the way the entire staircase lifted up to access the basement at the press of a latch. I always expected Herman Munster to come walking out. But this time I held on to the banister and took one baby step after another. I stepped right over the latch and pushed open the screenless screen door.

I stepped out unnoticed onto the warped porch. I stared at the crowd that surrounded Dad as he lay mangled in the bushes below the window while Mom held his hand and stroked his forehead. She whispered that everything was going to be all right and that we were going to be a family once he came back home. She spread his hand over her belly and moved it in a circular motion.

Dad's hardened cold eyes met hers, went down to his limp hand on her belly, then up to her face again. He moaned and his eyes turned empty.

Then I heard Mom profess her love. She sprinkled kisses across the back of his hand and his face as an ambulance drove up. Our neighbor, Mrs. Woods, spotted me peering over the banister and whisked me back upstairs as I began to absorb what I later came to know as a strange kind of love—an inevitably bitter kind of love that surfaced when you stayed with someone long enough. That sick, bitter love that I came to know as the gift of any marriage that lasted beyond seven years. That gift of eternal misery.

One

"OKAY, WE CAN STAY at the Marriott or the Roney Palace again. Or, we can do the Hilton," Alton said to me as he browsed the Internet.

Even though we'd already been to South Beach at least six times and designated it as "our spot," Alton became ritualistic whenever we decided to go again. He'd break out the legal pad and mechanical pencil, park himself in front of the computer, and check out every single hotel on the strip. He'd examine the size of the hotel, parking services, nearby restaurants, attractions, clubs, and whatever else crossed his mind. That was his thing, and I never bothered him. I absolutely loved it. Except for the times when he shook me awake or called me after midnight to check out a hotel room on the Internet. That's when his enthusiasm for the perfect trip made me want to take away his paper and pencils and ban him for life like Pete Rose.

"Honey, really, any hotel is fine with me. You know we never stay in our room anyway," I said from my soft-side bed, where I was sorting through a week's worth of mail—mostly bills. Working ten hours a day and some weekends hardly left enough time for even the essential things that I needed to do, like writing checks.

"Well, what do you think you'll be in the mood for this time? At the Marriott we'll be right on South Beach. If we do the Roney on Miami Beach, we'll have some quiet time. We can always walk down to South Beach when and if we feel like it. The small hotels in the Art Deco district are another option."

"Um, we're not going through this again, are we?" I looked up at him and smiled. Alton didn't even notice. The travel wheels in his head had already started to burn rubber like Evel Knievel. He sat at the computer desk gazing at the nineteen-inch flat-screen monitor, completely mesmerized as he read the amenities of different hotels, all of which he could probably recite from memory.

"Go through what?" he asked.

"Looking at the Internet sites of every hotel on the strip, choosing either the Marriott or the Roney, and then getting there and spending all of our time on the beach, shopping, and at clubs." I chuckled.

"Well, you never know. There could be a new hotel that's opened since the last time we were there. Maybe it's plush, the way you like it, and reasonable, the way I like it."

He put the mechanical pencil between his full lips and used both chiseled hands to type on the keyboard.

Envying the pencil, I plopped the stack of mail on the espresso-colored nightstand. I deviously slipped behind Alton for a Sunday-morning attack and began massaging his massive shoulders as I peered first at the computer screen, then down at him. His solid shoulders were a result of consistent dedication to the gym a few days a week. He had managed to carve out a well-sculpted body that was not too bulky and, most important, wasn't supported by the birdlike stems that seemed to be common around here. I'm sure I loved touching and massaging his body more than he loved feeling my touch. I hopped at any chance to caress his maple skin and soothe his muscles into relaxation.

I moved inward to the base of his neck and used my thumbs to gently knead and stroke from top to bottom. Alton immediately released the tension in his neck, willing his muscles to surrender and let my hands have their way. I moved a hand to each side of his neck and stroked in circular motions. He leaned his head to the right side, which signaled to me that the left side of his neck could use some extra attention. Using both hands, I kneaded the pressure out of his neck and shoulder. He let out a low moan of approval, put the pencil and legal pad on the computer desk, and let his arms fall limply to his sides. His head rolled back and, with his eyes closed, he smiled at me.

Continuing Operation Seduction, I took my thumbs and stroked his right eyebrow first, then the left. Alton has thick eyebrows that add depth to his high cheekbones and ruggedly squared jawline. His brown eyes are narrow at the inset, open abruptly, and end with a slight slant at the outside corners. As I ran my fingers over his eyes, his lengthy lashes tickled my fingertips. He pushed out a long, approving breath through his nose as I traced the sides of his face and caressed his smooth skin. He has the smoothest skin that I've ever seen on a man. Whenever I mentioned this to Alton, he would always laugh and say, "That's because I got Haitian in my family."

I glided my fingertips from his cheeks to his full lips and thought about kissing him. I loved kissing him. I leaned over and planted tiny kisses across his forehead.

"Oh, see, now you know you're trying to start something."

"Uh-huh," I replied as softly and seductively as I could.

"You know that drives me crazy," he said with his eyes still closed.

"For sure, no doubt," I said, playfully using his favorite phrase against him. He laughed when I said it. Alton always used that phrase as his way of saying yes.

I held his head between my hands and continued to tenderly kiss his forehead in random spots.

"Okay, that's it, Vanella. I warned you." Alton stood, picked me up, and gingerly lay a giggling me on the champagne-colored Egyptian-cotton comforter. He straddled me, brushed my hair off my face, and passionately kissed my impatient lips. Alton was a master at kissing, and he knew it. I knew it, too, which is why I loved kissing him. He would start with small, quick teasers, then gently lick, kiss, and suck my lips before completely driving me crazy. He combined slow and medium strokes to enjoy tasting me before allowing me to give his mouth the feel and taste of heaven.

I slowly lifted off his sleeveless undershirt, gave it a quick toss, and ran my hands across his powerful chest while he suspended his five-foot-eleven-inch frame over all five feet five inches of me. Mmmmm . . . he smelled of just a hint of cologne. The fragrances he chose mixed well with his natural scent and always made my body simmer with excitement. Whenever he was at my place, Alton would lightly anoint his body with cologne after a shower. He knew I loved to snuggle against him and let his sexy scent lull me to sleep. I slowly pulled him closer to me and buried my face in the crook of his neck, feeling the crests and depths of his firm shoulder blades and spine. I moved my hands to the back of his head and ran my fingers over his low-cut hair as he worked artful kisses down to my neck.

Now the getting was good. Alton moved his strong hands down my neck, across my shoulders, and began to . . .

The phone rang.

Damn! I hate intrusions. The telephone, doorbell, it never fails. Especially when he's doing it well. Oh, so well.

We both paused and groaned at the same time—Alton, perhaps because he knew he had gotten into a groove and was about to experience one of our most intense encounters of the day, and me because I knew it was probably somebody in the family, which meant nothing but more drama.

Alton grunted. He rolled his luscious body off me and ran the palm of his hand down his face, as if to wipe away the intimate moment and snap his mind into football mode.

"Well, I'm going to shower and start setting up for the game." He pecked my lips, grabbed his undershirt off the top of the headboard, and headed for the shower.

I couldn't resist watching his bare backside as he walked away. Boy was a walking poem. Alton already had a well-built and perfectly proportioned body, but I loved it when planning one of our beach trips compelled him to prepare more by putting in extra time at the gym. The product was simply scrumptious.

"And quit looking at my ass!" Alton said without looking back. He knew me too well.

I pulled myself up on the bed and looked at the imposing phone as it rang for the third time. What is it going to be this time? Who is it going to be about now? Is it my sister, Jaelene, calling to borrow money again? Or is it Kizaar and Dad this time? Dad forever complained and instigated his own hypertension about either something Kizaar said, did, or didn't do. It beat me as to why Kizaar kept trying.

Or was Mom calling to tell me how insensitive Dad had been to her again? She constantly calls to tell me how Dad yelled at her, put her down and demeaned her, missed her birthday or their anniversary, or made a bedroom out of his home office and refused to sleep in their bedroom with her anymore. She told her children about all of these things but she begged us not to say anything to him because she feared that it would only make the situation worse. Frankly, I didn't know how she put up with it. I felt sorry for her, and sometimes wished I could slip her the backbone she needed to stand up to him and his disparaging remarks—and maybe even kick a little ass every now and then.

I picked up the phone. "Hello?"

"Hey, Van. How are you doing?" It was Mom. I knew she wasn't calling to see how I was doing. Mom rarely calls just to chitchat. There's always a purpose. I could have told her that I'd just been hit by a semi, she would have said, "That's nice," then rolled right into the reason she was calling.

"I'm fine. Alton's here and we're gearing up for the Browns-Steelers preseason game."

"The who?"

"We're about to watch a football game," I said. Mom isn't into sports, so there was no use in taking an extra fifteen minutes to try to explain the football teams to her. Besides, I knew she didn't really want me to anyway. "How are you? Is everything okay with you?" I asked.

"Well," she drew out the word with a heavy breath, which let me know that I needed to buckle up because I was in for a long ride. "Your father is refusing to give me money to take that personal-finance class that you told me about, and the class starts tomorrow. He says that since I don't have a job, there's no reason for me to learn about finances and that I probably couldn't learn, so it would be a waste of good money anyway."

I rolled right past the condescending remarks because no matter how much you told her not to take the mental abuse, she would continue to do so without a word. She would be scared to death if we even mentioned telling the man off for the way he talked down to her. Scared like he would beat her or something. I'd never seen any signs of physical abuse and she never spoke of any, but I wondered about that possibility sometimes.

"Mom, every woman should know about finance. At a minimum, everybody should know about bill management, investing, and handling retirement funds. What if something happens to Dad, God forbid? How would you know about handling insurance, income taxes, household debts, and everything else?"

Mom sighed. "I know. I told your father everything you told me. He just said it was nonsense and that I would know what to do when it happened. He said I wasn't going to handle any bills or money, and it didn't matter since he wasn't going anywhere and that I shouldn't worry my thick head about it anyway. Then he left the room before I could say another thing."

As if she would have said another thing, I thought.

"I'm going to talk to him. It's important for all married women to know how to handle finances, even if you aren't bringing an income into the household. This class is important for you. That's why I told you about it. You need to go. I'll talk to him," I said. I knew what was coming next.

"No, no, if you talk to him it would just make him more upset that I talked to you about it. Then things would just get worse over here." She heaved a sigh as if she'd just been hit with the heaviest burden of her life.

"Mom, we go through this all the time. There's no reason you should be this unhappy. I wish you would say something or let me say something for you. This is ridiculous."

No answer.

"Well, look," I said, "I'll go ahead and send you the money for the class." I knew that was the solution she was waiting to hear.

"Oh, would you? That would be great because I really do want to take that class. I really appreciate it."

"Of course I would, Mom. I don't have a problem with that. I just hate to see your life like this, and I don't understand why you want to keep it that way."

"It's not bad. Not as bad as you make it out to be. He's bitter because of James's death."

"Mom, I'm really sick of hearing the excuse about Dad's twin brother. That was twenty-five years ago."

"They were really close and—"

"I know," I interrupted. "They were close, they were inseparable, they were in the Marines together, and they were starting a business together until Uncle James died in a motorcycle accident," I recited. "You know what? I've heard the whole story a million times. Uncle James died years ago and I know it was extremely painful, so I don't mean to sound insensitive, but Uncle James's death over twenty years ago doesn't give Dad the right to treat you like shit today. There's no reason for it, and I wish you'd stop making excuses for him." I could feel sweat beading on my forehead and between my breasts.

Again, no response.

"I'll put the money into our account tonight and you should be able to get it out tomorrow."

"Thanks, Vanella, baby. Well, I'm not going to hold you. Tell Alton I said 'hi.'"

"I will. Love you."

"Love you, too." She hung up the phone.

I put the phone back in its cradle, shook my head, and growled to myself. As I sat on the edge of the bed, I ran moist hands down my thighs, trying to ease away the frustration. I love my mother dearly, but her passivity with my dad drives me absolutely insane. My stomach turns sour, and I always feel a tightening in my throat whenever we talk. I wanted to shake Dad, but mostly I wanted to shake some sense into Mom for allowing him the freedom to trample on her spirits. I didn't understand why any woman today would stay in a marriage with a husband who didn't appear to love her and made her life as miserable as he possibly could. I am far from a proponent for divorce. But I am less of a proponent for sticking around someone who abuses you— mentally or physically, man or woman, husband or wife, girlfriend or boyfriend. I didn't know how long I could grant Mom's wishes and be a passive listener. She had perfected being passive and was damn good at it, but I'm not and don't want to be.

Alton had finished his shower and the aroma of microwave popcorn from the kitchen saturated my condo and made my mouth water. I glanced at the clock on the nightstand, jumped up, and showered quickly so I could be ready in time for the start of the pregame show. Since the Browns were away, I went to my walk-in closet and grabbed my "away games" Browns jersey to wear—and nothing else.

I scurried into the den, where Alton had just finished setting up for our Sunday ritual. He'd changed into his Browns jersey and a pair of drawstring shorts. His legs were looking too good. He had arranged a small spread of finger sandwiches; bowls of popcorn, snack mix, baked potato chips, and fruit; a couple of beers for him; and a bottle of Chardonnay on ice for me.

It was an overcast day in Cleveland. Cleveland skies can be overcast quite frequently, especially the closer it gets to fall and winter.

My three-bedroom, garden-style Shaker Heights condo faces east. On a sunny day, the natural sunlight seeps in and bounces off the cathedral ceiling, thoroughly illuminating my simply furnished unit. Although there was no direct sunlight, Alton turned the blinds down to minimize the soft daylight radiating on the wall-mounted TV.

I stood in the doorway for a second and peered at Alton. I loved him and our relationship. I didn't want it to change, and I didn't want him to change. Most of all, I didn't want to end up a divorced mess like most of my girlfriends or in a loveless marriage like my parents. I'd grown up watching my mother endure verbal abuse and not being touched or kissed at night—or perhaps at all, for that matter.

I refused to do that.

I looked at Alton and realized that at some point Mom and Dad had to have been right here where we were. Perhaps they started out with a deep love for each other, and somehow, somewhere, through the passing of time, their love evaporated and left the scum of a marriage that it was now.

As I stood there watching Alton, I thought about that and resolved not to let it happen to us.

"So are you just going to stand there, babe? The pregame show is about to come on." He looked around the room. "What? Did I forget something?"

I smiled. "No, you didn't forget a thing."

I headed toward the blue couch, where he was propped up on pillows with one leg on the floor and the other stretched out along the length of the cushions. I took my place between his legs and tucked my legs under me. I grabbed a fistful of popcorn and began feeding him three or four kernels at a time. Alton used the remote and turned up the sound on the TV as James Brown, Terry Bradshaw, Howie Long, and Chris Collinsworth began talking. I turned my head to face him and stared.

"What?" he asked, feeling my vibe.

"I love you," I said.

He squeezed me tight and said, "For sure, no doubt," knowing good and well that his response would not suffice. He held a playful smirk on his face for as long as he could, watching the television and pretending to ignore my stare. I patiently held a steady gaze and waited for the proper response that I knew was coming.

"Okay, okay." He laughed and wiggled his nose into my cheek. "I love you, too. Can I have some more popcorn?" he asked, then kissed my forehead.

I reached over to grab another fistful and felt him rub his hand along my backside.

I jumped. "Hey! The game's about to come on. No time for freaky stuff."

"I'm just checking. After all, it's only preseason." He grinned his devilish, sexy grin.

"Uh-huh." He didn't have to tell me. I knew what I was doing. I was always one step ahead of him.

Two

I WOKE UP AS Alton tried to ease out of bed without waking me. He hadn't planned on it, but we had watched a few more games and he had stayed overnight after the Browns lost to the Steelers. Being a native Clevelander and a devoted inmate of the Dawg Pound at the Browns Stadium, he claimed that he was in shock and needed to be consoled afterward, since the two teams were longtime rivals. Actually, it was pretty much over for the Browns at halftime and my strategically fitted #30 Jamel White jersey had begun to run interference with every play after that anyway. Like I said last night, I knew what I was doing.

When I heard the sound of shower water, I got up and made a pot of coffee. I tiptoed out of the bedroom into the stark white living room and past the frequently used fireplace that needed to be cleaned. I had never cleaned it. Alton usually did it before I ever thought to ask. I opened the blinds.

The hostile sun pushed its way through gaps in the clouds and cascaded over the black-and-white framed prints on the walls. From there, the rays of light trickled down to my Monarch sofa and matching maple tables. The greenery that laced the room yawned and stretched its leaves when the sun hit its sweet spots. The light felt like fire on my face and made me notice the chill bumps prickling down my arms, my nips at full attention. I turned down the A/C as I thought about a drenched Alton emerging from a balmy bathroom.

On the wall across from the thermostat and next to my bookcases, the large black-and-white professional portrait of Alton and me caught my eye. I scanned the rest of the portraits of us on the walls: a St. Louis summer under the Arch; in front of the Cleveland Rock and Roll Hall of Fame; South Beach last fall; South Beach last summer; South Beach two summers ago.

My heart glowed.

I poured a cup of coffee for him and added two packets of Equal and a bit of his favorite French vanilla creamer. Alton rarely drank coffee because he didn't like all the extra caffeine— that is, until I introduced him to French vanilla creamer. Now, he loves coffee, and that's the only way he drinks it.

He was still in the shower when I slipped into the sweltering bathroom and placed the cup of coffee on the marble vanity top, then crept back out again. I anxiously snuggled back between the warm sheets, shielded from the still-frosty A/C, for my last hour of sanity before heading to the stressful office of Kawamichi Finishes.

A short screech ended the waterfall, and I heard a deep "Mmm" about a minute later. Alton opened the door wearing a fluffy, white towel around his waist and holding the steaming cup of coffee. He leaned over and pressed his moist lips against my forehead.

"You are something else," he said.

He paused for a moment, sat next to me on the edge of the

bed, and stroked my arm. The breaking daylight peeked through the heavy drapes, and fluorescent lights from the adjacent bathroom outlined a silhouette of Alton's features.

I started to feel flushed as I watched the expression on his face slowly turn solemn. It deepened into a look that made my heart pump faster and a sharp chill surge up the back of my neck. When his lips parted, I felt an abrupt impulse to try to stop his words before they were even spoken. I was scared to death of what he might say.

He said, "I love you, Miss Lady."

"I love you, too," I said as I put my hand over his, suspending his strokes. I held his hand tightly as the comforter seemed to pulse up and down to the beating of my heart. He turned to place his cup of coffee on the nightstand, and then dropped his other hand on top of mine.

"I want you to know that you are the best thing that's happened in my life in a long time, Miss Vanella Morris. You have made the last six years heaven for me. You know what I'm thinking?"

He hesitated.

I swallowed hard.

"I'm thinking that I don't want to have to live without you—ever."

Alton's face revealed more love than a mother goose being followed by her little goslings. There was more love there than I had seen in his face over the last six years—and he's shown a lot of love. I felt extremely uneasy and apprehensive about where he would go with this. I was afraid that this lovable moment could turn into the beginning of the end for us. And I didn't want that to happen. Not yet at least. I wanted more time. Wanted more happiness. Wanted more of this before it was over.

My throat felt thick. I felt cornered and decided to try to lighten things up a bit. I needed to take control of the situation and redirect it to safer grounds. "What? Am I going somewhere? Am I going on a little trip?" I joked. My laugh trembled though, and my eyes shifted.

"No, you nut." He smiled and slipped his hand from under mine and fondled my cheek. Alton's touch always makes it seem like I have silk for skin, and I unconsciously began to lean into his hand. "I just want to make sure you know how special you are to me and how much I love and appreciate you and all the little things that you do. Just like the cup of coffee. I mean, here it is almost five in the morning, and you get out of a warm bed to make me a cup of coffee when you have to be up in another hour or so. You didn't have to do that. It's the little things that I love about you," he said in a baritone whisper.

My heart pounded frantically as I continued to try to drive his passion down a level. "Wow, all this for a cup of coffee? And what do I get for toast?" I asked with a slightly edgy chuckle.

Alton hesitated before speaking. "You're exactly like what I imagined my wife to be: strong, thoughtful, caring, and generous. You know, before my father died, he showed me what it was like to be a husband, a man, and a father. I was only seventeen. But by then, he had taught me what family was all about. And when he died . . . when he died, our family was cut short. I always wanted a family like we had before my father died. And I promised myself that when I found a woman, the woman who would partner with me in building that type of family, that I wouldn't let her go."

I felt my right leg twitch, and quickly tried to stop it before Alton noticed. I failed.

"You're nervous," Alton said, as if it were a new revelation.

"Baby, I'm not nervous," I lied. I wiggled my way up to a seated position to prevent my stool pigeon of a leg from telling on me again and leaned back against the headboard. I faked coolness. "I love you, too, and you are definitely the best thing that's happened in my life." I paused.

"Believe me, I don't want to lose you either, and there's nothing I wouldn't do to make sure that doesn't happen."

His eyes tightened in on mine. "Good. I'm glad you feel that way because there's something I've wanted to ask—"

"Um, baby, it's getting late and you still need to go home and change." I nudged his leg and dipped my head toward the clock on the nightstand. "You don't want to get caught up in traffic on the way to Avon Lake. You know Cleveland has only one lane leading from the east to the west side," I nervously joked again as coolly as I could.

He looked at the clock. "See, that's why I love you. You're always looking out for a brother." Alton leaned in and quickly kissed me again before he picked up his cup of coffee and took a sip. "And this is good, by the way."

"Really?"

"For sure, no doubt."

Alton put on his spare athletic gear that he kept at my place before he headed to his home in University Heights, the closest suburb to mine. Alton's house was close enough to my condo to allow him time to switch into his VP of finance attire and get to the Eveready Company in Avon Lake by 8 A.M.

As Alton's titillating scent slowly faded, I lingered in my bed a few minutes longer and wrapped my arms around the down-filled pillow that had cradled his head only moments ago. I couldn't help but think about how Alton had made the last six years my happiest ever.

That I couldn't deny.

He was definitely my best friend, my shoulder to lean on, a great lover, a great teacher, a great learner, a generous giver, a humble taker, a great supporter, and my biggest fan. I was all of those things to him as well. We mixed well, like strawberries and cream. We had grown together, played together, laughed together, cried together, raised hell together, and made love together over and over. With all that was right, I didn't want to see it all come to a blinding halt. Yet, from what I'd witnessed in relationships, I believed that was exactly what would happen if we got married.

After all, observations don't lie. Statistics don't lie.

The snooze alarm went off for the second time. I finally dragged myself out of bed and poured myself a cup a coffee before taking my turn in the shower. It was time to shake everything off my mind and prepare for another day of long meetings, tough negotiations, male posturing, and defending my worthiness as the general manager of quality engineering, which is a daily challenge that I never look forward to doing.

After I showered, I followed my normal routine of critically scrutinizing my abs, hips, and thighs to see if any of them had stepped out of line within the last twenty-four hours. I carefully ran my hands across my curvaceous hips a couple of times before feeling the width of my stocky thighs. I turned to the side to view the reflection of my middle in the full-length mirror. My dark brown skin glowed while my chin-length dark brown hair hung limply down the sides of my oval-shaped face. The large round eyes that I'd inherited from my mother could use a bit of soft brown eyeliner on the upper lids, but I wasn't criticizing my face just yet. It currently wasn't my main focus.

After a thorough examination, I concluded that I had gained

at least an eighth of an inch in the hips and thighs—or at least it felt like it—and that the madness must stop now before it got too out of hand. I decided to have a strawberry Slim-Fast for breakfast and promised myself that I would have just a salad when I met Synda today for our weekly lunch date. Not feeling confident that I could keep that promise to myself, I popped an appetite suppressant just to ensure that I could make it without any difficulty. Then I packed my gym bag so I could go directly from work to the gym to make the 7:00 advanced step aerobics class. As a matter of fact, I'd try to get there early enough for forty-five minutes of free-weight training before class. I made a mental note to call Armando so I could start up my personal training sessions again.

I got dressed in my standard business-casual black pantsuit with a light blue pullover blouse that hugged me at the waist. After several mishaps in my career, I had learned that my body works best with a basic black bottom and any top that doesn't have buttons trekking down the middle of my breasts. Let's just say I had given several presentations where I had every male colleague's undivided attention. Unfortunately, it wasn't for my incredibly engrossing and stupendous report.

I grabbed my cell phone off the dresser on my way out. Damn! It wasn't even 7:15 A.M. and I already had six messages waiting. I could already tell that it was going to be a dillydally of a day.

Synda and I slid into a booth at Panera in Tower City for lunch. Tower City Center is composed of offices, three levels of retail, and a restaurant area. The mall sits in the heart of downtown

Cleveland, stretching the east and west banks of the Cuyahoga River, and connects to Jacobs Field and the Gund Arena—homes of the Cleveland Indians and the Cavs. At any given time of day, you can find all walks of life strolling and wandering about the Avenue of Tower City Center. Tower City attracts everyone from businesspeople using cell phones and PDAs to truant youngsters in saggy, baggy jeans, trying unsuccessfully to avoid the CPD, who just love this style of clothing, which slows down the flight time of the deviants and makes them easier to apprehend.

As usual, the café was crowded with a well-mixed and moderately loud lunch crowd. Since Synda and I each had extremely busy schedules during the week, we had a standing appointment to meet for lunch somewhere in Tower City every Monday. Synda works as a computer programmer for a communications company in the Higbee Building and my company's headquarters are in the Terminal Tower. It feels nice to have someone that I've known since childhood working in the same area.

She asked me how the day was going.

"Same ol', same ol'. Just watching the testosterone fly and the backbiters hate as they all take orders from a female. Every day I truly think it's the funniest, saddest, and most tiring sight ever. Watching grown men twist my exact words to make it seem like what I said was a new, brilliant idea that they just thought of. They need to feel like it was their bright idea and not mine. To that, I say 'whatever.'"

"You're not worried about someone stealing your credit?" Synda asked as a couple of women slowly cruised by our table and studied our plates. From the looks of things, they were calculating how much time it would take us to finish our lunch and whether they should camp out by our booth or not.

"No. I'm not trying to break the glass ceiling or work my butt off all nights and weekends to beat out the next guy for a promotion. Playing the corporate role and kissing up to the boss so that he can remember me for the next prestigious position is just not my thing. And for some reason, being chief of car-paint quality issues just doesn't make me salivate."

I chuckled to myself at the thought of all my male work associates who obviously had not been used to having a female boss in such a male-dominated field. Early in my career, I even had an older male coworker whom I beat out for a promotion tell me that women don't know anything about making a durable coating for an automobile and that if I wanted to stay in auto finishes, I should consider being the secretary or somebody's assistant. Yeah, old Mr. Thurman. But he decided to take early retirement after I decided to share his lovely point of view with my boss, who then shared it with Human Resources. It seemed that ol' Mr. Thurman had expressed his perspective with a lot of women with prominent positions.

"Girl, you know men have trouble having a black female as a boss, especially in engineering. There just aren't many of us out there," Synda said.

"Oh, you don't even have to put the black part in there. They're first just trying to swallow the female boss part. Women can be just as bad as men, if not worse. Men will try to show you up in a meeting, outdo your presentation, or try to upstage you in front of the boss. But afterward, they're done. Now women . . . humph. Women will make it their personal career goal to make all ten to twelve hours of your days a living hell at the office and will formulate a life-long vendetta against you, your mother, your kids, and your ex-husband's pet dog, Hoover." We both laughed.

I looked up as two young mall shoppers bulldozed their way

into a booth that was taken by one elderly white man, and he seemed to enjoy the company. His wrinkled mouth and hands were moving at Porsche speed until the girls spotted an empty table, got up, and left. The old man watched them walk away with longing eyes.

I mixed the light honey mustard dressing into my café salad. With the help of the diet pill I'd taken that morning, I'd kept my promise to myself and ordered a light salad and a Diet Coke. As a matter of fact, I wasn't feeling too hungry at all. But to make a good lunch date, and to keep Synda out of my business like she always is, I decided to nibble at it anyway.

Synda got her usual Tuscan chicken, mocha café latte, and a thick slice of chocolate fudge brownie topped with cream-cheese icing. Just looking at that fudge brownie made my mouth water and the blood in my veins coagulate. But that was Synda. For as long as I've known her, she's always been slender with curves. The girl can eat just about anything and never blow up. Her mother's the same way, although Synda does work out in the gym three times a week. I'll give her credit for that. She always talks about how just because you have a high metabolism doesn't mean you don't need to work out. Skinny people can be fat, too. She doesn't want any flab waving in the wind under her arm or dough rolls around her waist or on her back.

Synda has extraordinary features. Her long, light brown hair is naturally highlighted. It's probably a mixture from her fair-skinned mother, who had golden hair, and her Puerto Rican father, who had the blackest, curliest hair east of the Mississippi. Synda's hair complements her honey-toasted skin and draws your eyes into her face, which appears flawless except for a tiny scar on her forehead. Her eyebrows are naturally arched and seem to float over her sleek and slender hazel eyes. Her small but plump lips have a natural pink tone that makes her look like she is always wearing a hint of lipstick. She often forgos the lipstick and opts for a dab of gloss instead.

"How are things in the world of programming?" I asked as I took a bite of salad.

"Mmm," Synda said, flailing her arms as she tried to chew and swallow quickly, undoubtedly so she could relate the latest office gossip. Ever since we were little girls, Synda always had eager ears and loose lips. Girl couldn't keep a secret if her life depended on it.

"Girl, I knew something was up with Gene and that Ms. I'm-too-good-to-speak-to-you-today Esther. Turns out, they were both sneaking behind their spouses' backs and gettin' it on together after work, um-huh. We all knew there was something to the extra hours they've both been putting in during the last few months. Nobody's that dedicated. Well, now she's pregnant with his baby, sho' is." Synda leaned back, rolled her eyes upward, and pressed her lips together, all but too happy to relay the play-by-play of the downfall of her most hated office enemy, Mrs. Esther Watkins.

"How do you know the baby's not her husband's?" I asked.

Synda's honey-colored face turned maroon and her eyes drooped. "Well, I just happened to be in a stall in the bathroom." Her voice plunged as she spoke. "Someone came in crying and another girl, Tiffany, I think, came following up behind her asking her what's wrong. I peeped through the door crack to see who it was, and I saw that it was Esther. She didn't even check to see who was in the bathroom. The girl just came in and blurted out err-thang." She always seems to regain her midwest accent when she's in the throes of a good gossip episode.

She continued, "Girl, how many times they did it, what they did, whurr they did it, what she wasn't doing with hurr husband. Shoot. It took hurr forty-five minutes to pull hurrself together so we could all get back to work." She waved her right hand and rolled her eyes, as if *she* were offended.

I choked mid-gulp on my iceless diet cola. "You mean you stayed in the stall forty-five minutes listening to her spill her guts?"

"Yeah. Well, what else could I do? I didn't want to walk out and embarrass her. She was obviously traumatized. She was in enough pain already." She gnashed at her sandwich and wiped the corners of her mouth with a napkin. Her heavy St. Louis accent disappeared just as conveniently as it had appeared.

"Um-hum," I said. "Like you care. More like you wanted to hear all of her juicy confession so you could have more to gossip about."

"What are you talking about? I don't gossip. Ain't nothing worse than gossipy women. Can't stand 'em. Unh-unh. I can't stands no gossipy women," Synda said mockingly as she scarfed down a chip. Synda knows more than anyone else how she gets into the lives of everyone else just so she can have something to talk about.

"Serves her right anyway. Messin' with my chocolate fantasy man. Gene is as fine as he wanna be. He should have been having that affair with me instead of her," Synda added as she laughed aloud—alone. She looked at me and suddenly realized what she had said and who she said it to. She promptly dropped the smile that traversed ear to ear. "I'm just playing, girl. I love my man." She rubbed the scar on her forehead.

"You got a good one. Don't mess it up." I continued to mix the salad around my plate. Synda took a last bite of the cream-cheese brownie. It is amazing. No matter how much and what that girl shovels in, she always stays the same size. You have to wonder where it all goes.

"So, how's Alton?" Synda asked abruptly upon swallowing, not wanting to continue with the previous conversation. It was her usual tactic whenever our conversations even smelled like they were moving in the direction of her husband, Tucker Scott. In all actuality, I didn't want to talk about him any more than she wanted to talk about him with me.

"Fine." I debated how much I wanted to say to Synda about Alton.

"If he's fine, why did your face get all glum just now?" Another middle-aged set of sorry-eyed gawkers sniffed out our table, then left when we kept talking.

I thought for a moment, and then said, "I'm getting a little nervous about Alton and me."

"What do you mean? Uh-oh. Do I smell trouble in paradise?" No, she didn't. But she was trying hard as hell to smell something.

"Things have been going good and steady for a few years now. We're in love, we hardly ever argue or fight, we have great times together. . . . I mean . . . things are perfect."

"Okay, let me know when you get to the problem." Synda jutted her chin forward.

I thought carefully about what to say and what not to say. You don't tell Synda anything that you wouldn't want to see printed in the *National Enquirer*. "I'm pretty sure he's going to want to move to the next step," I said.

"Next step?"

"Marriage, Synda. I think he's going to propose, and sometime soon."

"And . . . that would be a bad thing?"

I exhaled from my gut and glanced around at the individuals bartering for space and tables. "Do you know that fifty percent of first marriages end in divorce within about five to seven years?"

"Well, I guess TC and I should be signing divorce papers right about now since it's been seven years, huh?"

"Look at all of our friends from high school and college. Most of them are married and already divorced, or on the verge of divorce. The rest of them are unhappily married, cheating on each other, or practically living as roommates. And you know about my mom and dad. At this point, I think a happy marriage is the illusion of a delusional woman."

"Who says you got to be like everybody else? From what I understand, you and Alton really love each other. It's been six years and you're still together. If that's not a good sign, then I don't know what is."

"Yeah, but everyone goes into it in love and with the intent of living up to 'till death do us part.' But somehow, 'till death' equates to an average of five years. Then comes the messy divorce and dividing things up, fighting over who bought what and who can have what, fighting over this, that, the cars and the kids. I'm not going through all of that. And I'm certainly not going to live the rest of my life in an unhappy marriage like my mother."

"Whoa, whoa, whoa!" Synda threw one hand up in the air. "Slow down. Van, the man hasn't even proposed and you're already dividing up the house, kids, and tropical fish. None of which you have yet, might I add."

She was probably right. I had already taken Alton and me through divorce court without him even presenting me with a ring and the lovely honeymoon trip to Aruba. At least that's where it'd better be.

"You know, you always throw out these figures from time to time. Where do you get all this stuff?"

"Books from the library, magazines, the Census Bureau's Marriage and Divorce Statistics . . ." I trailed off and twirled my fork in my salad.

"Oh, I see. So, you're going to base your future with Alton on statistics? Well, that's mighty engineering of you," Synda said, with no attempt to disguise the sarcasm. I didn't like her little remark, and she knew she was starting to irritate me.

Syn knew me so well that she was able to see just how much I didn't appreciate her words. "Look, Van, I'm not going to kid you. Marriage ain't no joke. Sometimes I want to wring TC's neck, and I'm sure he may want to do the same to me. I certainly wonder if we're going to make it sometimes. We've even gone to marriage counseling before." She looked directly into my eyes and the tone of her voice begged for understanding. She reached her arm across the table, grabbed my hand, and rocked it from side to side. "You just got to work at it. And you know what? It's worth it. In the end, it's worth it." She squeezed my hand and smiled.

"You're just saying that because I told you in college that if you ever messed TC over, I'd beat your ass."

Synda looked down at the table. I rolled my wrist toward me while her hand was still on top of mine and looked at my watch. "Time for both of us to get back to work," I said, trying to help her save face.

"What? Not finishing your salad? I hope to God you're not on another diet. You look better than half these wenches walking around here in dresses that look like they should be tank tops, as barely there as they are."

"Easy for you to say," I said as I looked at her honey skin and long, shoulder-length hair. "You're a natural size four, got rounded hips, long hair, beautiful skin, and gorgeous eyes—"

"Yeah, and a big brown scar on my forehead." Synda removed her hand from mine and ran her finger over the barely visible scar on the right side of her forehead.

"Syn, you can hardly see that. It wouldn't be there if you hadn't decided to celebrate getting accepted to Case the way that you did. You'd just better be happy that's the only damage you have."

Synda ignored my comment—something she was good at. "Well, anyway. You don't need to be on yet another diet. It seems like you work out every day. You got a tiny waist and thighs like Gail Devers. I only wish I had your thirty-four-double Ds." Synda nodded toward my breasts.

"Okay, enough of us flattering each other. I'm just trying to take off five pounds. Maybe ten. Then I'll be okay."

"You're already okay. And girl, you *know* I would tell you."

"Let's get out of here and get our butts back to work," I said. "I've still got to prove to the old men up there that I'm good for more than just birthing babies."

Syn reminded me of ladies night out this Friday at Alexandria's on Main and Spy Bar. We got up and had barely exited the booth before a couple of mannish-looking women in double-breasted suits ran toward us and laid claim to our booth. The short woman reached it first and frightened off all the other predators who were charging the table. It's always the short ones.

I gave Synda a hug before we headed up the escalator and back to our offices.

❀ ❀ ❀
❀ ❀ ❀ Three

I JUST WANTED TO slap his ass once. *Just once, Lawd, and I swear I won't ask for any more favors. Ever.*

Dexter McKleon is the most irritating person in the office. He always tries to compete with me and show me up at meetings, especially in front of the president and VP. Personally, I think he starts each day with a cup of coffee and strategizes how best to appear superior to Miss Vanella Morris—the woman who had effortlessly beat him out for the general manager position. I could count on him to challenge my perspective in every meeting, ask the VP to share his *most notable* thoughts, and elaborate endlessly on a good point until everyone was ready to shoot themselves in their faces. Dexter wears designer suits and a tasty cologne, and keeps his nails manicured. His main purpose at Kawamichi Finishes is to fulfill the role of company tool in the making of automotive finishes. He often volunteers to take the big American bosses out to lunch—the Japanese bosses aren't into that sort of hazing. He always laughs hard and long at their thirsty jokes, jogs and works out with them at lunch and before or after work, and golfs with them on weekends. Dexter studies the boss's patterns and times his own workday to begin ten minutes before the boss arrives and five minutes after he leaves—*whatever* time that might be.

Dexter makes sure to avoid me in any way possible, except for sneaking peeks at my breasts when he needs a rise, along with his coffee, to get him going in the mornings.

And in the afternoons.

I'd be as lucky as a vulture spotting fresh, succulent road kill if Dexter ever returned even one of my e-mails or phone calls requesting information or guidance. Since he'd been in the department two years before I came, I mistakenly thought I could refer to him when I had questions. It didn't take me long to figure out that he wasn't interested in showing me the ropes when, on more than one occasion, he provided me with false information, then conveniently corrected me in a meeting or in front of the boss. Once or twice, I thought it was a mistake or that maybe, just maybe, he was a little stupid. But after the third time, I realized he was one of those people who wants to be the only successful African American in the history of the company, and he certainly didn't want to be shown up by a woman. Especially an African American woman. He longs to keep the rest of us at barrel-scraping level if he can't keep us out of the company altogether.

During my report, I noticed that Dexter spent most of the time flipping back and forth through the pages. Looking for errors, no doubt.

"Are there any questions on what I've reported thus far?" I asked the Kawamichi senior management team as we sat at the conference room table.

Everyone looked at his watch, then at Dexter.

Dexter didn't let the team down. "Uh, Miz Morris, I was just looking through the report here. The data on page four seems inconsistent with the graphs and conclusions on page ten and . . ." He trailed off, which suggested that he was waiting for an explanation. The room was serene except for the sound of rustling papers.

"I'm not sure what you mean, Dexter," I said as I, along with everyone else, examined the data more closely, as Dexter had indirectly commanded us to do.

"Well, on page four the data shows a significant improvement in appearance, specifically in smoothness and gloss. Improvements are well beyond target. Yet, if you turn to page ten, your conclusion states that we need to level up on smoothness and gloss and you go on with projections." Dexter carefully leaned back in his chair so as not to wrinkle his designer shirt, which had probably been ironed by one of his trophies of the month. His frigid eyes scanned the room for comrades, then settled on me. He had that "I finally gotcha now" look on his face.

Before I could respond, Mr. Taguchi, the division manager, asked in broken English, "Vanella san? Is information correct? If inconsistent, we must correct. We must clarify our position."

Dexter picked up his copy of my report and pretended to read it silently with a confidently smug grin. "I agree, Taguchi san." He customarily reciprocated in broken English. "When we present report to president, we must ensure all information correct. If not correct—"

"Taguchi san?" I interrupted Dexter. The petite Japanese man looked up from the report with flat, wide eyes.

I replied slowly in broken English to make comprehension easier. "Taguchi san, data on page four shows improvement beyond target on smoothness and gloss. But data is only on five panels. Five-panel report too small to make judgment. Previous six months data shows smoothness and gloss to be no good. Does not meet target."

Mr. Taguchi took his left hand and rubbed the left side of his neck. He sucked in air between his teeth the way little girls sometimes do when their mothers get too close to their necks or ears with the scorching hot pressing comb. Over the years that I'd been with Kawamichi, I had come to recognize that as a sign of contemplation.

I continued. "If you look on bottom of page, you should see note that states information is based on small data pool. We need more data to show smoothness and gloss good."

"Ah! I see. Very good, Vanella san. I see." Mr. Taguchi smiled and nodded his head.

"I understand data pool is small, but report shows a very big improvement," Dexter said to Taguchi, hoping to lure the division manager back over to his side of the Pacific.

"No. Vanella san is correct. We cannot judge condition to be good on small amount of data. We must verify with more data." Taguchi looked at his watch. "I must go. I have other meeting. Thank you, Vanella san. Very good information." Mr. Taguchi got up to leave and the other Japanese managers followed suit behind him.

Dexter said nothing as I turned off the computer and began to collect my pages. With the smugness washed from his face, he picked up his report and started a conversation with the manager of safety. I heard him boast about how I benefited from advice he'd previously given me. What advice? Oh yeah, he did tell me to make colorful graphs for my presentations. I almost forgot.

I shook my head and continued to bring the meeting room back to order. Dexter was definitely the most animated competitor in the office, and one I was growing more tired of day by day.

Breaking the glass ceiling in somebody else's company had never been my goal. I'm all for seeing more women and minorities in engineering and management positions. It's just that becoming vice president or president of Kawamichi Finishes, and ruler over the making of car paint, had not been my goal. If it were my own company, then it would be worth working my ass off for.

I rushed into my cubicle and caught the ringing phone before it went to voice mail.

"Vanella Morris."

"Hey, babe. How are you doing today?" Alton's voice surged through the receiver and immediately calmed my irritated nerves. No matter what time of day it was or how annoyed I was with people at work, just hearing his voice would smolder the flames in my veins. His soothing calls always made everything better.

"Better, now that I'm talking to you," my voice dragged as I whispered into the phone. The Japanese prefer cubicles with low walls rather than enclosed offices, so privacy was not possible.

"Hmm . . . sounds like somebody had another run-in with Dexter Brownnose," Alton said. That's what he called him. Alton had attended a few company outings and Christmas parties with me. He noticed Dexter's suck-up personality before I even had a chance to mention anything. Dexter is a very tall, handsome, light-skinned, muscular, and sexy man. Most of the time, he came to company functions alone or he brought a stunning trophy—and they were always stunning—who would end up standing and nursing a glass of wine in the corner while Dexter investigated how far up each executive's ass he could insert his head. It was kind of hard for anyone not to notice.

"Yeah. I had another manager's meeting today, and he showed out as usual. I'm really getting sick of this game. I'm not even trying to be a player."

"Sounds like he really got under your skin today. You want me to rough him up for you? You want me to get this one for you, huh?" Alton made a karate sound. I visualized him posing in the "Karate Kid" stance and laughed. He could always pull a laugh out of me. Sometimes he would catch me off guard. I'd be so angry, utterly furious at something. The next thing I know I'm rolling around on the floor with his crazy butt, laughing my thong off about who knows what.

"It's not like today was any different from other days. And it's not like he's the only ass-kisser here, or the only one who's in a race for the brass ring. I think every day I get more and more fed up with people trying to pull me into a dog fight and the expectations associated with being a female on the rise to the top and breaking barriers."

"Tell you what," Alton said. "Why don't you come on over. Stay at my place tonight. I'll cook something—"

"Uh, Alton—"

"Something light, although I don't know why you're watching your weight anyway, but since this is your night I'm not going to get into that again right now," Alton ran on, over my objection. I was forever trying to lose five, ten, or fifteen pounds and Alton always objected. I thought he was just trying to be nice. "And I don't know what yet, but I'll throw something together to make sure we have a relaxing evening. We can talk and de-stress together."

"How about a movie?" I sat down and propped my elbows on the desk, then balanced my stressed-out head on my palms.

"How about a life-sized dart poster of Dexter?"

"Can we fling axes instead of darts?"

"Nah. Remember I just had the walls painted."

"Oh, yeah. That's right." We chuckled. "Well, it sounds good. I'll be right over. But I think I'm going to make a stop first."

"You got to pick something up from the store? What do you need? I'll go out and pick it up for you."

Wasn't he sweet?

"No, actually I want to pick up some information at one of the offices out here. I'm just going to make a quick stop on the way out and come right over. So, I'll see you in a few minutes."

"All right, baby. Oh, and how about the Marriott at South Beach?"

"Sounds great like always."

We said good-bye and I picked up my purse and left.

"May I help you?"

"Yes," I said to the receptionist. "I would like to pick up some information on—"

"Can you hold on a sec?" She picked up the buzzing telephone before I could reply. While I was the only one in the lobby at the Greater Cleveland Growth Association's COSE office, the phone was lit up like Times Square and had the young receptionist's fingers hopping. I imagined the young girl behind the desk to be a second- or third-year college student, working her way through college, as I had. She sat before a framed picture of Cleveland's skyline, complete with all three tall buildings downtown.

I walked over to the seating area behind me and to the right of the elevators. Inspiring business portraits on the walls, a matching black table set, and a television tuned to CNN complemented the bright orange contemporary couch on chrome legs. The coffee table held a spread of information provided by the Consortium of Small Enterprises (COSE). I took a seat on the end of the couch, picked up a magazine, and began flipping through articles about people who had started out with half a piece of lint and built it into a multimillion-dollar lint conglomerate—big, expensive balls of lint that they created, nurtured, and cultivated with their own hands.

"You needed information on starting a business?" the receptionist asked as she peered over the counter.

I snapped out of my thoughts, stood, and walked toward her. "Yes," I said. "I knew this office was here, so I just wanted to stop by on my way out and pick up information on small-business ownership and what services COSE offers."

"Your name, please?"

"Vanella. Vanella Morris."

She stared hard, then quickly looked away. "Okay, Ms. Morris. I'll have someone out to speak with you in a moment."

I was familiar with the pause that my name, as that of any dark-skinned African American, often solicited.

She spoke into her headset, then said to me, "Please have a seat in the lobby. Samantha Parks will be with you in a few minutes."

I walked back to the lobby and resumed flipping. I don't know why, but I felt excited just being there. Like I was a rebel about to pull off the most unexpected caper of the century. I really wasn't absolutely sure that this was something I would do. Leaving the corporate world and branching out on my own had been on my mind for the longest. I had previously dismissed it or brushed it off. What business would I start? How would I fund it? What if I failed? What did I know about owning a business? Absolutely nothing, which is why I was there: to find out. I wasn't telling myself that I was going to do it, but sometimes things will keep buzzing inside your head and you have to go check them out just to shut them up.

"Ms. Vanella Morris?" A strong female voice brought me back to the present. She was a white woman of medium build with shoulder-length reddish brown hair, smartly dressed in a standard blue suit with a white blouse and navy blue pumps. I sized her up to be about a size twelve.

I placed the magazine on the coffee table, stood, and extended my hand to greet her. "Yes, I'm Vanella Morris."

"Pleased to meet you. I'm Samantha Parks with Member Services here at COSE. I understand that you're looking for information on starting a business? What type of business will you start?" she asked with a cheery voice.

My leg twitched in response to her question. I suddenly felt foolish for wasting this woman's time. I didn't know what type of business I would start or even if I would start a business. I just wanted to see what it took to be in charge of my own destiny like the lint people in the magazines.

I followed Samantha's lead and took a seat next to her on the couch. She held an emerald folder with COSE on the front in gold lettering.

"To be honest, Ms. Parks, I'm really not sure what type of business I would like to start," I said, making an effort to still my leg. "I have a few ideas, but I haven't pinpointed anything yet. I don't mean to waste your time. I just wanted to pick up information to see how people do it." I started to stand, but Samantha placed her hand on my forearm and motioned me to stay.

"You're not wasting my time. A lot of people start out this way. Quite a few people start off not sure what they want to do or how, but they know they want to leave corporate America and do their own thing. It's the entrepreneurial spirit that drives a lot of people into this office. It's a starting point. If you want to go into business, you've got to start somewhere."

I smiled at her assurance.

"Let me explain our services for the small-business owner." She opened the folder and went over several documents with me, then directed me to the National Small Business Association for guidance on starting a business. Samantha handed me her card as we shook hands. I took a complimentary copy of the magazine with articles about the lint people and headed to Alton's. Who knows, maybe I'll become one of the lint people myself.

Four

IT WAS AN OVERCAST day in Cleveland.

Alton's quaint little four-bedroom bungalow brightened the block. The two-story tan stone house sat in the middle of the stretch of homes with perfectly manicured lawns. Alton lives in an old-fashioned neighborhood—the kind where neighbors look out for each other and call the cops if they see suspicious characters loitering about. Summers, you were sure to find Mr. Coleman sitting on the porch watering his lawn.

I rang the doorbell, waited a few seconds, then used my key to enter his house. We both had keys to each other's places, but we still called and rang the doorbell before we came over and entered. That was our agreement.

I walked into a candle-lit house. Mmm . . . scented candles. The house had a juicy tropical scent that made my nose dance like a kid who had just bought a popsicle from the Bomb Pop man on any given St. Louis August day. Alton was nowhere in sight. A soft Boney James jazz melody was playing on the audio system that he'd wired throughout the house.

I set my purse down on the table in the foyer and let the tropical scent escort my nose into the living room. Alton's place has a metropolitan feel. The living room is outfitted with tightly buttoned brown leather furniture and cherry-stained tables that contrast with the off-white carpet. His walls are sparsely dressed with framed black-and-white prints in the living room, an abstract in the foyer, and Picasso prints in the dining room and hallways. The artwork was compliments of his oldest sister, Gwennie.

Alton had left a vase of roses on the dining room table with a card attached. I slipped one red rose out of the bunch and brought it to my nose. I inhaled as I read the card: "For the love of my life. Just because you're you." I laughed because he had signed it "All Good." All Good was a nickname that his college buddies had given him. For a while, nerdy Alton tried to use it as a line to meet women. Had even attempted to use it on me back in the day. When I first asked him his name, he said it was Alton Goode but to call him "All."

"All?" I asked like he wanted me to, and he replied, "Because I'm all good."

I didn't laugh.

Then I laughed because it was truly the corniest thing I had ever heard. He'd tried as hard as he could to sound cool when he said it. Poor Alton's feelings were really hurt, but after admitting to himself how corny his line was, he ended up laughing with me.

All Good. That was truly how he made things for me. That was how he made me feel from the very beginning.

I met Alton a little over six years ago at Case Western Reserve University. His major was finance; mine was material science and engineering. We crossed paths in a humanities class, and I remember that I wasn't up for meeting any new friends— male or female. Plus, he was looking to get over some girl named Robin who left him for a quarterback. A few months earlier, I had broken up with my first *real* love, whom I had met my freshman year there at Case. My ex and I dated for about a year and a half before he gave a college football victory and Boone's Farm Strawberry Hill wine the power of attorney to make decisions for him. And they chose to make him celebrate by sleeping with another female—who knew he was dating me, but obviously didn't give a damn—and getting her pregnant. After that incident, I stayed to myself and wasn't up to hanging out or meeting new friends.

Alton saw that my welcome mat had been put out on the balcony to dry, but he was determined to melt the ice that girdled my heart. He said he had seen me before at a couple of baseball games at Jacobs Field. His parents had season tickets. I had the sweet-talk-the-stadium-guards hook-up. Cleveland is a sports town. The Indians were a hot team in the American League, and the new Browns Stadium was under construction. The Cavs . . . well, they were the Cavs. So we talked a lot about the Indians and the new Browns Stadium and team over lunch, after class, and, eventually, over the phone and at each other's dorms.

When Alton shared with me his love for motorcycles, he opened me up for good. Alton was pretty much a gear head and loved buying old bikes, taking them apart, fixing them up, riding them, and then selling them. I had never ridden a bike myself, but had wanted to ever since I saw pictures of my uncle James on his many different bikes. Since he lost control on suicide hill in St. Louis, hit a telephone pole, and died, talk of motorcycles was never again allowed in our house. B-Momma, my dad's mother, said that his twin's death was the reason Dad seemed so distant and so uncaring at times, so none of us wanted to say anything that would remind him of Uncle James. Just the mention of motorcycles would do precisely that.

Alton immediately picked up on my interest in bikes and invited me to ride behind him. He took me through the Cleveland Metroparks—a series of interconnected parks that weave through Cleveland and Akron—down Highway 90 and on the road alongside Lake Erie. I wrapped my arms around Alton as we glided down Lakeshore Boulevard on his custom-built cruiser. We rode at dawn and at dusk. Whenever there was a full moon, Alton would swing by and pick me up after midnight and off we'd go. We'd have the road mostly to ourselves as we sailed down the highway under the spell of the moonlight, being led to the promised land. Riding with Alton was the best thing ever. Feeling the wind. Feeling Alton.

He knew he had me.

"Come on in here, girl," Alton called from the den.

As I walked past the kitchen to the den, I could taste the rich Italian spices in the air. They tingled on my tongue and caused my taste buds to jiggle. My mouth instantly watered and my stomach yelped as I swallowed the thick, rich sauce in the air. The oregano, sage, and tomato blend primed my tongue with a thin, tasty coating that I could not wash away. Mmm.

Alton sat on his black suede couch with a glass of white wine. There was another glass of wine on the coffee table for me. "Come, sit down and relax." He patted the seat cushion next to him.

I took a seat next to him without picking up the wine. Alton placed his on the table, turned me around, and began to massage my shoulders.

"How was your day?" I asked.

"Just typical. Another day of battling the worthiness and unworthiness of the latest acquisition recommendations. Some people just don't understand that company growth is not measured through numerous acquisitions."

"Sounds like your coworkers are cousins of my coworkers."

"Look, don't let 'em get to you. Work is just that—work. It's what you do to pay the bills. If you don't like it where you are, you can always go somewhere else." Alton paused and captured a thought as he continued to rub my shoulders. "But, you know, if we got married, you wouldn't have to work unless you wanted to."

Alton was good. Oh, he was good. Scented candles, soft music, roses—he buttered me up and got me to let down my defenses. Dammit! Was he about to propose? *Come on, come on. Not now, Alton. Not now.*

I shifted, then heard my cell phone singing a tune from my purse in the living room. "My phone." I jumped up and ran before Alton could speak another word. Thank God. My hurried steps were muffled by the carpet until I hit the parquet floor of the foyer. Then I sounded like a Clydesdale breaking away from the herd.

"Hey, Babysista," I said after I retrieved the phone and saw Jaelene's name on the caller ID.

"Hey sis, what's up?"

"I'm at Alton's hanging out. Nothing's wrong, is there?"

Her squeaky voice held no sign of trouble, but with Jaelene you never knew. Sometimes she called in need of money. Sometimes she called to tell me about something that was going on with the family, sometimes she actually called just to chitchat. Jaelene has her problems with money and men and gets on my nerves about it, but we're still sisters and we act like sisters—close sisters.

"Well, I'm not going to hold you since you're at Alton's. I was just excited and I had to call someone. I got two plasma TVs like you and Alton. Just had mine delivered and put up in the bedroom."

"Two? Where'd you put the other one?"

"Oh, that one's going up in Cyrus's bedroom in his apartment." Her voice was laid back, mellow.

"You bought what? An eight-*thousand*-dollar TV for a man who's not even your husband?"

"Got a deal for five grand each," she said. Her tone was still just as nonchalant, like she was Janet Jackson or Lisa Marie Presley and need not be worried about price. I didn't think Anheuser-Busch paid *that* well.

I paused as I gathered my thoughts. "Wait a minute, wait a minute. Babysista, doesn't Cyrus live, uh, in uh—"

"The projects? Yeah. Look, Van, everybody don't live like you or have the type of job you have. Cyrus is going to school. He's premed. It don't matter how late you do it, just as long as you do it."

"Hold on, now, Babysista, don't get me wrong. I'm not knocking where he lives. But if the man lives in the projects," I spoke slowly, hoping that something would click in her head, "and is a full-time student, does he really *need* a five-thousand-dollar plasma TV? And not that you should be doing it, but if you wanted to spend five grand on Cyrus"—*five grand?* I thought—"wouldn't you think that it might be more useful toward his education? That's my only point."

Silence.

I exhaled hard. I don't understand my little sister sometimes. She is the most beautiful girl in the family and somehow she feels the need to constantly buy expensive gifts for whatever man is in her life at the time, despite the fact that she can't afford it. She makes a damn good living as a product manager for Anheuser-Busch, but she's always giving her money away to every Tyrone, DeShawn, and Hakeim in St. Louis, trying to keep a man by her side.

"Cyrus is going to pay for half. So don't go lecturing me about buying things for men."

"Oh, he's going to pay half, huh? Okay, let me get this right." I shifted my weight from one leg to the other. "Cyrus, a full-time college student living in the Blumeyers, is going to give you twenty-five hundred for a TV?"

Dead silence.

She was giving me a headache. Again.

"You know, if he does pay you, I'm not so sure you should take that money because only God knows how he would get it. It's been what, Babysista, about ten or eleven months that you've been seeing this one?"

"Six. And there you go stereotyping again." She was as serious as airport security. By now, excitement had left her voice and was replaced with annoyance at me for not sharing her joy.

I shoved my fingers through my hair. How was it possible that a Morris girl, who had a career that required so much thought, could be so incredibly dense when it came to her personal life?

"How's everybody else?" I asked, not wanting to delve further.

"Well, Mom's fine, even though she said Dad refuses to let her make flyers on his computer while hers is in the shop. And, let's see, Dad had to go to the hospital briefly. He started having chest pains after he got into it with Kizaar again. He was in and out though. They gave him some medication and sent him home. Afterward, he had one of his nice spells and took Mom and Kizaar to the Lake of the Ozarks for the weekend. Didn't last long. Seems that on the way back home, he transformed back into Mr. Grouch."

"What did he fight with Kizaar about?" I asked, as if I really wanted to get into that right now, after the day I'd had.

"You know Dad. He'll find anything. He accused Kizaar of throwing a plastic bottle in the aluminum can receptacle. Of course, then he started pulling out stuff from the past, especially that Kizaar didn't want to take a job with him in his real estate business. You know Dad never lets that go and brings it up in every argument they have. But hey, two days ago he had another one of his turnaround moments and took us all to dinner. We haven't done that since you were here."

"I don't understand why Kizaar stays with them."

"Well, you know he wouldn't if it weren't for Mom. If it were up to Dad, he would probably be out on the street somewhere. Dad hit the roof and threatened to throw me out of this house when I told Kizaar he could stay with me. It is technically Dad's place—"

"Technically?" I scoffed. "What do you mean technically?"

No answer.

Mom and Dad let her live rent-free in the house that we grew up in after she filed for bankruptcy a couple of years ago.

"Well," she finally said after a long pause, "I'm not going to hold you. Tell Alton I said 'hi.'" Her voice was low and totally dismal now.

"Sure thing," I said and ended the call. At some point I knew I was going to have to take the time to go hang out with her a bit.

The light in her head seemed to click on for at least a little while when I last visited her for a few days.

I jumped as Alton came up behind me, startling me as he slipped his arms around my waist and pulled me into him. His broad chest pressed hard against my back and his warm breath whisked across the back of my neck.

"Didn't mean to scare you," he said softly into my ear. "I've got a good idea. Slip into your gear and meet me by the garage."

"Oh, you kinky thing you. You want me to slip into my Victoria's Secret best?"

"If you want to ride like that, hey, I don't have a problem with it," he joked as he continued holding me from behind, swaying side to side. "Let's go for a ride, then come back for a light spaghetti and salad dinner, okay?"

"Sounds good to me, All Good," I said as I turned to face him. Alton held my waist and firmly slid his hands up my body, slowing as his hands climbed over my breasts. He moved his hands up to my face and held it securely in place as he kissed me. I felt his thin mustache and facial hair growing in. I thought it made him look even sexier, if that was possible.

I changed into a pair of jeans and a black pullover shirt from a stash of clothes that I kept at his place. We met in front of the garage, where he had pulled out his motorcycle and our helmets. We geared up and I took my place behind him, anxious for a chance to get close to him and wrap my arms around his thick chest. Damn, I was lucky.

It was a comfortably warm evening as we rode to Edgewater Park. Alton didn't tell me where we were going, but I didn't mind. I was enjoying riding behind him under the Cleveland moon. We rode up Warrensville Center Road to Mayfield. Cruised over to Chester and took I-90 to Memorial Shoreway.

Alton slowed his speed and we cruised alongside the lake. I leaned my head on his back and watched the waves roll in and fold against the shore.

Alton pulled into a parking space at Edgewater Park. A few couples walked leisurely hand in hand: some were sitting and holding each other, while others were kissing. It was early evening, and all of the tiny tots that usually besieged the park had gone home. Alton secured his bike and we strolled alongside Lake Erie and took a seat on one of the large boulders. We sat in pleasant silence for a few minutes, looking over the lake and listening to the waves collapsing against the rocks in the distance. This was another of Alton's stress-relieving tactics that worked well for us.

"Thanks. I really needed this today."

Alton rubbed my thigh.

After a while, I spoke again. I told him about my conversation with Jaelene and the TVs.

"Doesn't she still owe you about four grand?"

"I don't count on seeing that money again, but I let her think I'm waiting on her to pay me back. Otherwise it wouldn't even cross her mind. Not like it does anyway." I rested my head on Alton's shoulder as I told him about Dad and Kizaar.

"What's up with Pops? He switches back and forth, doesn't he? Seems like one minute you're telling me about something nice he's doing for your mom and brother. The next minute he seems mean and ornery as hell."

"Well, I really do think this is his way of dealing with Uncle James's death."

"Like you said before, that was twenty-some-odd years ago."

"Yeah, but do you ever get over losing your best friend? Your twin brother? From what I understand, they were practically joined at the groin. They were fraternal twins and best friends and hardly had any friends outside of each other. They were starting the real estate business together that Dad has. Dad's never been able to utter a word out loud about him since his death, so no one ever tries to get him to talk about him. They were total opposites, but stuck to each other like . . . like Vanella on Alton," I said with a smile, happy with my twist on a cliché.

Alton gave a small chuckle and said, "I can understand that then. But have you noticed that he's sour only with your mother and Kizaar? He treats you and Jae like you're both . . . well, like you're both All Good." He rubbed my back.

"Still corny!" I exclaimed. "But, actually, no, I never thought about that. You're right, come to think of it. My guess is that it's because Mom and Kizaar are the ones closest to him. I'm states away, and Jaelene lives a few miles away. Mom and Kizaar live in the same house with him, and that's probably why they get the brunt of his mood swings. His mood swings with Kizaar have been picking up and getting pettier each day. I'm getting a little worried about it."

"I don't know. I think there's something else there, but, hey, I could be wrong." Alton shrugged and leaned his cheek against the top of my head.

We sat quietly again. I watched and listened to the lake as the waves ushered in thoughts that washed over my brain.

"What would you think about my leaving Kawamichi and starting a business of my own?"

"Mmm," Alton said, without as much as a wince. He fell silent for a long time before he continued, "What type of business?"

"Well, that's what I'm not sure about. But the idea that's been rolling around in my head the most has been a bookstore with multicultural titles and a café that would offer different ethnic treats. It wouldn't be a full restaurant though."

"It would be a risk."

"You know I'm a risk-taker. That's not the problem."

"And you'd have to work your butt off even more than you do now for Kawamichi. Can you handle that?"

I leaned my head back so that I could see his face and stare at him, because surely he was joking. "You know I could handle that. I love working hard. I know I would love it even more if I were working for myself. It would have much more meaning and give me a sense of purpose. And no Dexter McKleons to deal with, either? Yeah, I think I could handle that. With a bookstore, I would create literacy programs for children and adults and hold literary events like spoken-word sets and open-mic sessions, host book signings and—"

Alton laughed softly. "Listen to yourself. Do you *really* have to ask me if it's a good idea?"

"Well, I'd have to give up a steady paycheck from Kawamichi and scale back on my lifestyle. Like sell the Lexus and maybe pick up a used Corolla or Cavalier or something for cheaper car payments. At least until I get the business off the ground."

"Like I said, it's a risk, and you have to be ready to take that risk. Me? I think you can do anything that you set your mind to. You are an outstanding, ambitious, generous, courageous, and strong woman. God knows I wouldn't want to be on your bad side." He faked a block with his left arm. "And you know I'm always here for you, babe."

I knew he was.

"Thank you," I said as I squeezed his arm tightly. "Thanks for being my best friend."

"And when we get married you won't even have to do that if you don't want to. Work, in your own business, that is," Alton added. He nudged me with his shoulder. "I think we'd be able to manage off my salary, you know."

I didn't say another word. I just sat next to him, listening to the waves harmonizing to the beat of Alton's heart.

Five

"JUST LIKE BITCHES TO be late," Synda said as she sucked down more than half the loaf of bread that the waiter brought to our table.

I looked at my watch. "Late? What are you talking about? It's only a quarter to six." I reached for my glass and took a sip of Pinot Grigio.

"Well, I'm hungry as hell. All I know is if they don't get here soon, I'm going to order and start eating without them." Synda took a sip of her Long Island Iced Tea. "Excuse me," she said to the waiter as he passed our table. "Can you bring us some more bread, please?" She dangled the empty cloth-covered basket at him and forged a smile.

He hesitated for a split second, as if reminding himself that he was at work to serve customers—even the uncouth ones—and replied, "Yes, I'll bring that right out for you, ma'am. Can I get you ladies anything else while you're waiting for the remainder of your party?"

"No," I said. "But thank you." The waiter graciously nodded

and walked toward the kitchen with the empty bread basket. He was a cutie.

I had already planned for meager eatings tonight. The plan was to search the menu for light fare, but something other than a salad. I didn't feel like hearing a bunch of lying women with near knockout bodies asking me if I was on a diet and telling me that I didn't need to be.

I was doing great at it again—the goal of relosing the ten pounds that I had gained for the umpteenth time. I had resumed sessions with my personal trainer, who basically told me that my body went to hell without him to push me through my workouts. Armando had thrown his hands up in the air when he saw me, as if to say that I'd ruined all the good work that he had done and that he would have to start over from scratch. Now, I wasn't happy with my body, but I knew it wasn't *that* bad. Personal trainers could always be counted on for the slanted truth when their well of cash has been sucked dry.

This morning, I'd gone to the gym feeling great. As had become my routine over the past few weeks, I swallowed a few Hydroxycuts and two cups of water to get me pumped up for the workout. After the workout, I took a Metabolife, drank a Slim-Fast shake for breakfast, then ate a meal bar and another Metabolife pill for lunch. A revisit with my reflection in the mirror early this morning told me that the work had paid off already. I eyed a loss of somewhere around three-eighths of an inch around my hips—or at least I thought I did. I didn't want to ruin my pace now with a good Southern-style meal, even if it was the mouthwatering, tantalizing, and lip-smacking cooking of Alexandria's on Main.

I spoke to Synda to keep her hungry lips from slurping up

the tablecloth. "Synda, don't start anything with Sherron to-night either."

Synda tilted her drink, almost to the point of spilling it. "Miss Thang does not like me. She didn't start with the jabs until after you told her that . . . that . . . well, until you told them about . . . about *that*."

"She doesn't dislike you, just what you did. And you know how women can be. We all look out for each other."

"But it's none of their business. If you decided to let it go, then what's it to them?"

I understood how Synda felt, but, to be honest, I really didn't have any sympathy for her. My only concern was to smooth things over so we could have a good time without Synda and Sherron bickering like they usually did, although the more they drank, the better they got along.

"I truly don't feel like seeing the two of you go back and forth at each other's throats tonight."

"If she starts in on me, I'm not going to just sit here and take it while she finds reasons to go off on me." She lowered her lids and rolled her eyes slowly as she pulled the glass up to her lips. "Humph! Speak of the devil." Synda took a deliberately long swig and stared at the entrance behind me.

I turned around and saw a smiling Sherron gracefully making her way through the restaurant. She was dressed in a form-fitting black pantsuit with glistening silver accessories. She blended well with the tranquil surroundings of the room. Sherron wore her hair natural and cropped closely to her head, and the large silver earrings she donned sandwiched her face like bookends. She looked like an African dignitary, or at least some important person with a lot of power. I could have sworn that each candle flame on the tables bowed in her direction as she strolled by.

Sherron was the oldest of our girl group. When I first met her at Case, she had just enrolled her youngest child in kindergarten and was looking for something constructive to do with her life. Her husband, Daylon, was a sports agent and had a handful of Cleveland Indians and AAA players. He was constantly on scouting trips and entertaining current and prospective clients, so Sherron stayed home to raise the girls. One day, six years into the marriage, Daylon came home and asked her for a divorce. Sherron said she didn't know what she'd done to make Daylon take up with a younger woman. She was crushed, and that's when we'd gotten closer.

After Daylon moved out, I went to her Beachwood home on a daily basis and cooked and cleaned house for her and the girls. I talked with her, listened, and basically offered the support she needed. It wasn't the first time I had done something like that for a divorce-distraught girlfriend, and I was sure it wouldn't be the last. I just wanted to make sure nobody would have to do that for me. It took about seven months for Sherron to be able to open the blinds and let the sun in again. She'd been a mess.

"Hey, girl," she said to me as she reached our table. She leaned over and gave me a tight cheek-to-cheek squeeze, then looked down at Synda, munching on a fresh slice of buttered bread.

"Synda," Sherron said, after draining her voice of all emotion.

"Sher-*ron*," Synda returned, heavily emphasizing the last syllable.

"Look," I said, "can we get through one night without you two getting into it with each other?" I alternated a glare between the both of them. "Need I remind everyone that we are grown women here?"

"Yes," Sherron said as the waiter pulled out her chair. "I'll leave that high-school nonsense to my three girls at home."

"Hey, just in the nick of time," I said to Medena and Zandra as they arrived at the table. The pair looked back and forth between Synda and Sherron, who locked eyes like two razor-tagged cocks in a cock fight.

"Are these two starting up already? Can we all get a good drink down first?" Zandra said. The waiter seated her and Medena, then took their drink orders.

Medena, Zandra, and I met five years ago while building a house for Habitat for Humanity. Community service was something that kept me grounded, and it was great working with other women who had the same drive. We began doing volunteer work together, and I found out a few weeks later that Sherron was already good friends with Medena. Zandra and I discovered common roots back in North St. Louis—hence, the formation of our little girl group.

"A couple of apple martinis, and I might be putting that waiter in my back pocket tonight," Zandra joked as he went to retrieve our drinks. "You never know when Darien or Kenard might start acting up, and I'll need a new little thing on my arm."

"Oh, I hear you, girl. He looks a little young, but you know that's a good thing," Synda said. Everyone giggled except Sherron, who merely smirked. I made a mental note to myself to buy her another drink.

"All right, girls," I said, and ventured to change the mood. "We might as well get started. Football season is upon us and once again it's time for—Football 101."

"I still don't see the purpose of this," Sherron said. "Why should women have to bend over backward to learn football just to please a man? I mean, even after we did this last year, I still didn't want to waste a Sunday watching football. I don't care who it's with."

"Oh, great. Coming from a woman whose husband divorced *her*," Synda jabbed at Sherron.

"Yeah?"

Sherron placed her right elbow and forearm on the table and slowly leaned forward toward Synda. The rest of us looked away because we knew what was coming next. It always did.

"Well, at least I didn't get drunk in college, sleep with and get myself pregnant by my so-called best friend's man, and then go off and marry him. That's probably why you lost the baby. God knew your trifling ass didn't deserve to raise any kids." Sherron's words were sharp and distinct to be sure that they pierced the target.

"God knows you got enough kids for all of Cleveland." Synda was ready to fire back. She crossed her arms in front of her chest. "And why you gotta keep bringing that up? If Van forgave me years ago, why do you keep bringing it to the surface?"

Medena picked up the bread basket and offered it first to me, then to Zandra, who took a piece and buttered it. We knew it was best to let them get a little bit out now, and then agree to stop talking to each other as they usually did. Only then and a few drinks later could we all finally have a good time. Even the two of them would have a good time with each other—until they realized it, of course.

"Because for the life of me I can't understand why Vanella decided to forgive you and let you back in her life. If it was me, you can best believe that you wouldn't be sitting here at this table dining with me. Hell, you wouldn't be sitting anywhere had it been me. Unh-unh. There's no way I would let your trifling behind back around so you could do that shit again. Once a ho, always a ho."

Zandra nibbled on a piece of buttered bread and added, "Give Van some credit now. Ol' girl ain't all that stupid. Ask Synda if she's even met Alton." Zandra smothered a laugh and tapped the side of her face with her freshly French-manicured nails. Synda ran her fingertip back and forth over the scar on her forehead. I cut Zandra my best pissed-off look for being the best little instigator she knew how to be.

It was true; I forgave Synda after I found and fell in love with Alton. I felt I had to. We'd been friends since childhood and in two different states. You can't drop a friend who's been your friend for twenty years.

Synda and I had grown up together in St. Louis and had been inseparable hellions on foot. We did everything together. After my family moved next door to her family in North St. Louis, we became practically joined at the aorta.

Synda played the role of protector in our friendship. Girlfriend had a loud, fast mouth and a hell of a punch. I was the shy one back then and Syn took it upon herself to shield me from the playground bullies. She seemed to enjoy it, like it gave her something constructive to do with her fists. Some of her boldness eventually rubbed off on me, which became handy when I went to Sumner High without the enforcer at my side.

We went to Herzog Elementary and Northwest High School together. Then my family moved and I transferred to Sumner High. But that didn't stop us from being close. When I chose

Case Western Reserve University in Cleveland for college, Synda picked computer science as a major and decided to follow suit. I didn't think she really cared much about Case or Cleveland, but she just didn't want to go to any school without me. I was glad she had—at least at the time.

We did have a lot of history behind us. But just because you forgive someone doesn't mean you throw all your God-given senses out the window. The Synda/Tucker fiasco became just another stone in my wall of disbelief in long-lasting and loving relationships. Tucker was my first love, and he had said that he loved me, too, but I guess love wasn't enough to make him resist my best friend.

Synda knew he was my first love, too. I had never talked to her about why she did it because, to me, there was no explanation. Talking about it would only make me angrier. Plus, after I fell in love with Alton, it didn't matter. I forgave her and told her that after all she put our friendship through to get him, she'd better treat him good. I even promised to beat her ass if she didn't. And I meant it.

I invited Synda over only when I knew Alton would not be there. I trusted Alton; that wasn't the problem. I didn't know if I was afraid that it could happen again. Maybe I was.

"Well, thank goodness there are more forgiving people in this world. Everybody makes mistakes, Sherron. You of all people should know that," Synda responded, ignoring Zandra's comment.

"Getting pregnant by your best friend's man is not a mistake. That's reflective of an inherent personality trait. In other words, you're a screwed-up individual. Obviously you got that from your daddy. If I recall, he's got eight kids and your mother has two, right?"

Medena glanced at her watch and faked a yawn. Zandra quietly extended her bread across the table to Medena, and they toasted their toast.

Sooner or later my girls were bound to take it to the street and pummel each other to death, so I decided to end it.

"All right, I forgave her, Sherron, and that's that. It wasn't immediately. We didn't speak for what, two years?" I gestured toward Synda, who nodded in agreement. "You know, we women are always getting mad at each other and dismissing each other for life. Ever notice that guys don't do that? They do the right thing and just consider the girl a slut and it's back to the court for B-ball."

"You can forgive and forget, but that don't mean you gotta let a trifling wench back in your life," Sherron countered.

"Synda's not a trifling wench and she's not a ho," I said, as if I were saying it for the thousandth time, which I was. "She made a mistake, but should she be shot for that? Never mind," I quickly added before a ready Sherron could whip out a Nine. "Everybody makes mistakes, and I believe that she's a good person today."

The waiter brought our drinks to the table. We quickly glanced at the familiar menu, gave him our orders, and then it was back to business.

"Well, why don't you start Football 101 off for us, Medena, with a football play?" I said.

Synda and Sherron both retired to the backs of their chairs, waiting for the bell to ring for round two.

"Okay, this week, I learned all about the defensive blitz play," Medena said in her best schoolgirl show-and-tell imitation. "A defensive blitz play is when a defensive player rushes across the line of scrimmage in order to attack, uh, tackle, the quarterback. They have more men at the line of scrimmage than the offensive team can block."

"Very good," I said in my best teacher imitation as the girls softly clapped at the table. The low-decibel claps still drew stares from those within earshot of us.

"Okay," I said. My eyes played roulette around the table. I purposely stopped on Synda to rescue her from the funk swamp that she was drowning in. "Synda, why don't you tell us about a football player you learned about this week. Who is he, what position does he play, and what have you learned about him?"

"Well, Miss Morris," Synda said as she reached down in her purse and pulled out a magazine clipping and slowly displayed it around the table. Zandra tried to snatch it out of her hand, but Synda pulled back quickly as if she was expecting such a move. "My player is Jamel White. Number thirty of the Cleveland Browns. He's a running back and he is *fine*. This is his second year in the NFL, so that means I still consider him a rookie."

"He's only a rookie if it's his first year playing," Zandra said, elated that she knew what a rookie was.

"I know. But he's still rookie fresh, meaning I can make a move and put a hurting on him. Next thing you know, I'm living large! I'm paid! Hmm . . . five-nine, two hundred and some pounds. Mmph! I can live with that. I can teach him a few plays myself and have him swinging in the trees." Synda laughed as she and Zandra exchanged high fives.

"Okay," I said, "so you think he's cute. But what does a running back do?"

"Who cares? As long as we're getting paid." Synda gave Zandra another high five. Sherron uncrossed her arms, looked at me, and laughed.

"Synda, I think you're missing the point of Football 101," Medena said. "You're supposed to learn a different something about the game each week so you can surprise your man with your knowledge of and interest in football, instead of complaining about him watching the game every Sunday. So you can curl up and share the game with him from time to time. I really don't think your man is going to be interested in how rich and fine you think Jamel White is."

Medena became interested in football last year. She'd been married two years, and was already sharing *Cosmo* articles with us on things like "new ways to please your man in bed." She actually believed in the "until death do us part" line of her wedding vows, and funneled more energy into her marriage than lightning to a rod.

"Or the fact that you're scheming on how to get into the pants of a rookie and get paid," Zandra added.

Synda shrugged and looked goggle-eyed as she sipped her wine.

"Let me show you how it's done," I offered to an uninterested Synda. "My player of the week is Marshall Faulk. He's a running back for the St. Louis Rams, number twenty-eight. He's a leading rusher in the NFL and had several seasons where he rushed for over a thousand yards. He's the second player in history to surpass a thousand yards rushing and receiving in the same season. He's been invited to the Pro Bowl five times already . . . boy is bad!" I finished excitedly.

"Yeah, but is he fine?" Synda asked. Medena, Zandra, and even Sherron smothered laughs at Synda's shallow question. They were probably interested in the answer more than Synda.

"Is he fine? Being fine don't have a thing to do with being a badass player in the NFL," I said.

"So that must mean he's not fine." Synda looked over at Medena. Medena and Zandra laughed at Synda's mindless antics.

"No, I'm not saying he's not fine. If that were the point, I'd say the brother looks good. But that's not the point." I hated giving in to the expected shallow female point of view when it came to football. "We're trying to learn tidbits about football so you all can share in your men's likes and impress them," I said.

"See, now why can't our men impress us? Why do we always have to bend over backward to get into what they like?" Sherron asked the group.

"Well, humph! Nothing wrong with bending over backward for your man. I don't see what the problem is," Synda said with a sneer in her voice.

"And you're a crazy Rican wench, too. Did I say that earlier? I meant to." Now Sherron had laughter in her voice when she spoke to Synda. Then she addressed everyone: "I don't like football and I'm not going to pretend that I do just to please my man."

"What man?" Medena asked in jest.

"Screw all you shrews," Sherron replied. She looked around the restaurant. "Where's our waiter? I'm getting hungry sitting here smelling everybody else's food."

She was right. The restaurant was filled with savory spices that tingled my taste buds and teased my nose. The aroma of sage, lemon pepper, and cayenne hovered in my nostrils and had fun taunting my empty stomach. But I still had my eating plan.

"Finally, we agree on something," Synda said to Sherron.

As if on cue, the waiter brought our plates out in two trips and disappeared when we assured him there was nothing else we needed at that time.

"Okay, ladies, a football tip, and then we'll end this week's session. This is for next Sunday. Before you settle down to watch the game with your man, I want you to go out and buy yourself the jersey of his favorite team and, if possible, his favorite player. But get either a woman's cut jersey, or go to the boys' section and buy a jersey that hugs your body. Make sure it fits snug now." I painted a picture with my hands as I spoke, framing my breasts and smoothing down to my waist. "Snug enough to the point where you almost have to wiggle into it."

Zandra demonstrated and gave her healthy body a wiggle in her chair. I think the chair submitted its approval.

"Make sure it wraps around the body tight and hugs all your curves and stuff," I said.

"I like the sound of that," Medena said. She nodded and chewed.

"And before you wear it on game day, shower, put on his favorite smell-goods, and slip on nothing but the football jersey. Nothing. And make sure it falls short, like just below the cheeks there. But not up around your waist . . . *Synda*." I looked at her pointedly.

Synda nearly choked on a piece of chicken. She patted her chest, took a sip of wine, then held her mouth open and gestured innocence with her arms.

"Mmm, all right, girl. Now you're giving some tips," Zandra said as she cackled and tossed her head from side to side.

"Why do we have to sex ourselves up in order to please our men?" Sherron dared to go there again.

We all huffed at the same time.

"I mean, we're all professional women—" Sherron began.

"We?" Synda asked. "The last I heard, you were sitting at home collecting alimony and child support." She leaned against the table. "Does it really take fifteen grand a month to raise three kids?"

"Don't you talk to me no more tonight."

Synda raised both hands as if to surrender.

Sherron continued, "*We* are engineers and managers. Why then should we go home and have to lower ourselves and become Miss T and A just to please our men? Why can't they learn to respect us as the professionals that we are and learn to tame that perverted desire to have a woman on display at all times? We're more than just walking vaginas, you know."

"As professional women, why can't we have balance?" Medena asked. "I admit that I like a little spice in my sauce, too. What's wrong with doing our thing at work, coming home, and getting a little kinky in the bedroom? Because we're professional women, we can't loosen up? We got to stay uptight and be hardened bitches or stuck-up snobs twenty-four hours a day?

"Honey, I have no problem putting on a little strip tease for Aneaus from time to time. I kinda like the football tips. Aneaus definitely noticed last year and even started teaching me a little about the plays when we watched games together. No offense to you," Medena said, looking at Sherron, "but I believe all that uptightness is one reason why a lot of us end up divorced."

"Oh? So I have to become a trick to please my man? If I have to degrade myself to stay married, I guess I'll just be divorced then."

"And so you are," Synda said in violation of their agreement.

"What's up with this trick thing?" Zandra asked rhetorically. "You seem to have a thing for tricks."

"That's because it was a trick that ruined my marriage. My no-good man dumped me for a trick, so I'll be damned if I become one."

Medena twisted her mouth as she chewed her food. "I'm not

even going to comment on that one. Come on, everybody, eat up so we can get to the Spy Bar before it gets too late."

We finished our meals and I succeeded in getting through it without anyone noticing what I was eating, or rather how little I ate. We left the waiter a sizable tip and Zandra blew him a kiss that put a smile on his pretty-boy face, then we headed to the Spy Bar in the Warehouse District.

Six

WEST SIXTH STREET IN the Warehouse District was buzzing with mostly twenty- and thirty-something socializers. The street was congested with Mercedes Benzes circling the block futilely in search of parking spaces; double-parked Lexuses with fresh tickets from traffic police; bumper-to-bumper BMWs that successfully found real estate for the night; and taxis with flashing taillights, anxiously awaiting the next ride.

Clusters of people stood on the sidewalks laughing, talking, macking. Couples strolled the street looking for a venue: Sixth Street Down Under for jazz; Liquid/Fusion for conversation and eye candy; Cafe Van Gogh for a drink with a sweetie and the chance to impress or fool her with knowledge of art; and the Spy Bar for expensive drinks, a seductive atmosphere, and getting your groove on across the dance floor. Cleveland doesn't have as many spots as big-time New York or sunny L.A., but what it does offer makes your body hum when there is a need for a tune.

The large wooden door at the entrance of the Spy Bar belonged at the entrance to somebody's castle somewhere. Just inside the club, the room was darkened with a mystic appeal. The comfy design of little coves was closed off enough to afford guests with privacy, yet open enough for inclusion. Near the dance floor, cool leather couches rested in front of brick fireplaces; tall, sleek stools dotted the bar area.

The ladies and I took a seat in front of one of the sultry fireplaces. Medena and I perched on the plush leather sofa while Synda, Sherron, and Zandra sat in the single leather chairs across from us. A waitress, dressed in a tasteful black minidress, came by and took our drink orders. She returned with apple martinis for all of us, except for Synda, who'd ordered another Long Island Iced Tea.

I heard my cell phone ring in my purse. It was Alton. He was out with the boys, but he'd called to arrange a little rendezvous at my place later that evening. I could barely talk to him without the ladies acting like little schoolgirls teasing me.

"So, how is Mr. Goode?" Medena asked after we ended the call.

"Oh, he's fine," Synda butted in. "The man is about ready to propose, but Miss Morris here is scared. She's going to turn him down if he does," Synda said matter-of-factly.

"What?" Medena asked. Her leather skirt made a raspy sound against the couch as she shifted her body in my direction. "Alton proposed and you said no?"

"Are you crazy?" Zandra chimed in. "Now, Alton's one man that even I would say yes to." Her voice rose an octave in amazement.

I gasped, not quite prepared for the immediate interrogation that I'd been thrown into, thanks to Synda. "I—"

"She's been quoting marriage and divorce statistics again."

"It's not only that. I—"

"And you all know the thing about her parents still being

married but her father treats her mother like shit for nothing," Synda said.

Sherron said, "Well, men will be men."

"I just—" I began again.

Synda cut me off. "Sherron, she was with you through your divorce. She also went through divorces with a few of our college friends and folks back home in St. Louis. Let's see, there was Allison and Dauntae, uh, Monya and Isaac, Layne and Jerametrius. Come to think of it, none of them even made it five years. No, I take that back. Layne and Jerametrius. Layne and Jerametrius got married right after I did. And—"

"Synda, um, can I talk about me and my reason for not wanting to get married?" I was used to Synda's intrusive personality, and I only told her what I didn't mind the other ladies knowing. If I did mind, Synda always ended up telling them anyway.

"Oh, by all means," she said.

All conversation stopped, and the ladies had all eyes focused on me.

"The O Theory." I sipped.

"Oh, Lord. Here we go again." Synda pursed her lips tight and rolled her shoulders.

The girls looked puzzled. "What the O?" Medena asked.

"Isn't it Obvious?" I asked.

The ladies stared, each looking as if they were waiting for some valid reason, some reasonable explanation that would explain why I didn't want to marry a fine specimen like Alton. I already knew that there would be no explanation good enough. Not even the O Theory.

"The best way to ruin a good relationship is to marry the man you love." I waited. Waited for somebody to say something. But they were all obviously trying hard to make some sort of sense out of what I said. "First of all, Alton has not proposed. Second of all, I love Alton and I want to be with him forever. That's why I don't want to marry him."

Medena's eyes widened. "That makes absolutely no sense at all. You love the man, so you *don't* want to marry him?"

"And y'all talk about me being crazy," Synda said and flipped her hand in the air.

"Oh, you *are* a crazy Negro," said Sherron. "Excuse me, a crazy Rican Negro."

"I've never seen anything happy about marriage. I don't have many friends, besides Synda, who have been married beyond five years. Those who are still married are cheating, thinking about cheating, talking about divorce, or are just plain miserable. And let's not even get into the divorces. People spend all that money on a wedding ceremony, then they're ready to cut each other's throats in the courtroom a few years later. I can do without all the drama."

"Okay, Van, so how does not getting married guarantee you a long relationship?" asked Zandra.

"I don't know, but it does. Seems like there's something about that piece of paper that makes relationships go bad. Ever notice how people can be in a relationship for years, but as soon as they get married, they're off to divorce court?"

"Hmm . . . Jackie and Mark Jackson come to mind," Zandra said, speaking of a couple we had all met while volunteering at the Urban League.

"Exactly," I said. "They were together what, fourteen years or so, then got married and wound up in divorce court a couple of years later?" I looked at Synda. "And Monya and Isaac. Monya and Isaac were together seven years before they got married. Here it is two years later, and they're getting a divorce."

"You don't really know what happened in those marriages. Even so, that doesn't mean that will happen to you," Medena said. "You and Alton couldn't be more made for each other than anybody I've ever met. Two motorcycle-riding, beach-hopping fools." She laughed.

"I'm kinda liking the Oprah thing," I said.

"Oprah thing?" they asked simultaneously, their faces puzzled.

"Yeah, Oprah. Look at her. Oprah is just chilling with Stedman. Seems like as far back as you can remember Oprah, you can remember Stedman by her side. But do you see her begging Stedman for a wedding ring?"

"Uh . . . I don't think Oprah has to beg anybody for anything," Sherron said.

"Got that right," Synda said.

"Is that the 'O' in O Theory?" Medena asked.

I hesitated. "Umm . . . marriage is just Old and Outdated. A thing of the past," I responded.

"I'm feeling that," Zandra said. She directed her eyes upward as if she were reading her thoughts in the air. "Women are always looking for a man to marry them. That's so 1950-ish. Really. Why are we women so unhappy with ourselves, or feel so inadequate without a man, that we push men into marriage or marry the first one who proposes?"

"So what are you saying, Little Miss Zandra? That women should let men have all the pussy they want and let them decide if they want to keep us around or not? I can tell you what would happen, all right. We'd have a bunch of pussy-happy maniacs running around from spread to spread, getting pussy-full until they all just welled up and died. None of them would marry any-body at all."

"Sherron, I think you're a little too bitter right now to be talk-ing about men and marriages. I don't think you'll be happy unless they cut off the dicks of every man in Cleveland," Zandra said.

"That would be a good start, yes," Sherron said, and nodded. She paused, then added, "Marriage is just a contract slanted in the favor of men. Women give up their identities, work full-time jobs, and still come home and do all the cooking, cleaning, and taking care of the kids, then they want you to stay up and give them some before they go to bed. I tell you. The first time I mar-ried for love, but if there's a next time, it will most definitely be for money," she scoffed and leaned to the side, scoping the room for possible financially qualified candidates.

Synda waved her arm and snapped a "Z" in the air. The music drowned out the snap, but we laughed at the motion anyway.

I said, "My point is that we as women are always the ones chasing after a ring and trying to get a man to marry us. It's like the ring and the ceremony are the actual prizes. I like being happy with my life as it is. Finding someone to share all this hap-piness with would be just another sweet potato for the pie. So, I can get into what Oprah is doing. I like it. It's the Oprah way."

"Hell, if you think about it, why do we have to get married at all unless we're ready to have children?" Zandra asked.

We call Zandra Miss Independent. As the youngest of our bunch, she took pride in being able to take care of herself and to choose the man that she wanted to be with, unlike her intention-ally welfare-dependent mother. When Zandra's relationships moved to the comfortable stage and her man, or men, stopped doing the things he'd done when he first met her, girl was gone without a word. It was a sight to see sometimes. The poor little souls would still have their feet propped up on a coffee table, with dropped jaws, as they tried to figure out what happened in the wake of the breeze she left behind. And with Zandra, once you were dumped, there was no coming back.

Zandra is slightly left of a beauty queen. She is an average-looking young woman with a thick, but not fat, build. Her medium-length charcoal hair hangs loose to her chin and the only makeup she wears is eyeliner, which suits her small oval-shaped face just fine. There is nothing really special about her, but she obviously doesn't need the extras like the rest of us. Perhaps it is her confidence that draws men to her. She charms them like nothing I've ever seen.

Synda said, "I'm feeling you on that one, girl." They stared at her. Hard. Synda's input on anything about marriage or children is a pill to take. Living down a marriage to your best friend's boyfriend is not an easy thing to shake off among girlfriends. A tougher thing to do for Synda. She noticed all eyes on her, took another sip of her drink, and started bopping to the music. "I think I'm going to find a dance partner."

"Good idea," Sherron said. Her voice droned. The ladies laughed and Synda got up and slithered to the dance floor.

"I swear, Van, I'll never understand why you're still friends with her. But that's your decision, and I respect that." Sherron lifted her right eyebrow and gave up half a smile.

"Well, I'm going to add my two cents," Medena said. "People don't take marriage seriously anymore. It's a commitment, and people today get married and give up at the first sign of trouble. That's why a lot of marriages end up in divorce. People just don't give it a chance."

"Good speech," Sherron said. "Come back and talk to me in

about four more years. Let's see if you're still talking that shit then."

Medena waved Sherron off.

"Van's absolutely right, though," Sherron said. "It's the paper. As soon as you sign that paper, the good times are over, honey. Marriage don't benefit women. Daylon treated me like a queen until I signed that piece of paper. Then all of a sudden, he wasn't doing the nice things he'd done before. I moved in and he treated me like an instant maid. I gave up my management job, too. What you say about being a roommate? Hell, that's what I ended up feeling like. A damn roommate."

"So, why did *he* divorce *you* then?" Medena asked with a raised eyebrow.

"We're out here to have a good time. I'm not getting into all that tonight."

"Mmm-hmm. Good answer," Medena replied.

"Alton is a good man because he's got money. I will say that much," Sherron said. "With that said, I'm going to walk around a bit." Zandra decided to go with her.

"I agree with Sherron," Medena said. "Alton is one of the good guys. If he does propose, I don't think you should turn him down. Girl, you better look around. Look at what's out there. When you find a gem, you don't just toss him back."

"That's the point, Dena. I know he's a gem and I don't want to lose him. Just trying to figure out a way to make it last forever."

We talked for a little while longer before I spotted Sherron at the bar talking to a tall, handsome gentleman in a dark suit. He wasn't speaking though. It didn't look like he had a good chance to either. I saw Sherron's lips moving and him standing there. She stood stiffly with tight eyes. Then I saw him nod and walk away. He stretched his eyelids toward his hairline. He ballooned his cheeks, then slowly deflated them, blowing through his extended lips. He walked a few feet and shook his head before he struck up a conversation with what seemed to be one of his boys. He pointed Sherron out and laughed as he expressed absurdity with his face. Sherron had a scowl on her face as she tilted a wineglass and took a long swig.

"You can't base your relationship on your friends' or anybody else's relationships because you never know the truth. You know only what they tell you," Medena said.

"I got eyes," I said. That was all I could say. "Well, I'm going to get out of here. I'm meeting Alton tonight."

"I'm getting out of here, too. You go on and I'll let the others know."

I looked up and saw Synda on the hardwood dance floor jiggling and shaking between two men, one staring as if he were looking at half a crumb between her cleavage and the other keeping a watchful eye on her backside as if making sure that it didn't fall off.

My gait was slow on the way to my car. I wondered if any of my divorced friends told me a slanted story. Not that their marriages were any of my business, but I had placed heavy weight on their failed marriages. It was never their fault. It was always the fault of their husband, his job, his mother, his mid-life crisis, his infidelity, or something other than my girlfriends. I wondered.

I came home to Bob Marley, tropical flowers scattered about my condo, and a warm tub of bubbles in a candle-lit bathroom with a glass of sparkling apple juice on a tray. Two white chenille robes hung on a hanger behind the door. I peeled off my clothes and tested the water with my toe—nice—then I lowered myself into the tub, allowing the bubbles to rise up and swallow me. I leaned back and closed my eyes. Bob Marley suddenly grew louder as he pulled me into a dance with him on the beaches of Jamaica.

After a few minutes, a dark, naked figure entered the bathroom and joined me in my steamy soak. Alton pushed the power button and the Jacuzzi's jets pushed the inviting water into and around us. He lifted my feet, one by one, and gently massaged and kissed them before placing them back in the water. Silently he changed his position to move behind me, then he beckoned me to lean back and rest my head on his chest. We soaked there quietly. Amid the bubbles; amid the candles; and amid the music.

Seven

I FREAKED. I HAD never been furious at Alton, so I didn't quite know what to do. I sat frozen in my beach lounge chair after Alton picked up my ringing cell phone, twisted his body to the left, and pitched it into the Atlantic.

"Are you crazy? What the h— What did you just do?"

Alton didn't look at me. He didn't even respond. He glanced down, retrieved his *Motorcyclist* magazine, and backed his sexy tush into the beach lounge chair next to mine. He grunted loudly as his back hit the chair, but he still didn't say a word. He gracefully flipped through the magazine, looking at Suzukis, Harleys, and Ducatis like nothing had happened.

"Boy, have you lost your mind?" I stood wistfully before the ocean that had swallowed my phone as I tried to decide whether to begin my own search-and-rescue mission, flag down the nearest lifeguard, or curse Alton out. The latter I knew I'd have a hard time doing, no matter how angry I was. I managed a half-step toward the ocean before my instincts brought me to a grinding halt. I couldn't swim.

Alton pinched his lips together and masked a laugh through

his nose. He pursed his mouth, whistled an unrecognizable tune, and bobbed his head from side to side.

"What are you laughing at? What's wrong with you?" I was hot. Mad hot. But I had a hard time coming to a boil, even though I was trying. I needed to get angry at Alton so I could yell, scream, say something to him. My nostrils flared, and I clenched and unclenched my fists repeatedly.

Alton tried his best to look dumbfounded. "Oh, are you looking for this?" He reached down into the sand on his right and retrieved my silenced cell phone. The sun glazed his bouncing shoulders, and his hearty laugh was at full throttle. He just tickled himself to death. He held his left arm over his ripped stomach as if trying to keep his laughter from spilling out of his guts.

I stood frozen as I looked blankly at the cell phone in his hand, at the ocean, then at the cell phone again. I struggled to comprehend. I dug the toes on my right foot deeper into the sand as referees in my mind reviewed the instant replay reel and tried to make a call on the play.

"That was just a shell that I threw into the ocean. Old sleight-of-hand trick I learned as a kid." Alton blew across the top of his fingernails, buffed them against his toasted chest, then held them up as if he were examining the gloss. "Didn't you notice how much smaller it was than your cell phone? Pay attention. Geesh!" he added, in his best nerd imitation.

Realization finally ensued. My anxiety dropped, and I rushed Alton. Rushed him hard. Tackled him right in front of the lounger. We tumbled over the lounger and hit the hot sand, laughing and giggling. We wrestled playfully on South Beach, yards in front of the Marriott Resort and next to other raunchy vacationers, some of whom acted like they had placed bets and began whooping and jeering for one of us to be pinned.

"Come on, babe," Alton said as I eased off him. "I'm sorry." We were both holding our stomachs now. His hair was embedded with tiny white grains that gave me a glimpse of him as a seasoned gray-haired gentleman. "But why did you have to bring your cell phone to the beach? We're on vacation. If Kawamichi calls, what are you going to do? Pack up and take the next flight out?"

Kawamichi had already called earlier this morning. I had a message from Dexter, who let me know that he was there with the VP and that they, or most likely Dexter, had concerns over the Toyota account and needed to quickly discuss it with me as soon as possible. There was also a message from the paint manager, explaining a new and urgent quality issue with the waterborne paint that "was urgent and must be addressed immediately." Everything was urgent to them, while it had lost its meaning for me. They were well aware that I was on vacation for five days. As always, it didn't matter.

Alton suggested that we leave our cell phones behind. "No Kawamichi, no Eveready, no family problems. We're on vacation, okay?" His deep voice lifted as we brushed sand off each other. I dusted the age from his hair and the remaining sand from his back and legs. Alton started at the tip of my head and worked his way down, dusting sand from my hair, ears, cleavage, and belly button. He even blew in my middle for extra assurance.

"I think I can agree to that," I said. I turned my backside for a dusting and Alton obliged. Without giving it a second thought, I dropped the intrusive cell phone in my bag, retrieved my O magazine and plopped back down on the lounger.

"I'm going to the bar to get a piña colada. What can I get you?" Alton asked.

"I'll have the same."

"Two piña coladas. Coming right up, ma'am." Alton put on his sunglasses and shirt and headed to the bar. Boy was looking good. His hair was freshly cut, and the recently grown stubble on his face and his brown-tinted sunglasses completed his sexy, brazen look. I saw several women licking their lips as he strutted by. Asian women licked their lips. White and Latina women licked their lips. African American, Jamaican, and Haitian women all licked their dry and thirsty lips. But no way were they getting a taste of my man. Alton paid none of them any mind.

The September Miami sun was basting and roasting all of us. Summer's final laughter hung over the SoBe strip as people played volleyball, Frisbee, football, and Hacky Sack. Young college-aged beachers tossed around rainbow-colored beach balls and inflated footballs in the shallow waves while they drank from plastic cups and forty-ounce bottles.

That loose, carefree atmosphere was what Alton and I like about South Beach. We could hang out and be ourselves without having to worry about the bourgeoisie turning up their noses at us for being real. Although we both do pretty well in the financial department, neither of us suck up the urban yuppie image. Okay, maybe we aren't about tossing up forty ounces ourselves, but, if we wanted to, here we could and we'd blend right in.

I stretched my legs and yawned as the heat seared every follicle on my body. Before leaving for this trip, I'd lost a full inch off my hips and ten pounds. I admit that I still wasn't fully satisfied, although I had reached my goal of a size six, so I decided to keep dieting for another five to ten pounds and go for a size four. I knew from experience that once I went off the diet, I was going to gain back at least three pounds anyway. So, my strategy was to compensate for that three-pound gain by taking off an extra ten. That's the new female math.

I pulled two beach blankets out of my oversized bag and spread them atop the sand. I draped myself over one blanket and dipped my foot in and out of the hot sand as I studied the bodies of other women on the beach.

I reached behind me and unhooked my bikini top. The straps slid down the tops of my shoulders and I slipped my arms out one by one. I put the top in my bag and rolled my neck as a breeze whisked under my arms and around my breasts. The best feeling to my double Ds was to be able to sit in the sun and have the wind go where it rarely had the chance to go. They were too big to go braless under a tank or a tube top in the summer time like A and B cups. Running or going down a flight of stairs would hurt like hell.

The twins looked up and thanked me profusely.

I turned my head to the side as two more women walked in front of me further up the beach. One was Latina and the other was black. Both had smooth, flawless skin and well-toned, curvaceous bodies. The black girl's stomach was engraved with muscles, as if she did at least a thousand sit-ups a day. I looked at her stomach, then ran my hand across my fleshy abs. *Gotta do more sit-ups. Maybe a little less carrot cake and banana pudding past midnight might be good, too.* Damn, they looked good. *Yes, I've definitely got to lose ten more pounds. Maybe even fifteen.*

Another breeze from the ocean licked my nipples as a group of college-aged young men seemed to appear from nowhere. The first one passed me, abruptly whipped around to face his boys, and lost his footing. He wrapped his arms around the nearest of his friends to steady himself, causing his friend to topple backward and sending half the group tumbling to the sand in front of me like dominos. They quickly dug their faces out of the sand and scrambled back to their feet. Youngsters.

I reluctantly reached into my bag and pulled out a sheer black scarf and draped it over my shoulders. Sometimes the twins caused too much damned commotion.

"Look at you. Causing guys to trip and fall all over themselves. You're going to cause a medical emergency down here." Alton handed me a drink and sat down beside me on the towel.

"Oh, you saw that, huh?"

"Yeah. Saw the whole thing and cracked up. Young guys aren't as smooth as us older gentlemen folk."

"Is that right?"

"You know young guys can't watch breasts and do anything else at the same time." We laughed.

It was nice that Alton understood the boulder issues and had no problem with my taking off my top when we came here. Anyway, I think Alton kinda liked it. I suspected he got a kick out of watching guys try to get an eyeful. Perhaps he liked knowing that I was his prize and others could only dream.

"Don't I know it," I said.

Alton and I sat on the beach, sipped piña coladas, and talked. We stretched out and chattered about people on the beach, what we wanted to do in the next ten years and when we retired— seemingly everything. Alton loves listening as much as he loves talking. We could talk about anything at any given time. This time he seemed a little more talkative and deeper than ever.

We spent the next four days as usual: water skiing, playing beach games, shopping on the Strip, club-hopping, enjoying massages at the spa, and just plain relaxing and having a good time. We left our cell phones in the hotel room as promised, although we did spend fifteen minutes a night listening to messages. We needed to make sure there were no deaths, kidnappings, or anything of that nature, but everything else could wait until we returned.

On more than a few occasions, Alton's conversations skirted the matter of marriage. But when they did, or when I assumed that's where they were going, I steered them in a different direction. I could tell that he knew what I was doing. He would pause, smile a knowing smile, and then follow my lead.

"Let me see." Alton put aside a bike trade magazine when I returned from the surprise manicure and pedicure appointment that he'd made for me. After I showered and put on a white Victoria's Secret teddy, I snuggled up next to Alton on the king-size bed. Alton ran his warm hands over my fingers, brought them to his lips, and kissed them. His fingers trickled down my arms and I drew in my stomach as he continued over to the middle of my body and down to my toes.

"I love the French manicure on your toes. That is so sexy to me." He kissed my toes one by one. The touch of his lips shot sparks through me that lit my biddies on fire. He prowled slowly and kissed my ankles, then lifted my legs to touch his lips to each of my burning calves. My breaths quickened as he worked his way up to my knees and my outer thighs before coasting over my inner thighs, inching closer and closer to my warm spot.

He blew a cool breath across me and I released a helpless squeal as I impatiently pushed myself into his face. Alton grabbed my thighs, skewed my teddy, and pulled me closer into him while I anxiously pushed. His savory tongue tended to my powerful throbs and added a rising thunder that caused my lips to moisten. My back constricted and arched relentlessly. I moaned as Alton unsnapped my teddy and went at me with a force that squelched my moans and caused me to beg for a moment to catch my breath. My eyes flicked wide open several times, and I could only stare at the faint ceiling, unable to focus.

I reached down for Alton's head, but his unyielding strokes paralyzed my arm just above him. A slow-rising, bold rush took over my body. My arm tightened over my stomach and my legs quivered and shook hard. I closed in on Alton's head and embraced him. Then, little by little, I relaxed.

I tugged at Alton's firm shoulders and he pulled himself up on me, grazing my damp body as he came up. The cool room had grown hot, intensely hot, and my body felt drunk. My muscles tingled, relaxed, and succumbed to Alton as he filled me. I moaned. Alton moaned. I groaned. Alton groaned. My legs widened to accept more of him. He gave me more. He ran his tongue over my nipples, kissed my neck, and went deeper as my softness had asked him. Deeper. Together we rocked back and forth to the rhythm of his passion until my thighs attempted to choke Alton around his waist, gripping him in a tight, merciless squeeze and digging into his middle as his pace quickened. Then, fatigued, my legs fell limp.

Alton slowed and began to kiss me again. "You feel so good. I just can't stop," he whispered in my ear. His kisses lengthened and grew more determined. He stared into my eyes and gradually increased his pace again. His passion dripped onto my already wet cheeks. Alton closed his eyes. Another long moan radiated from his throat as his face narrowed and he achieved his goal.

Our hands clasped as we climbed together, higher and

higher. Finally we reached peak and yelled out in victory to let each other know that we had both arrived.

We harmonized together in the explosion.

"I love you," Alton whispered, out of breath and trembling.

"I love you, too," I said as the most pleasant feeling of exhaustion blanketed my body.

Tuesday was quiet. Most vacationers ended the last summer holiday on Monday night and packed up and returned to reality. Alton had planned it this way so that we could end our vacation with a quiet night to ourselves. That was Alton, a planning fool.

For our last night, Alton wanted to get slightly dressed up for a romantic oceanside dinner. That was so typical of him. When we were at home, Alton would cook dinner from time to time and have us dress up. Sometimes we wore formal gowns and tuxes; sometimes ethnic wear. He even had us dress in traditional Indian garb one evening when he prepared Indian dishes for us.

Alton was dressed in an off-white silk shirt that was opened to display an unassuming rope necklace. He wore off-white pants that accentuated his backside, which I loved. I dressed in a simple ankle-length black silk dress with spaghetti straps that was fitted on top but flowed in the breeze from my hips to my ankles. Alton insisted that we not wear shoes with our outfits—perhaps that was why he made that appointment for me to have a manicure and a pedicure at the hotel spa yesterday.

I ordered a garden salad, but Alton insisted that I eat a full meal. So, he ordered a filet mignon for me, medium rare, and lobster and clams for himself.

"I don't know why you keep dieting. If you ask me, you could put on a few pounds," Alton said.

"You're just saying that to be nice."

"No, I'm dead serious. I keep telling you that a man likes a little meat on his woman. We like a little something to hold on to at night." He grinned.

"Yeah, but not rolls and butter."

"All right now. You keep on and I'm going to have to find me a Star Jones. If I wanted a bone, I would have just picked one up right here on this beach."

"Yeah, that's what you say now. Let's see if you'll say that after I'm pregnant."

"Speaking of . . . We're going to have to negotiate on the kid deal, you know," Alton said.

"Negotiate on the kids?"

"Yeah. You want two. I want six."

"I'm not having six kids. You can forget that, my brotha."

"Like I said, we'll negotiate. I'm willing to drop down to five."

"Five? Okay, then, I'm willing to drop down to one."

"Wrong direction."

"You trying to tell me how to negotiate?" I put a little cute attitude in my voice as I fluttered my eyelashes at him.

"I go down, you go up. That's the way this thing works," Alton said, not budging.

The waiter brought dinner salads. Alton gazed into my eyes and gave me a gentle smile.

"Okay, I'll go back up to two kids," I said, just to please him. Alton was silent. He stared as I took a knife and began chopping the salad leaves.

"Hey, I'm not budging anymore. I'm the one who has to pop them out, not you," I said. Alton just licked his lips and smiled.

"That sexy lip-licking thing will not work on this one. I would have two—" My knife staggered against a solid mass. I moved the knife between the fork's prongs once more. It stalled. My heart stalled.

Alton smiled.

"What the—"

I pushed the field greens around with my fork. My heart suddenly dropped as my mind went through a list of possible causes for the blockage. I looked up at Alton. My throat fell to my stomach as he continued to quietly gaze and his smile seemed to confirm my guess. *Not yet, Alton. Please, not yet.*

I felt moisture rise on my hands and lubricate the knife and fork I held. I wrapped my hands around the utensils tighter and used the knife to toss the leaves that hid the culprit. I looked at it.

A broccoli stem.

"Something wrong?" Alton asked.

My heart hurt from its vigorous pounding on the walls of my chest. I wanted to keel over.

"Uh . . . no dress . . . no dressing. He forgot to bring our dressing on the side."

"Hmm. You're right."

Alton motioned to the waiter and brought his attention to our missing dressing while I coaxed my heart to take its place back on the left side of my chest. A breeze swooped in and dried the beads of sweat on my forehead. My heart calmed and I was about normal again when the waiter returned with a tiny covered serving tray.

"My apologies, madam." He bowed over the serving tray and lifted the top.

I didn't even see him coming. In a swift movement, Alton swooped down by my side on bended knee faster than Michael Johnson on a fast track with the wind blowing with him. "Vanella Morris," Alton said. His voice was low and determined.

He grabbed my quivering left hand as the waiter removed the diamond solitaire ring from the silver tray and handed it to Alton.

The air suddenly turned cold. My arms were covered with goose bumps and my naked toes curled under beneath the table. Every single hair on my body stood at attention while my mind went as limp as a wet leaf of lettuce.

"Vanella Morris, I love you. You are my world and my life."

The air felt thin. Cold and thin. My head was light . . .

"The last six years have been heaven with you. You are my best friend and my lover. I would want nothing more than to share the rest of my life with you."

. . . light as if it were about to fall from my neck. And my neck. My neck was thick and heavy. I couldn't swallow. Aw, hell.

"Vanella Morris, will you marry me?"

And with that, the rope began to unravel. With his stinging proposal, the tip of our relationship began to unwind. My mind began to undo all that we'd done in six years. It began to unwrap what was once tight and to unbind the bonds that had taken so much time to build. It had begun. No matter what I said or did from this point on, I could not undo what had just been done. I would not be able to stop the unraveling, the unwrapping, nor the unbinding. From here on out, it was finished.

If I said yes, then I knew that there would be a time limit on our happiness before our relationship died as half of the matrimonial unions had before us, whether it was like the countless divorces or the marriages that fizzled to a relationship of roommates or enemies. If I said no, the tension from then on would surely be insurmountable and would tear us down until we finally grew apart and went our separate ways. We were essentially doomed from this point forward. There was nowhere for our relationship to go but down. It was the beginning of the end.

The air droned in the channels of my ears, then it was quiet. I stared past Alton and imagined I could actually see the wind twirl and ebb like the ocean below it. The sun had abandoned me, leaving me alone in my mind to sit in my gloom.

The waiter retreated to the background and stood next to a glass door. Two sappy-faced waitresses stood behind the door, dabbing their eyes with napkins as they watched Alton and looked as if they wished he were proposing to them instead. One held her hand over her heart like she was reciting the pledge of allegiance. Goldie next to her stood with watery eyes and a hand covering her mouth. Both were ringless.

I took Alton's face in my hands. How could he do this to me? I loved him. I would have never proposed to him because I loved him so much and I wanted us to last forever.

Forever doesn't come with marriage. Not these days. Not in the new millennium.

My vision blurred as tears welled in my eyes and my legs bounced ferociously. I couldn't believe that we had reached the top and were now about to begin our slow decline. I looked into his eyes, which were filled with tears of excitement that I knew I would have to disappoint. His precious dark brown eyes searched my face for my answer. His lips—those lips that I have always loved—were slightly parted, coercing me to say yes.

I pulled Alton close to me as tears spilled from the corners of my own eyes. I held him tight and pressed my cheek into his, wishing never to let him go. I kissed his cheek first, then the lips that I loved to kiss. I pressed into them hard and tasted him for what I thought would be one of the final times. His tear-stained lips tasted like strawberries to me—the sweetest, ripest strawberries ever grown.

The waiter and other patrons began to clap.

"Way to go!" I heard.

"Aww, Herb . . . isn't that the sweetest thing you ever saw?"

"Congratulations!"

Alton lifted me from the chair and swung me around. The people clapped louder and rose to their feet with smiling, sniffling faces.

"Baby, I promise I will make you the happiest woman alive. I will make you feel the way you've made me feel all these years. I love you, baby. I love you."

"I love you," I said.

Eight

I WANTED TO DIE right then and there.

I asked Alton if we could go to our room and have our dinners delivered to us there. I told him I wanted to be alone with him.

I excused myself to take a shower as soon as we got to our room. I needed time to think. While drying off, I heard room service bustling in our meals and Alton offering his appreciation before the door closed.

I felt flushed as I slipped into a long transparent white nightgown, one of Alton's favorites. He always loved seeing soft white against my chocolate-mousse skin.

Maybe I should just go through with it. Maybe I should just marry Alton and hope for the best. Hope that we could beat the odds and that he wouldn't fall out of love with me. I knew I would never fall out of love with Alton. That was one of the things that scared me the most. I could control myself, but not Alton.

It would certainly make me feel a whole hell of a lot better if I could put my finger on exactly what to watch out for. Hell, I can fix anything if I know what the problem is beforehand.

A clothed cart with two covered dinners rested against the wall. On the table in the sitting area was a cake with one candle in it. I walked closer and saw that the restaurant had written "Congratulations" on the cake.

"Compliments of the restaurant," Alton said. He wore a grin plastered on his face that dared to be removed.

My legs felt numb, as if they were going to collapse, but Alton just beamed with excitement. I imagined how that beam would eventually change over time and be replaced by utter disgust. His expression would begin to look like my dad's face. I imagined us living together and getting tired of each other; having that I-got-you-now-so-I-don't-have-to-do-shit-else-to-impress-you feeling; and the final parting along with all of the bullshit that came with it at the slam of a judge's gavel.

I thought about Oprah.

As long as there's an open door, we'll do anything in our power to keep the other person from leaving.

"Alton, honey," I said in a soft, timid voice.

"Yeah, baby," Alton said.

"You know I love you, don't you?"

"For sure, no doubt."

My legs carried me over to the bed where he was seated. "Alton, we need to talk and you're not going to like what I have to say."

Alton swung his legs around and sat on the edge of the bed. He pulled me by the waist and positioned me between his knees. "Baby, there is nothing you can say to me right now that I wouldn't like." He held my hips with his hands and looked up at my face. He was still all smiles, as though there was nothing that could pry that smile off his face. But I knew there was.

"What's wrong, babe?" Alton asked. His smile decreased

thirty degrees. I suddenly noticed the reggae playing softly in the background.

"Babe, I don't think I can get married," I said. I felt my voice and hands tremble. My spine shook.

Alton's face held firm in its positive position, as if my words hadn't registered. As if he didn't hear what I said or was waiting for me to yell, "Psych."

"I can't do it. I can't marry you. I don't want us to get married."

"What do you mean? What's wrong?" Alton became motionless. The smile finally dropped off his face and his gaze rested on me. This time my words broke through the fog and settled on his brain.

"I love you and I want things to stay the way they are."

"I don't understand, babe. Are you nervous? I think you're just starting to get nervous about getting married. That's all." He caressed the small of my back. His voice was somehow soothing and unperturbed.

"No, Alton. I've been thinking about this for a couple of years now, really."

"But you said yes in the restaurant."

"Well, no. I didn't say yes. I was crying because I felt like your proposal was the start of the end."

"Why?" Alton's expression changed. He went into a mode of trying to understand me. I knew in the back of his mind he was still thinking that everything would be all right. It wouldn't.

"Marriage is a fantasy. People get married and two, four, five years later, they end up divorced and go through a lot of bullshit to get there. I don't want to lose you now, or five years from now. Frankly, I don't want to go through all that hassle and turmoil. Divorce can break you down and truly mess you up real good. I've seen it happen too many times."

He grabbed my waist again and his smile returned as if he understood the problem and that it was nothing to fret over. "Miss Morris, won't be no divorcing here. I know a good woman when I see one, and you are a damn good woman. Believe me, when we get married, it will truly be until death do us part."

"Everybody says that. What makes you so sure?" My fear lodged in my throat.

"I told you. I want a family. I believe in family, but with the right woman. Even before Dad died, I knew I wanted to be like my father. My father was a very strong man and he loved us all. He gave us so much love, structure, and support. I miss that. His time was cut short with us when he died in that fire, but that's the kind of man he was." His eyes softened and shifted downward as if he were placing himself back at that day.

Alton's father had moved his family from New York to Cleveland when Alton was fifteen. The year following, a neighbor's house caught on fire, and Alton's father went in to try to rescue the frantic mother's six-month-old baby. Mr. Goode never came out. Once the fire was extinguished, the firemen found him in the foyer five feet from the front door with the baby buried in his chest. They both died of smoke inhalation. Even though Alton was the youngest, in his mind he took his father's place. He assumed the role of protector of his mother and two older sisters, Shirley and Gwennie.

"Family means more to me than any job or any amount of money. I vowed that when I found the right woman, I would marry her and be the man that my father was, have the family that we had, and love the way we did." He repositioned himself to get a better grip of me and a better view of my pupils.

"Van, I love you more than anything in this world. You're my best friend and I want you for my wife. I want you to have my children, I want us to raise them together. I want to grow old with you. There's no way I'm letting you go. You're going to be stuck with me forever." Alton continued to rub my back as he spoke. My spine began to settle as my muscles relaxed. His eyes were confident and steady. His voice made direct contact with my heart, but to no avail.

"This is our first marriage. Do you know that fifty percent of all first marriages end in divorce within five to seven years? It's even worse the younger you are."

"No statistic is going to run my life for me." The words rolled right off his tongue as if he was prepared for my statement. No hesitation.

I said nothing.

"We're going to have things to work out like anybody else. My mom and dad had disagreements, but they worked them out."

I was still speechless, not completely convinced.

"Look. As far as I'm concerned, you can quit Kawamichi now and start your business. Work on your bookstore. I'll take care of everything. I don't want you to have to want or worry your sexy little body about anything anymore. I got you. From now on, I got you."

"Alton, statistically, a woman's standard of living significantly decreases in the event of a divorce, while a man's increases." I paraphrased from a book I'd read. "Not working is what put other women in that situation after divorce."

"We won't get divorced."

"Do you know how many friends I have who have been happily married over five years? None," I persisted. I knew single girls everywhere would slap me if they were here. I felt like I was in a movie theater and could just hear people screaming at me on the screen, "Marry that man, fool!"

Alton released a long heavy sigh, yet he managed a subtle curve to his lips. "You're nervous. I noticed before that every time it looked like I was broaching the subject, you would get nervous. Your leg would start going fifty miles an hour like it is right now."

I distributed my weight on both legs to dispel the fidgeting.

"Tell you what," he said after a moment, "you take a little more time. You think about it and give me your answer in a couple of days." I could tell that Alton thought that was all I needed. As if time would bring me to my senses or I would sleep off the fear like a young college kid sleeps off a hangover after a fraternity party.

"Just like that? You're not angry?"

"No, because I know this is just nerves and I *know* that you love me as much as I love you. I knew you were nervous before and I put you on the spot in front of all those people. So, maybe that was my fault and I apologize." He brought my hands before his face and kissed them. His gaze was deep. "If this is going to work, we both need to be one hundred percent sure. We both have to want this on our own. I don't want to push you into anything. You think about it and give me your answer later. No rush."

And with that, he hugged me tightly for what seemed like heaven. He calmed my body.

"Come on, we'd better eat dinner before it gets too cold," Alton said.

I forced down a few bites of dinner while Alton ate nearly everything on his plate. We cut the cake together, like the bride and groom do at wedding receptions, and fed it to each other. Alton's idea. "For practice," he said. He smeared icing on the bridge of my nose and that lightened me up. I smeared cake on his face, too, and we ended up chasing each other around the room, threatening each other with vicious pieces of cake. We landed on the bed and played. First, play wrestling. Next, play rolling. Then, making love. For real.

Nine

IT WAS AN OVERCAST day in Cleveland.

I needed to think. So I did what I always did when I need to think: walk. I didn't want to walk alone in the neighborhood and be stopped by chatty neighbors, so I hopped into my SUV and drove to the Flats.

I drove through the city and down Euclid Avenue. Passed Cleveland State University as the night students walked around campus toting books and backpacks. Drove past the Cleveland Playhouse Square where Alton and I had seen countless plays after eating dinner to the sounds of live jazz at Fat Fish Blue.

Alton. Why was this so hard for me? This whole thing seemed so silly. What was I putting myself through? I loved this man . . . he is a good man. Do you know how many Oprah, Sally, Ricky, Jerry, Maury, Jenny, and Montel shows there have been about women looking for good men? I had one. I knew I did. I had a man who was dying to have a family and thought I was the queen of Africa. A man who believed I fit the role and wanted to give me the world.

My thoughts took me past Superior Avenue and to the East

Bank of the Flats. Drove and thought. Everywhere I went, there were Alton and I, together. I drove under the viaduct, past Diamond's Men's Club, over the drawbridge, and past the Nautica. I ran past the Mirage on the Water. Alton and I would go there only when we wanted to be entertained by the younger clientele on certain nights. Alton would go to the bar or something and sneak up on me with corny pickup lines. And I'd have fun playing the role of trying to find out what kind of car he drove or how much money he made before agreeing to talk to him—but only because he looked good.

I wanted nothing more than to love Alton forever. How could I make forever happen?

I drove back around to the West Bank looking for a place to park. Passed BW3, the Odeon, and Hooters and parked in the parking lot near Fagan's. I got out and started walking and my body went on autopilot while my mind tried to figure out what the hell to do.

I walked around a bit and tried to figure out a solution to the damned-if-I-do-or-don't situation I was in, before I found myself back in the car heading to Synda's house in Ohio City. I rarely dropped by Synda's house unannounced since I never had much to say to Tucker. We were cordial, but since college we were no longer friends. I wouldn't let that happen.

"What's up, girl?" Synda asked. She came to the door dressed in a number thirty Cleveland Browns jersey. It was snug—very snug. The jersey gripped her around the waist and fell just below her butt cheeks, leaving her café-latte legs on display. I dared not ask or look to see if she had anything on under there. I know I shared that little tidbit of advice over a month ago, but I really wasn't up to seeing it on display right now. Mention anything that has to do with her or a tool she can use to get what she wants, and Synda will quickly heed your advice. Her light brown hair was pulled back into a ponytail, and her lips had a touch of wine gloss that was smudged beyond her lip lines and drier in some places than others.

I walked in and followed her to the forest green leather sectional. We sat down before a wall garnished with a more than generous offering of Synda Manzano portraits: Synda's nursery school graduation pic, her high school and college pics, her and her family, her and Tucker's wedding pic, then more portraits of Synda alone.

My eyes scanned the room and found familiarity in Synda's trophies and plaques from high school, college, and her job. I looked around and there were more uniquely framed pictures of Synda. If it hadn't been for an old Mutant Massacre comic on the coffee table, I would have sworn that Tucker didn't live here at all. The house was screaming, "Tucker who?"

"I see you're taking me up on that tip, huh?" I said. "And a Jamel White jersey?"

"Jamel's my man. Oh, and listen to this. Jamel White, like Marshall Faulk, also plays running back. Last season, his rookie year, he had forty-seven rushes for a total of one-forty-seven yards. He also received thirteen times for a hundred yards. He was just getting his feet wet in the NFL. He'll be up there with Faulk in no time." Synda pushed her shoulders back and jutted out her chin. Her eyes sparkled in her new knowledge.

"Oh, so you've looked at more than just how fine he is?" I absently forced a smile. I wasn't there for idle chitchat.

"What's up, girl?" she asked.

"Alton proposed."

Synda squealed, jumped up from the couch and then up and down. She grabbed her breasts and pressed them into her chest while she continued to celebrate for a few more vertical propulsions. "Oh, congratulations, girl! I'm so excited for you." She stopped jumping long enough to run to me and wrap her Twiggy arms around my shoulders. She gave me a tight hug.

Tucker came rushing down the stairs in the wake of Synda's screeching yelps. Hot damn! The brother had on a pair of black drawstring pants and no shirt. I'm ashamed to say how good he looked. I was already begging Alton's forgiveness in my mind. *Alton, forgive me for noticing how fine Tucker is looking right now.* He'd obviously been working out since the last time I'd seen him. His caramel chest was smooth and defined. His pecs were cut sharp, casting a hard shadow over his tightly packed abs that begged to be touched as he ran down the steps. Just a dab of oil, and damn.

"What's going on?" he asked. Our eyes locked for what was a split second but seemed like a century. For some reason it felt weird, as though I were standing there naked and sandwiched between the both of them.

"Alton proposed. Vanella and Alton are getting married!" Synda gleefully announced to Tucker. She hugged me again and pressed her cheek so hard into mine that I was sure that at any moment, we would swap spit.

Tucker pressed on a smile. He cracked an opening between his lips, but said nothing. His eyes seemed to ask if that was what I really wanted to do.

"Congratulations," he finally said. Synda turned to me again. I couldn't help but watch Tucker over her sharp shoulder. His left hand strangled the wooden banister. He looked as if he'd just taken a bite of double fudge cake and someone had gulped down the last drop of milk. He stood there motionless before he stuttered, "Uhh . . . I'm uh . . . I'm going back . . . upstairs. Oh, um . . . congratulations."

"Thanks," I said, determined not to drool or look at his back as he marched back up the stairs.

I thought Synda's nose was trying to sniff out that little moment between us, but evidently her mind convinced her that she was obviously tripping since I was in love and about to marry Alton—or something like that.

"Where's the ring? I know he gave you some gigantic ring." She examined my bare left hand.

"I only wear it when I'm around Alton."

"What? Why?"

"I told him I needed to think about it."

"Oh, lord." She dropped back in her oversized chair and crossed her legs as she exhaled through her nose, as if to say "here we go again." I sat on the couch like a little girl in the principal's office.

"I'm just scared to death," I babbled. "I'm afraid of getting married. I don't want to lose him."

"He proposed, Van. In my book, that means he wants to be with you. Not leave you."

"You don't understand."

"No, I don't."

I growled and ran my hands along my temples. Synda gave a soft chuckle.

"Women are dying to find a good man." She held her hand out toward me, palm up. "Here, you got one, and you're about to throw him back to the vultures. Humph! Well, you don't have to worry about it though. As good as he sounds, there will be plenty of women out there to snatch him up when you let him go." Synda's voice held that irritating drawl it had when she knew she was right and she was saying, "Quote me." Her straight talk pissed me off sometimes.

"You won't be happy unless you're just living together with him forever, not ever getting married," she added.

My head snapped to attention at her comment.

"I have to ask," she said, "will I be invited to the wedding? You know, since I'm not allowed to see Alton and all. Since I might take off with the groom before you walk down the aisle." She looked down as if she were asking for a presidential pardon.

"Shut up," I said and left her hanging.

I hugged her and dismissed myself from the "Shrine of Synda." My mind was reeling now from the idea that Synda just gave me, and I needed time alone again. I thought I finally had the solution to my and Alton's problem.

Well, *my* problem.

Ten

MY HOME OFFICE WAS a scattered mess. I had the contents of the COSE folder dumped all over the mahogany desk along with information I had picked up from the Small Business Administration. The floor was cluttered with balled up sheets of paper from a yellow legal pad on which I'd scribbled and discarded ideas for the bookstore and the beginnings of a business plan. I had been all through the literature and around the block with different ideas for the bookstore. Nothing had quite jelled yet. I didn't know how the lint people made sense of it all when they started out. It seemed to me that I needed to take a class or something. Maybe I wasn't cut out for being an entrepreneur. It wasn't for everybody. But then I thought about Dexter and all the other little *Dex-ettes* like him and decided that I was, but I would just give it a break for tonight.

It was 8:45 P.M., and the ladies and I planned to meet up at Club 75 for a little jazz and conversation. We had decided on this at the last minute that afternoon, while doing volunteer work for the Urban League and discovering that none of us had any plans for the night. Alton was going out with the boys and I had planned to curl up with a good book: *The Abolition of Marriage*.

"You are crazy. I can't believe you said you had to think about it" were the first words out of Medena's mouth as I approached the table where they were already seated. The jazz band, Horns 'n' Things, was on a break and had slipped off to the side to sip beer and wine while sampling plates of hot dogs, mac and cheese, and fried chicken wings. Contemporary jazz—Rick Braun at the moment—was being piped in from speakers overhead to keep the jazz spirit flowing.

"I guess I don't have to ask how you found out," I said. I looked over at Synda, who smothered a smile while she sipped her Long Island Iced Tea through a straw and sheepishly rolled her eyes from side to side. She whisked a stray strand of hair from her eyes.

"You did the right thing, girl," Sherron said as she pinched the corners of her wine-colored lips together so that her cheeks poked out. "Marriage benefits nobody but men. Hell, I'd get married again if I could have a wife."

I hoisted myself onto the pleather-covered bar chair and hung my lined leather jacket and my cashmere sweater on the back of my seat. It may have been October, but this was a Cleveland October, which felt more like St. Louis in early December. I wouldn't give Cleveland up for the world though. I ordered a glass of Pinot Grigio when the waitress came over.

"So, what's the deal?" Zandra asked. She made a come-hither motion with her fingers and tried to lure words out of my mouth.

"And you ladies are looking fine, too, I might add," I said, intentionally prolonging the appeasement of their curiosity. "Syn, perfect makeup as always. MAC, is it? Zan, you're naturally stunning as usual. Love those shoes, girl. Sherron, sista, you always do black good. And, Dena—"

"Let's hurry this up because I got to be home in a bit. Aneaus is watching Cornell for me tonight," Medena said before I could finish my sarcastic statements.

"Uh-knee-us," Synda and I sang after cueing each other with our eyes. We teased her about still being in honeymoon mode with her husband.

"Watching him *for* you tonight? Isn't that his child, too?" Sherron asked. She animated her words and twisted her face so that her upper lip nearly met the tip of her nose.

"Yes, but—"

"See, that's what I'm talking about," Sherron said. She pointed and wagged her index finger up and down in Medena's direction. "Why is it that when women get married they take on two jobs? Okay, now we're bringing in just as much money as they are—sometimes more—but we still do seventy, eighty percent of the housework, plus take care of the kids ninety-five percent of the time. That's not right." Her finger steadied on Medena now, who sat looking like a victim while her lawyer, Sherron, was giving her closing statements. "Here it is she can't even have a full night out with her girlfriends because she's got to rush home and relieve him of his fatherly duties. What the hell is that?" She huffed and threw her hands up in disgust. "I'll never get married again. I tell you that much."

The table of late twenty- to early thirty-something women behind us peeped over at Sherron and nodded in agreement. Sherron's statement provided them with a much-needed topic of discussion. They lit into a lively exchange while their eyes scoured the room for "even if just for one night" potentials.

"I enjoy being with my little boy. Besides, you leave things to a man and he'll mess it up for sure every time. You might as well do it yourself," Medena said. She shifted and crossed her legs.

"Uh-huh. That's exactly what they want you to think. That lets them off the hook from doing anything." Sherron planted her eyes on me. "Girl, you doing the right thing. You think about marriage and think about it hard. Being a wife? You're not doing anything but doubling your responsibilities with no increase in appreciation or pay and no extra benefits." She tossed back a gulp of wine to emphasize her point.

"You are just too much," Synda said to Sherron. She turned to me and added, "Now you, on the other hand, I think you're being an absolute drama queen. You know you're going to marry that man, so you need to cut all the drama. And if you don't marry him, then you're a fool. Plain and simple."

"So, what's the deal?" Zandra repeated.

"Exactly what Syn told you. Alton proposed and I said I needed to think about it."

The waitress came back to the table with my drink and waited as I pulled out my wallet to pay her. I glanced at her, putting her at five foot seven and a size four. I looked at her small waistline and hated her.

"Why?" asked Medena. "I hope you're not listening to this crap Sherron is flinging. She's just getting bitter in her old age."

Sherron scoffed.

"Marriages just don't seem worth the paper they're written on anymore. They never last. Or even if they do, the love doesn't."

Zandra continued the conversation. "Well, I say there's noth-ing wrong with not getting married, especially if you're not going to have kids right away. Hell, I may not have kids at all because I'm really not all that crazy about 'em. Since that's the case, why would I want to tie myself to one man? As long as I'm not married, then I can trade the one I got in for a new model when he starts acting up. And he will. They all do in time."

Medena said, "Alton is a good man. And *fine*, too. I can't believe you said you had to think about it."

"Alton's fine? How fine is he?" Synda leaned over and asked Zandra. Zandra leaned away from her and looked at her like she was crazy.

Synda's cheeks flushed from the burning eyes of everyone at the table. Her body jerked as she picked up a cocktail napkin and dabbed her nose. "Y'all excuse me. I see somebody I know." Synda grabbed her purse and stood up. She tugged at the ends of her black miniskirt, smoothed the fabric of her red sleeveless sweater, then glanced at the back of each calf to examine her jet-black stockings for runs before disappearing to the area behind the bar.

"Look, everybody ain't trying to be Miss Happy Homemaker like you, Dena," Sherron said to Medena without missing a beat. "Personally, I don't see why you're so happy. You work a full-time job, come home and cook for your husband, do the laundry, clean the house, take care of your son, then have to ask permission to go out. On top of all that, you're running yourself ragged playing dress-up every night like somebody's drag queen just to please him sexually. I'm exhausted myself just talking about it."

"It's called marriage, Sherron. Besides, I love doing all those things for Aneaus." Medena's face turned warm and fuzzy.

"Okay, and all that. But tell me, what does a woman get out of marriage? Sounds like nothing but extra work. Hell, if I were a man, I'd get married as soon as I was twenty-one. I'd jump right from Momma's house to my new momma's house."

"Marriage is give and take, Sherron. Aneaus and I have a fifty-fifty marriage."

"A fifty-fifty marriage? Where's his fifty? Sounds like an eighty-twenty marriage to me. Pareto analysis at its best. As with most marriages, eighty percent of the work is handled by the wife. Mine was like that, which is why I'm divorced now. I found the light. Wise up, Van."

"I hear you talking, Sherron," I said. "But that's not exactly Pareto analysis."

"All right now. We won't have no shop talking up in here tonight, okay. Pareto analysis. Y'all better take that somewhere," Zandra said, darting accusing eyes between Sherron and me. Accusing us of bringing work outside of the office.

"No, that's not why you're divorced. But anyway, Aneaus is a good man. He spends time with me and Cornell. I know he's not cheating on me," Medena said.

"It's not a matter of whether he's cheating or not. Women think if their man's not cheating, they have a good marriage. Like that's all a man got to do is not cheat, and boom he's a good man. The man volunteers to baby-sit his *own* child for two hours and that makes him a king of a man." Sherron huffed. "See, in marriage, husbands get pampered and wives get another child to take care of. Hell, my man didn't cheat, but he wasn't a good husband."

"I thought you said he cheated with the little Jamaican woman, Orenthia?" I asked.

"Oh . . . yeah, but that was later. I was talking about early on when we first got married." She cleared her throat. "But anyway, it's not about a good man or bad man. It's about the one-sidedness of marriage."

"Ever wonder why married men say their wives are their best

friends, but married women say their husbands are like another child to look after?" Zandra asked.

"Uh-huh. See. That's what I'm talking about. Van, you'd better listen up, honey. Save yourself before it's too late." Sherron reached across the table and pressed both hands against my forehead and anointed me.

Horns 'n' Things had resumed playing. I looked around at the bobbing heads and closed eyes of people who were absorbed by the saxophone and the bass guitar and swept up by the smooth, mellow beat. The bass entered my body through my toes, rocked its way up to my thighs and added a bounce to my shoulders. By the time it reached my mind, Alton and I were already dancing there. Holding each other. Catching the beats.

"Well, that's really not a concern. Alton does more in our relationship than I do right now. The man comes over and cleans my fireplace, does maintenance on my bike, and checks my furnace and A/C without my ever asking him, not that I would. He loves to cook for me—although it's for him, too, since he complains about the light meals that I cook. He keeps his house cleaner than mine. Hell, if anything, I should be scared that he would out-clean me if we got married."

Zandra said, "Oh, girl, you're lucky then. Right now, I'm batting O for two in that department. Kenard always comes to my place looking for a cooked meal. He says his Italian momma told him that a good woman should always cook for him. Daylon claims he's not mechanical at all, so he can't even mow a lawn if he had to."

"Believe me, Alton's act is all for show," Sherron chimed in. "That shit will change before you can step foot out of wedding gown."

"How are you ladies doing this evening?" A tenor voice found space in our mix. We all looked up at a tall, handsome, bronzed-looking man. He was dressed in a dark gray tailored suit, smelled of Joop!, and spoke with carefully articulated words. The women at the next table halted their exchange and examined the brother's backside from head to toe. Their foreheads wore an array of lines; hope that he would turn from table number one and pick a contestant from table number two devoured their eyes.

"Well, hello," Zandra said and grinned.

"My name is Cedric," he said. "I was just walking around and happened to notice this table of fine professional-looking women and wanted to stop by and introduce myself." He held a goblet of red wine in his right hand. His left hand was ringless.

"You noticed that all by yourself did you?" Sherron asked.

Zandra extended her hand to him and introduced us from left to right. "I'm Zandra, and this is Medena, Vanella, and Sherron."

"Sherron?" he repeated, picking out his female of choice. "That's an interesting name. Does it mean anything?"

Sherron examined the threads of his suit and moved to his shoes, then his lightly salted hair. "Nothing in particular." She took a sip of wine.

Cedric cleared his throat, obviously undeterred. He'd obviously been at this point many times before. "May I join you ladies?" he asked in a tone that didn't seem to fit him. "You look to be having a spirited conversation over here." His fake enunciations were already coating my stomach with a fresh layer of bile.

Sherron perked up, probably at the thought of happening upon fresh meat to slaughter. "Why, sure. Why don't you pull up a chair? We're talking about how marriage benefits men and is nothing but a thankless job for women. Perhaps a fine young man like you can give us a male perspective."

Sherron reached behind her and lightly tapped the top of an empty chair at the table of hungry women behind her.

Cedric suddenly looked perturbed and his strong enunciations turned flat. "Uh, yeah . . . oh-kay . . . I'ma go on over here and get another drink. I'll git with y'all in a minute. A'ight?"

"A'ight," Sherron said, "that's a good idea. This might be a long one."

Cedric made a brisk retreat to the back of the bar and behind one of the columns to a location well outside our view.

"Fake ass," Sherron hissed.

We all laughed.

Zandra leaned across the table toward me. "Well, Cedric was quite 'The Entertainer.'" We chuckled.

"Well, Van, I will just say be careful about your decision. You could end up having to deal with that and more," Zandra said, referring to the likes of Cedric. "There aren't a lot of black men out there with your status, I mean, assuming that's what you'd look for, a black man."

"Zan, you're the only one looking for a rainbow of men making at least six figures. There're not a whole lot of single ones like that of any color," Medena said.

"I'm not looking for a man who makes six figures, but I would like him to be able to take care of himself, whatever responsibilities he has, and to be able to keep up with me. You all know I like to travel. Hell, excuse me for being ambitious, responsible, and for being careful of not having kids before I could afford them. When I want to fly from Cleveland to New York, then to L.A.," she mapped out the cities on the table with her index finger, "they want to give me sob stories about child support payments and high credit card debts. Then they have the nerve to look at me crazy when I say I'm going to go by myself and without them. Like I'm supposed to not go and miss out on life because *they've* got obligations."

"Well, they say that we are faring a lot better in our careers than our brothers," I offered. I decided to forego the statistic this time.

"Better reason for you to be thankful for what you have, Van, a beautiful man who's successful, smart, and financially stable," Medena said.

"And who loves you for some strange reason," Zandra added with a soft laugh.

I leaned against the back of my bar chair. I felt as out of place as a violinist at a hard rock jam session. "You all don't understand where I'm coming from."

"I understand all too well," Sherron said. "I think you're doing right by thinking it over. Lots of women don't do that. That's why they rush into marriage, look up, and find themselves knee deep in slavery with no Harriet Tubman in sight."

I looked up in time to catch a glimpse of Synda walking up the stairs toward the exit with someone who, from behind, looked like Cedric.

"Well, girls, I'm going to call it a night," Medena said.

Sherron looked at her watch. "Yeah, eleven thirty. You gotta stop staying out to the wee hours of the morning with us girls, you know. That does not a good marriage make."

Medena ignored Sherron's sarcasm, said her good-byes, and rushed to the exit with cell phone to ear.

The more I talked and the more I listened, the more I knew

that the decision I was leaning toward was the best decision for me, the best decision for Alton, the best decision for us.

I woke Sunday morning to the sweet sound of a motorcycle revving up. My motorcycle. I'd recognize that melodic purr anywhere. Alton's here for Game Day. The Browns were playing the Bengals. It would be an easy win today. After all, the Bengals probably had the record for the team with the most first-round draft picks year after year. I smiled as I felt my heart leap as if it had a crank start and the clutch had just been released.

I hopped eagerly out of bed and threw my white chenille robe around my bikini-panty clad, goose pimpled body. I caught a quick glimpse of my hips before tying the sash and promised myself that I would go back and do a thorough quality check later. I dashed down the stairs and outside to find my garage door open and Alton kneeling beside my bike. It looked like he had been there a while. He was surrounded by tools, oil cans, and darkened rags. His shoulders protruded from the white tank top he wore, and his thighs bulged in his worn pair of Levi's. I watched his strong shoulder blades rise and collapse in motion as he tended to the maintenance of my bike.

"Thank you," I said.

"You don't have to keep thanking me every time I work on your bike. I just want to make sure my baby's all right," Alton said without turning his head. "I know Moms and Pops are still worried about you riding this thing anyway, so I want to make sure it's always in tip-top shape." He probed the front tire and pressed an air pressure gauge to the valve.

"You're sweet, you know that?"

"For sure, no doubt."

I could feel his smile even though I couldn't see it.

"I'll go put on some coffee and make breakfast for us." I walked over to him and kissed him on the cheek. A wave of his cologne rushed up from his neck and took up residence in my nose. Rocked it slowly with a tranquil groove.

I hopped back up the stairs. I put on coffee and began to prepare breakfast: scrambled egg whites, English muffins with no butter, and strips of baked turkey bacon. One for me, six for Alton.

Alton came in and dashed into the bathroom for a quick wash-up before changing into a fresh pair of jeans and his Browns shirt. He took a seat at the table that I had set. I changed into my Marshall Faulk jersey before I served the warm eggs next to the bacon and muffins on our plates, then I sat across from him.

I took a bite of eggs and looked up to see if Alton's taste buds were at all as tantalized as mine. When I looked up, it was quite obvious that breakfast was the last thing on his mind. He sat motionless. His face appeared distant and his thoughts seemed to be on the other side of the world. His right wrist stiffened as he began to chop absently at his eggs as if to ensure they wouldn't jump off the plate.

"Alton? Is everything okay?"

He stopped chopping his now minced eggs. "Vanella, I was just wondering. It's been over a month now. You haven't said anything." He kept his eyes in East Egypt.

"Said anything?"

"About my proposal. You haven't forgotten, have you?"

"Alton, how on earth could I forget a proposal? Especially with this rock glaring in my eyes?" I held out my left hand to display the ring that I always threw on when I was at home or going over to Alton's.

"Well, you haven't said anything. Have you made a decision?"

My appetite faded. I set my fork down, too. My leg danced. "I was thinking that maybe we can live together rather than get married."

His forehead creased between his eyes as he stood straight up. The way he shot up made me nervous. My tongue felt dry and thick in my mouth. Parched.

"Live together?" He said it like the two words were part of a foreign language. He shook his head and sighed. "Live together?"

I tried to swallow, but my mouth was too dry. I picked up my glass. I needed a little bit of water to coat my mouth and to free my tongue, but I couldn't drink.

"Yeah. I think that would be the best solution for us, then we don't have to worry about divorce."

He didn't say anything for a minute, then he sat back down and asked, "You love me, don't you?"

"Yes."

"You know I love you, right?"

"Yes."

"You're my best friend. Am I your best friend?"

"Yes."

"We've talked about everything under the sun and we know each other well, right? We can talk about anything, right?"

"Yes."

"Then what's the problem?" He finally brought his head up and his brown eyes stroked mine. He put his fork down, placed his elbows on the table, and leaned toward me. His heavy voice dropped. "Help me to understand you."

I continued my weak explanation. "And it would be the same thing anyway. I mean, we'd be together in the same house, just like we were married anyway. And you—"

"I'm not interested in playing house, Van." Alton's gaze singed a hole in me before he stood up and backed slowly out of the kitchen. He looked as if he were grappling with my words as his feet moved him from the table and he headed toward the front door. I followed frantically at his heels.

"It's not playing house, Alton. I'm offering you a chance to live together instead of getting tied down. Most guys would kill for that."

Alton raised his voice. "I'm not most guys. And I'm certainly not looking for a live-in lover." His chest began to rise and fall at a faster pace. His nostrils flared. "I want a wife. I want kids. I want a family and I thought you did, too."

"We can still have kids," I said. My voice pleaded with him.

"You know me. Do you really think that's what I would want? As much as we talked about marriage and family, do you really think I would want a live-in girlfriend and kids out of wedlock?"

"I just thought it would be the perfect solution for us. We could have the family but not worry about a big split-up down the line in divorce court. You wouldn't ever worry about losing half of your assets to me."

"That's the difference between me and you. I'm not planning a divorce before we even get married." He shook his head and placed his hand on the doorknob.

"Don't leave," I said.

"I can't do it, Van. I don't want to play house with you. I want a family. A real family."

I felt him slipping away.

"Let me think about it more. I'm sure it's just nerves." I took his hand off the doorknob and pulled it toward my stomach.

"I'm trying to hang in there with you, but . . ."

"Can we talk about this tomorrow? Stay here with me. Let's watch the game and we can talk about it tomorrow."

His eyes dulled. "We can talk tomorrow, but I'm going to go home right now. I—"

The phone rang as his next word hung in the balance on his lips. I went to answer it before he could say anything more. It was a frantic Jaelene.

"Hey, what's up, Babysista?"

"I need you to come get me." Her voice was low and straight to the point.

"What do you mean, come get you? You're here in Cleveland?"

"No."

"Where are you?"

"St. Louis."

"Where are you in St. Louis?"

"Jail."

Eleven

ALTON WRAPPED HIS HAND around mine and held it securely as he drove us to Cleveland Hopkins International Airport, then stood by my side as if he never felt dissed. After Babysista's phone call, he saw the condition I was in, dropped his exit scene, and immediately went into take-charge mode. He made spur-of-the-moment first-class travel arrangements to St. Louis for us, then packed two overnight bags, got coffee, and stopped at the ATM while I showered and dressed. Now, as I stared out the window and imagined Jaelene screaming with her face pressed between the metal bars of a jail cell, my leg jiggled relentlessly.

"What can I get for you to drink today, ma'am?"

Babysista couldn't survive in anybody's jail. She didn't belong there. She could be a little off-center when it came to men, but that was nothing she should be locked up for.

"One Chardonnay and one Merlot, please," I heard Alton say. I felt his warm hand stroke my jiggling thigh to calm me. I replayed my conversation with Babysista in my mind.

"Jail? What do you mean you're in jail?" I asked Jaelene. Alton ran from the door and placed his hands on my shoulders from behind me, as if he knew I would need something to brace me.

"I really can't get into this now, Van. I just need help. I need you to come get me out. Please." The treble in her voice wavered at low scale. Her fear drifted through the earpiece and settled in the small of my back. I could never bear it when my little sister was in pain.

"Babysista, tell me what's going on." My legs, my arms, and my shoulders all tightened. My abdominal muscles tightened so much they began to hurt.

"They're saying I'm bouncing checks."

"They're saying? So are you or aren't you? How many checks? How much?"

"Van, can we discuss this later? I'll tell you everything you want to know. I really can't get into all the details here on the phone. Can you come bail me out?"

"Why don't you call Mom and Dad? It'll be much quicker. If it's a matter of money, I can wire it to them now."

"I don't want Mom and Dad to know. This is embarrassing enough and I don't need to hear a lecture right now."

Like I wasn't going to give her one. "What about calling Cyrus? I don't want you to be in there a minute longer than you have to be, waiting on me."

"I don't want Cyrus to know either, and I can't get out until tomorrow anyway. You can't post bail until tomorrow."

"I'll be there."

Before we left, I somehow managed to call Kizaar. Told him what was going on, not to tell Mom and Dad, and that I would pick him up at Babysista's house. The three of us had always been there for one another. When we were younger, we were like little line sisters and brother pledging "beatin'-phi-beatin'" together when one of us did something wrong. Sometimes that was the way it went down, too. We'd all stand together when Dad called one of us out for a whipping. We wouldn't break the line. Dad would take a step toward us, and together we'd move back. Arm in arm; arm to waist; hand to foot; whatever it took. Dad would try to pull one of us away and the other two would pull the chosen one back in. A couple of times, it actually worked. Dad put down the cracked leather belt and walked away mumbling, too tired for a battle. But more times than not, Dad would beat all our asses together.

Alton and I arrived at Lambert–St. Louis International Airport as the sun set on the St. Louis side of the Mississippi. We picked up the rental car that Alton had arranged for and drove across Highway 70 to the hotel where he had reserved a room. Alton tried his best to ease my nerves, but I could do nothing but think about Babysista's being locked up in somebody's jail.

Bouncing checks? The first thing that came to my mind was those damn plasma-screen TVs. That was ten thousand that I know she didn't have. Babysista could do some mindless things when it came to men and her money, but I didn't think she was senseless enough to pay for those with a bad check. That didn't sound like her. But then again, a man was involved.

I never asked how she paid for them. I just assumed that she used credit, but thinking about it now, I recalled that Babysista didn't have high-limit credit cards anymore. Not since the bankruptcy. I knew she had gotten a credit card to try to rebuild her credit. Damn shame: a thousand-dollar credit limit, 29 percent interest and initial fees totaling three hundred dollars. I never understood the logic of charging the highest fees and interest rates to those who obviously couldn't afford it.

The next morning, we picked up Kizaar from Jaelene's house, where he was waiting on her front porch. When I called, he was eager to ride with us to Clayton to pick up Babysista, I guess so that he could be certain that everything would be all right. That was us . . . The Three Musketeers.

Alton and Kizaar hung a few feet behind me at the courthouse as I posted Jaelene's bail. If that's what it took to get Babysista out, that's what it took.

A buzzing sound, a click, then Jaelene trudged through the heavy metal door. Her puffy eyes welled up when she spotted the three of us standing to the side. She looked a mess. Her midlength dark hair was unkempt; her eyes were red and swollen. She could have easily been mistaken for a domestic violence victim. The button-down white shirt that hung on her disheveled medium frame was painted with the hefty helping of makeup that she usually heaped on every day. With such a naturally pretty face, it baffled me that she felt the need to layer her skin with pounds of foundation, slather her lips with heavy lipstick, or cake her eyes with shadow, liner, and mascara. Her face had surrendered most of it overnight and had generously passed it on to her collar and the front of her shirt.

My skin chilled at the sight of her. Even with her ill-favored appearance, I saw her as prettier than ever. I ran up to her and grabbed her. Held her tight. I felt her body tremble as her tears broke loose and gushed south. Her trembles turned into intermittent convulsions as she let out gasps of relief.

"It's okay. It's over now," Kizaar said to her as he walked up behind me and took her out of my grasp. He hugged her tight and patted her back. "You're okay, right? I mean, nobody hurt you? They didn't put their hands on you, did they?"

Jaelene had covered her face with her hands and buried it in Kizaar's chest. She shook her head and let out a pitiful "No."

"Okay, well, it's over now." He swayed her from side to side. You would have thought that he was the big brother instead of the baby brother. "Let's get you home and get you cleaned up. You're a mess." He let out a chuckle. "I'll cook us all something to eat, too."

"Okay." She sniffed.

"What happened, Babysis—"

Alton stopped me in midsentence. He shook his head at me and mouthed, "Not now."

"Yeah, let's get going. We can talk when we get home," said Alton.

We walked to the car. Kizaar protectively wrapped his arm around Jaelene's shoulder and guided her outside. Alton did the same for me and kissed my forehead. He rubbed my right shoulder with "it's all right" strokes.

The ride back to Jaelene's was muted except for Tony Scott's voice blaring on 100.3 The Beat.

Kizaar stood before the kitchen counter whipping up a clumpy egg mixture for omelets. He's one of those men who can whip up a gourmet meal and have the house smelling like a smorgasbord after you just looked in the refrigerator and saw only a loaf of bread and half a jar of mustard. His short dreads dangled over his eyebrows and brushed against the diamond in his earlobe as he beat the batter. I peeked into his mixture to see what concoction he was throwing together this time, although it didn't really matter because I knew I was going to inhale it in an instant anyway. All diets were off when it came to Kizaar's cooking.

"Diced ham, green onions, tomatoes—"

"Say no more," I said. "Sounds good to me."

His wide mouth smiled under his neatly trimmed mustache and displayed a flawless set of snow-white teeth—teeth I used to despise him for since both Jaelene and I had to wear braces for two years. Kizaar's teeth had grown in perfectly. Just like Dad's and Uncle James's, from what I'd heard.

"So what's been up with you, Zar?" I asked. I used the name we called him when he was in grade school. Kizaar used to come home crying every day over kids teasing him about his name until Mom started calling him Czar and told him that it meant he was powerful. After that, Kizaar began to be proud of his name.

"Just trying to make it, that's all." He stepped a couple of feet closer to the stove, added butter to the hot skillet, and poured in the eggs. He walked over to the sink, rinsed out the mixing bowl, then wiped his hands with a towel. "I was thinking about culinary arts."

"Being a chef? That would be perfect for you. The way you cook? Mmph!"

"Yeah, I'm glad you think so." He said it like there was something lurking behind his statement. I bet I wouldn't have to wait long to find out what it was.

"How are things in the house over there?" I leaned against the bare kitchen wall.

His pearly whites slowly disappeared under the shadow of his broad nose. He pulled his lips in, moistened them, then released them. "It's still a little rough, but we'll work things out. Dad wasn't too supportive about my cooking career idea. He said it was women's work, or that it should be. Then, of course, he started bad-mouthing Mom, her lack of cooking skills, and her uselessness. You know he always has to get that in somehow. Anyway, he called my idea a career for women and sissies."

That was vintage Dad.

I watched Kizaar's body writhe with the discomfort that always surfaced when any reference to Dad entered the conversation. The number eighty on his chest heaved under his loose Isaac Bruce Rams jersey.

"The offer still stands on helping you get out of there."

"No thanks, sis. I can manage on my own."

"But you know it's not fair. Dad helped me and Babysista, but he refuses to help you start out."

"Aw, don't get started on Dad now. He just wants me to be a man and to make it on my own, and that's what I'm going to do. He helped you two out because you're girls. That's what he was supposed to do. That's what a father does for his daughters." He paused. "I don't know. Maybe he's trying to help me by pushing me into his commercial real estate business. Maybe he wants someone to hand the business down to."

I watched Kizaar in amazement. How did he do it? Every time the subject of Dad came up, his body always tensed, especially his jaws. But when he talked, he did nothing but defend the man who seemed to dream up ways to inch the hurdle just a little higher before each time he made him jump. Kizaar stared at the omelet before flipping it.

"Zar, Babysista told me about the plastic bottle in the wrong recycle bin issue. Was that to make you a man, too?"

"It was no big deal, Van." His voice stiffened. "And I think Babysista got things in her own life that she needs to be concerned with instead of what's going on with me."

"Why do you defend him?"

"There's nothing to defend. I know he really just wants me to be like him and Uncle James. So, maybe I should just go ahead and work with him. That would probably make him proud, give me the money to make it on my own, and certainly keep the peace."

"You shouldn't have to give up on your own dreams just to please him. Tell you what. I can—"

"I can work it out myself." He forcefully placed the spatula down on the stove.

"Okay, okay. I just don't understand why you try to impress him all the time. It's your life. Not his."

"You know a lot of my friends don't have fathers at all. Either shot, in jail, or just never was there at all. At least I got a father." His brow wrinkled. He brought his hand to his forehead, spread his thumb and fingers across his brow bone, closed his eye for a second and massaged. Suddenly he said, "Can you set the table for breakfast and I'll bring the food in?"

"Yeah, sure." I lifted my back up off the kitchen wall, grabbed the dishes from the cupboard, and set the table.

"As always, my man, this was good," Alton said. He rubbed his hand over his flat belly and gave it a soft pat. "You should come to Cleveland and cook for us for a bit. I don't know why this didn't rub off on your sister over there. Only thing she cooks is seaweed and bamboo shoots."

I threw Alton a sharp look and everybody laughed.

"I'm just playing, babe. You cook a mean tree limb. I love it."

I dipped my fingers in my water glass and flicked a few drops across the table at him. "If you're talking about the healthiness of my cooking, I don't see you over there getting too fat now, do I?"

Kizaar and Jaelene laughed as Alton wiped his cheek with his napkin. "Yeah, but neither are you. That's the problem. Zar, my man. Will you tell your skinny-butt sister over here that a man likes a woman with a little meat on her bones?"

"Hey, I'm not getting in this one," Kizaar said and grinned. He scooted his chair back and began clearing the table. "More coffee, anybody?"

We all said yes and Kizaar toted empty plates to the kitchen and returned with a pot of coffee.

"Look, I know you all are wondering what's going on," Jaelene said.

I looked up at Alton as I drained the last drop of coffee in my cup. "Yeah, you ready to talk about it?" I asked.

She released a nervous chuckle and rocked back and forth. She looked as if she were trying to get comfortable in an electric chair. "It was all just a big misunderstanding."

"Come on, little sis. What's going on with you?" Alton asked. He lowered his voice to her. Kizaar and Jaelene liked Alton and felt comfortable with him. It was as if Alton had become another brother to them.

"Did you write checks for the TVs? Is that what this is about?"

"Yes, I did write checks for them, but not bad checks. Not really. Well, not intentionally." She paused and retrieved her thoughts from space. "See, what had happened was . . . I had most of the money there and would be able to cover the entire amount on my next pay. It bounced before then, only I didn't know it. So, when I put money in my account, they had charged overdraft fees and below minimum balance fees, and whatever other fees they could think of, so I didn't know I didn't have money in the account and I was still writing checks. And I wrote a few bad checks here and there before all of this. And, well, the grocery store called the police on me when I was trying to write another check for my groceries and I was on their list. They said I had passed bad checks in their store already, and . . . well . . ."

Kizaar refilled everyone's cup. "I keep telling her to stop buying stuff for these knuckleheaded St. Louis men. They're only using you, Babysista."

"Cyrus isn't like that."

Kizaar said, "Yes, he is. You're so blinded by what you say are his good looks—although I don't see what's so special about him—that you can't see that he's really not into you. Not the way you are with him."

"Are you here? Are you around us? Him? How do you know?" Jaelene's voice climbed a notch.

Kizaar took a sip of coffee after stirring in cream and sugar. "Nope. Don't gotta. Know the type."

"Stay outta my business, Kizaar."

"Yeah, like you stay out of mine? Telling Van what's going on between me and Dad?"

"Well, talk about being blind to something. You're the one trying to win over a man who's done nothing but treat you like shit all your life."

Kizaar's jaw tightened. He gritted his teeth.

"All right, all right," Alton said. "Let's not turn this into a battle here. Baby-Jae, your sister flew . . . we flew here because we love you and we're concerned about you. Now, you've got to recognize that all's not right. Write a bad check, you get an overdraft fee and the store will send you packing elsewhere."

"They won't lock you up in jail and set bail at five thousand for writing a bad check for milk and butter," I added on to Alton's statement. "You know it was those TVs."

Jaelene huffed and got up from her chair. She paced the naked floor that conjoined with the bare walls before stopping in midstep. "Van, Alton, thanks for coming to bail me out. I really appreciate it. I'll pay you back, Van. I swear I will."

I lifted my eyes toward her in disbelief, but kept my head lowered.

"Kizaar, thanks for being by my side, as always." She stood behind him and patted his dreads. "But I got things under control here, y'all. I'll handle this in court. Everything's all right."

The phone rang and Jaelene left the dining room. She picked up the phone in the hallway.

"Hey, Cyrus, baby. What? Oh, I'm okay. Wait, can you hold on for a minute?" She covered the mouthpiece on the cordless phone. "Excuse me, I'm going to take this in the other room." She walked through the kitchen to the family room.

"This is all my father's fault," I said to Alton when we flew back to Cleveland and arrived at my condo the next day.

"Your father? How does he fit into Jaelene's writing bad checks?" Alton brought our bags in and set them down inside the front door.

"Everything that she does, that Kizaar does, and that I do all stems from our father. The way he related to us, his family, while we were growing up, and now, how he treats Mom, being so cold, mean, and vindictive for no reason. No reason at all." I headed to the kitchen and grabbed a couple of bottles of water. I emptied the bottles into glasses and handed one to Alton.

He took the glass from my hand and examined it. "So is your dad behind your not making a decision about us getting married?"

I picked up the empty water bottles and carried them to the trash can in the adjacent laundry room. Wondered how he was suddenly able to turn this conversation from Jaelene to me. He was always good for that. I really wasn't prepared to get into it at that time. I blew a breath outward as I turned.

"I love you, but I need more time."

"You need more time?"

"Yes."

Without giving me a chance to explain, Alton set the unsipped water glass on the kitchen counter. He walked over to me and pushed a dry kiss onto my cheek before he calmly walked out the door.

The condo was empty and quiet. I felt a cool drop of water fall from the glass in my hand, land on my sandals, and trickle down between my toes.

Twelve

I TOLD ARMANDO I wasn't feeling well and that I was skipping out on our workout session for the day. Didn't feel up to it. To make up for it though, I downed a protein shake for breakfast, and took a Metabolife pill before I gulped a strawberry Slim-Fast shake for lunch. I planned to fast for dinner or sip orange juice.

I slipped on my designated riding jeans and noticed that they were now whisking around my waist and thighs. *Almost there.* I would have been more excited, however, if I hadn't just looked in the mirror and skimmed my hands over what I considered to be obvious bulges around my hips and outer thighs. Five more pounds and I'd be there. I had to get rid of those unsightly things. Everybody else was crazy for not seeing them. They were just trying to be nice.

I went to the closet by the front door and grabbed my custom-made Rams riding helmet and headed down to the garage. The only thing better than walking to clear your mind is a motorcycle ride through the city. I had a couple of hours before Alton would be over. My mind went on autopilot under the purr of the engine, and when consciousness regained control, I found myself at Synda's, knocking on her door.

"You look sick," Synda said as she opened the door. She did some sort of gymnastics with her face. Her strained movement started with a slow sprint that moved to full speed before it seemed to do a high, double-back twist into a frown. "You're getting too thin again."

"I'm still bigger than you are."

"What? Is this a contest that I'm not aware of? Are you eating?"

"I don't know." I had stepped past her at the door and headed to the couch, where I dropped like a dead weight. I put my helmet on the coffee table and noticed that the *Cleveland Plain Dealer* was opened to an article on Jamel White.

"Oh, you are cut off," I said to her as I smacked my lips and turned my head away from the paper. "You are going too far with this Jamel White thing. You're not stalking the man, are you?"

"Very funny. At this particular time, no. Anyway, Jamel's a pretty interesting person. Did you know he also does community service work here in Cleveland? He visits kids at the Cleveland Clinic, and he's been a counselor for people with drug and alcohol addictions. I think that's so cool."

"Okay, whatever." I thought Synda was acting like a little schoolgirl with a crush on her favorite singer or TV star. Her face was giddy.

"Did you know that he could have played baseball with the Seattle Mariners, but decided to go with football? I don't know what was up with him going to college in South Dakota though. Humph. From L.A. to South Dakota? I didn't even know they had black people there."

I inadvertently glanced up the stairs. No sign of Tucker and I dared not ask, although, for some reason, I wanted to.

"So what's up, girl?" Synda asked when I didn't bother to respond to her raving over Jamel.

I leaned forward, resting my forearms on my knees. I propped my face between my fists and looked down at my Air Force Ones. "I asked Alton to live together instead of getting married. He didn't go for it." I heard a distant, but loud, clank followed by a series of lighter clanks. My shoulders hunched and I jerked at the sound. I looked at Synda.

"Shit!" said a male voice.

Synda's eyes widened. Her ponytail flipped wildly as she jumped up and ran to the door in the hallway. "T.C.? You all right down there?"

"Yeah, I just dropped a weight." He grunted. "I'm all right though."

Synda clapped her lips together. "Well, then keep it down. I'm trying to talk to Vanella up here."

A pause.

"Oh . . . okay."

Silence. Total silence. No sound of him resuming his workout.

Synda closed the hall door and sashayed back to the chair. She blew a hard breath that tossed her bangs upward. "That boy is going to kill himself trying to lift heavy weights by himself all the time. Humph. If I didn't know any better, I'd think he was making a move on some other woman on the job or something with the way he just started working out again all of a sudden." She plopped down across from me in her oversized chair and threw one thin leg over the other. "But that's not T.C. He's so damned predictable . . . I don't know what to do."

She began to examine her cuticles. "So you're still trying your damnedest to run this man off, I see."

I sat across from her and tried to comb my brain for why I had even come there. Why did I even try to talk to this girl? I'm usually able to talk to Synda about anything. But when it came to the subject of marriage, she seemed remote, not to mention that it seemed like her mind had been elsewhere lately. But right now I just needed to talk to somebody, anybody—even Synda.

"Apparently, living together was not the perfect solution to Alton that I thought it would be. It's actually the same thing. The only difference is the piece of paper," I said, more to myself than to Synda.

"Well, if it's the same thing, and only a piece of paper, then why not just make it official?"

"Because when it's official, that's when everything falls apart."

Synda dropped her hands to the side, rolled her eyes to the ceiling, and sighed. "You know what? You need therapy. You really do."

A muffled ringing emitted from Synda's midsection. She pressed her socked heels into the carpet and lifted her torso to retrieve a tiny cell phone from the front pocket of her worn jeans. She wiped the front with her palm, examined the number, then answered with a smile. "Heeyyy, how you doing?" Her voice tweeted. "Can you hold on for a second?" She drove the phone into her lap and whispered, "Van, don't go anywhere. I'll be right back." She sprung out of the chair and conquered the stairs two at a time before I heard her say, "Okay, I'm back." Then her chipper voice dwindled.

My mind began to wander as I waited for her to return. Leave it to me to have the one man in this world who wouldn't get excited about *not* being tied down. Or about having a woman who wasn't pressed about getting married and wanted to shack up instead. So many men out there were trying their hardest to dodge that marriage bullet, but Alton was just begging to be shot through the heart with it.

My woman's intuition was telling me that he'd come around. Alton loved me just as much as I loved him. He'd always been patient and understanding. When Alton felt he was making the right decision on something, and I wasn't on board with him, he was never one to force me to agree. He usually just kept explaining and continued being patient until we came together on it. Alton always listened, too. Always had an open mind. Even when he felt that he was right, he'd still ask my opinion, and had even changed his conviction a time or two after listening to me. I was feeling that this was one of those cases.

The hallway door opened and Tucker appeared. He stood there frozen, and our eyes made contact. His shaved head was covered with beads of perspiration that dripped over his bushy eyebrows and scuttled down his tapered nose. His shirtless warm brown skin glistened like chocolate crystals. Damn!

Tucker inched the door closed behind him. I passed a hastened smile, looked away, then picked up the newspaper and pretended to read. My neck grew hot and stiff, and felt uncomfortable. The heat climbed from my neck to my face, and they both began to itch.

"H-h-hi . . . Van."

I folded down the newspaper and looked in his direction. "Hi." Damn again. He had a six-pack now. He didn't even have that in college. His chest narrowed down to a chiseled waist like a funnel.

"How's everything going?" His eyes darted side to side, at me, and all around the room.

What? Is he trying to talk to me? We haven't spoken in years except for a cordial "hello" here and a nod there, mainly because I usually avoided him. "Okay." I snapped the paper back upright and began pretending to read again. I watched him indirectly over the top of the paper.

"How . . . how are the wedding plans going?" He twisted a comic book in his hand. X-men.

"Plans aren't being made right now."

He remained glued in one spot. "Oh?"

I looked up at him, then back down. His eyes were still darting around. He was giving me motion sickness. "No, um . . ."

Synda came bumbling down the steps. "Girl, I am so sorry about that. That was . . . oh, T.C." She looked startled when she saw him and her words stopped dead in their tracks. Her hand jetted to her open mouth.

"Uh, I just finished working out. I'm about to go shower," he said. Tucker charged up the stairs without saying another word.

I stood up. I felt freaked. Weird. "I'm going to take off, Synda."

"Girl, I'm sorry for taking so long on the—"

"No, that's okay. I got some errands to run and I want to hurry up and get my bike home before dark."

"Well, you can call me later if you want to talk."

"Yeah, I'll do that." I knew I wouldn't.

I picked up my helmet and placed it on my head. Synda gave me a hug before I zoomed off.

"Hey, how are you doing?" I said to Alton as I plucked off my helmet and placed it in the closet. I had seen his car in front when I arrived and had run up in excitement to see what he had waiting for me. He's such a romantic.

"Been riding, huh?"

"Yeah. Went out for a little bit." The room smelled bland and spiceless. I looked around and saw nothing new—nothing different, no surprises. The warm air chilled me. My ears were saddened by the sound of nothing. So unusual.

Alton held a glass of wine in his hand and sat on the living room couch. His shirt was tightly buttoned and his shoes were neatly tied, I noticed. I walked to the couch and saw a glass of wine on the coffee table; my soul sighed in relief. My shoulders loosened a little.

"So, you want to talk?" Alton asked. His voice was plain. Flat. Businesslike.

I knew what he was getting at. "Well, have you thought any at all about what I said yesterday?"

"Yes." He took a sip.

"And?"

"Were you expecting something different? Something different from what I said yesterday?"

"I thought you might have given it a second thought by now. Maybe realized that what I said made sense?" I ended up making a question out of it instead of a statement. Surely, he had come around by now.

He scoffed and put his drink on the coffee table next to mine. His voice was mild. "Van, nothing's changed in my mind since yesterday. I'm not going to change on that one. So you tell me what's up."

"Alton . . . I . . ."

All I needed to do was say yes. All this resistance that I was putting us through wasn't worth it. I tightened my stomach muscles and tried to pull the words out of my mouth. I almost grunted.

No, it wasn't worth possibly losing him now. But, then again, losing him later would hurt even more than now.

"Van? What is it? What's got you like this?"

I knew he was trying to make sense of all this, and that nothing I'd said up to this point had helped. It was clear only to me.

"You know the deal with my mom and dad. You know they've been married for years and how my dad is just bitter and evil for no reason. Plus, all my friends are either divorced or headed in that direction."

Alton opened his arms and pulled me to him. I relaxed under his breath as it trailed down my face. I loved being in his arms.

"I'm not going to leave you. I'm not going to get bitter for no reason like your dad. I will always love you."

He released his left arm to grab my chin and lifted it. Then I felt the sweetest kiss that he had ever given me. Those soft, full lips covered mine, lingered for a moment, then backed off. He blew a gentle breath across my wet lips and my back shivered. He lowered his right hand and stroked my shivering back as he continued to share his love with me.

"I love you, Miss Lady." I felt his broad smile against my face.

"I love you, too."

He pressed his warm, moist lips against the bridge of my nose, my cheek, my eyelid, then my forehead. He pulled me closer to him and held me tight. I swear we blended into each other and became one at that moment. "We're not going to be like your friends or your parents."

"Alton?"

"Yes?"

"Why don't we try living together for just a year or two? Then, if it works out, we'll get married?"

The moment broke.

Alton removed his arm from around me and sat straight up. His back was stiff. It slowly curved as he leaned forward, placed his elbows on his knees, and drew his hands down his face. He gave a cynical laugh and shook his head. His eyes were moist and he appeared to be reading something in the carpet. He lowered his head between his knees to read it more closely, I guessed.

I hadn't seen this type of reaction from Alton before and I didn't know what to think or do. I touched his back as he leaned forward. No response.

Alton finally raised his head. His thumbs held the weight of his chin as his fingers crossed his mouth and nose in prayer position. His eyes stared straight ahead.

I wished he would say something. I needed to hear him say something. Anything.

"I can't do this anymore, Van."

Anything but that.

Alton stood up and smoothed out his pants. He avoided my gaze, hesitating for a second before repeating aloud to himself, "I can't do this." He seemed to have erased me from the room. Alton stuck one leg out to get him started, and slowly dragged the second one behind.

"Wait, Alton!" I said.

"I can't. I can't do this. I'm sorry."

He was sorry? What was *he* sorry about? "No, I'm the one who should be sorry." I stood up and got in front of him before he could take another step toward ripping my heart out. Alton placed both hands heavily on my shoulders and peered into my eyes. He kissed my forehead.

"Van, it's obvious that you and I see things differently. We both want different things out of a relationship."

"No, Alton." My heart pounded in my chest. My palms began to sweat and my fingers froze. Air rushed in and out of my nose rapidly and dried its walls.

"I can't give you what you're looking for in a relationship, and I want more." He laughed that cynical laugh again. "I never would have thought this would happen."

"What would happen? What are you talking about?" I bounced up and down before I began to roll over on my ankle. Slowly at first, then faster.

"I've got to go. I can't do this anymore. This is killing me."

"Go? What do you mean go?"

He hugged me tightly, then released me and backed off. "I'm out, Van. I can't do this."

I felt a sharp pain in my gut that slowly began to rise. It crawled to my ribs, up through my breasts, and reached out to my nipples. The charge went through my shoulders, down my arms, up through my neck, and the next thing I knew, a downpour erupted from my eyes. I had known it would come to this. Had expected it. But that didn't mean I was ready for it.

"You can't leave me."

Alton's eyes were wet. His mouth had tightened. He pulled his arm from my grip and walked to the door.

My heart beat faster and faster. It began to hurt. It pounded through to my shoulder blades. I ran behind him as he got to the door and reached for the knob. "No, Alton, you can't leave me," I cried. Tears were rolling down my face like a rain storm.

I looked at Alton's face, but he wouldn't look at me. His eyes were fixed on the door. He didn't say anything more.

My cry turned into a heavy sob and I yelled out his name. I grabbed his arm again and held it tightly. He was not going to walk out that door. Woman's intuition told me that if he did, he wouldn't come back. I was certain my intuition was right this time.

Alton turned the knob with his left hand as I held on for dear life to his right, sobbing, crying, screaming.

"It's not going to work out, Van. I'm sorry. It's just not going to work out." He tried to wiggle free of my grasp, but I wouldn't let go. Wouldn't let him walk out on me. He wiggled harder. I held him tighter. He wiggled even harder. I wrapped my body around his arm and cried out his name.

Alton took his left hand off the doorknob and pushed me off his arm, gently at first, but I wouldn't let go. He pushed increasingly harder until he pushed so hard that I stumbled backward. My arm popped free of him and my hand flew back and hit me in the mouth, stinging my lip. I pressed my fingers against my bottom lip to block the pain. My face was drenched with sweat, and I gritted my teeth and cried between them. Alton still wouldn't look at me. I continued to step back, then I fell to the floor. Alton looked in my direction, but over my head.

"Alton, you know I love you," I cried. My voice was shattered.

He didn't return the response. His special way of saying yes. He didn't say it this time.

"Bye, Vanella. I wish you the best."

Alton opened the door and began to walk through, slowly dragging my soul with him. I was on all fours. In desperation I lunged for his pants leg and brushed against it as he carried it across the threshold and closed the door behind him.

My fingertips touched the front door that he had just walked through. I lay sobbing on the floor, face down, where I remained until the next morning.

Thirteen

DAY THREE WAS WHEN I finally got up out of bed. My joints were stiff as I stood at the foot of the bed. My body felt cruddy, and my head felt like the top of a high rise in the path of a strong gust of wind. I hadn't talked, eaten, or moved in three days. All I had done was lie in the bed facedown, trying to keep my heart encased inside my chest because I knew that if I got up, it would surely go tumbling down to the floor.

I pushed strands of hair out of my face and patted them into my dry, matted head, then wiped my face with my hand. My fingers skipped down my face over dried tears from waking up and crying every three hours, dried blood from the split in my bottom lip, and God knows what else. I pulled down the badly wrinkled, oversized T-shirt I wore—one of Alton's that I had pulled from his drawer after I finally scraped myself off the floor—and walked over to the blinds. The loose socks on my feet flopped like clown shoes with each stiffened step I took over the mounds of clothing that reminded me of the tantrum I'd thrown a few days ago. I opened the blinds to lighten the room. I hadn't seen the sun in the past three days. Apparently, I wouldn't see it today either.

It was an overcast day in Cleveland.

I lifted my face to the light behind the clouds, took a deep breath, then exhaled. I turned to face the room again and reviewed the aftermath of my tantrum. I'd snatched out everything he had in my drawers and closets and tossed it all onto the floor. I wondered if he was doing the same with my things at his place.

I walked through my condo to survey and extract the erratic scenes from my memory. In the kitchen, a broken glass—the last glass that Alton had touched at my place—rested in a puddle of water. In the living room, one glass of wine on the coffee table. When Alton walked out on me, I had opened the sliding door to the balcony and tossed his glass—Merlot and all—over three inches of fresh November snow. It left a spotted crimson trail that began on the balcony, skipped a path, then pooled in a small spot where the glass had landed.

My home office was clean. The wastebasket was filled with the COSE papers, Small Business Administration papers, and any and all other papers with ideas I had about opening a business. I had no energy and no passion to think about that anymore.

Completing the tour, I came across the front door where a finger-stroke of dried blood from where I had swiped my split lip, and then reached out for Alton, remained at the bottom of the door. I started to feel heavy once more and tears began to well up all over again. I leaned my back against the door and felt as if a heavy weight was slowly pushing down on my shoulders and causing me to slide to the floor. I sat there in pain with tears streaming down my face.

The phone rang. My legs trembled from lack of sustenance

and wouldn't allow me to stand again so soon. It probably wasn't Alton. Since I didn't feel like talking to anyone else, I let it ring. The answering machine picked up, and Synda spoke after my pleasant greeting from a different era.

"Okay, girl, that's it. I'm coming over. It's been three days now and none of us have heard a peep from you. We figured you needed time, but it's been long enough. I'm on my way."

Shit. I really didn't feel like going into the details about how I had screwed up the relationship I'd tried so hard to protect. But, on the other hand, I could use the company right about now. I felt small, lonely, and completely alone.

I summoned up a bit of energy from my gut to gain the strength needed for my legs to propel a wounded me upward. I trudged over to the phone and peered down at the flashing light. Ten messages, the display read. I picked up the phone and scrolled through the call list: Synda, Mom, Zandra, Medena, Kawamichi, Sherron, Armando, but no Alton. Not his home phone. Not his work phone. Not his cell phone. He hadn't even called to check on me. I wasn't used to that. I pressed play and skipped through the messages.

Zandra: "Hey girl. I stopped by Alton's to find out where you were and he told me that you broke up. What's going on? I told the girls because we were all worried about you. We called your job and found out you took the week off, but we saw your car through your garage window. We figured you probably needed some time, so we agreed to give you a little space first because we know how you are. But call me when you're ready to talk, okay? Love you."

Dexter: "Ms. Morris. This is Dexter McKleon. I know you called off for a few days, but I wanted to let you know that I had no choice but to handle negotiations on the Toyota account in your absence. Your boss came to me and summoned my expertise in your absence, so I couldn't say no. I'm aware that this job can be stressful, so it would be understandable if it was a bit much for you. Nothing to be ashamed of. It can even be a little stressful for me as a man." He gave a tool's chuckle. "I'm willing to provide you with assistance by taking something off your hands . . . like, say, this Toyota account. I'll discuss it with you upon your return. Thank you."

How nice of Dexter to offer to take the high-profile Toyota account. Actually, it was the highest. Especially since it was only Wednesday and supplier negotiations with Toyota weren't scheduled to begin until next Friday. Plenty of time for me to get back to work and get it going. Knowing Dexter, my boss probably only asked him after Dexter dropped mad hints and gave a presentation on how my absence could cause Kawamichi the loss of the account plus millions of dollars. What I wouldn't do to be rid of that type of job and that type of working environment.

Sherron: "Hey, Van. Zandra told us that you and Alton broke up. I hope you're not letting that get you down. Girl, this is a blessing in disguise. You are a beautiful, strong, and successful black woman. You don't have to take nothing from nobody. You hear me? You don't need a man unless *you* say so. But anyway, I'm there for you like you were there for me. Give me a call. If I don't hear from you soon, I'm coming by. Bye."

I skipped the rest. I wondered what Alton was doing, how he was feeling. Did he think about me over the last few days? Did he want to call, but couldn't? Why wouldn't he? Was this worth all the hell he was putting us through? Was living together worse than our breaking up? Than not seeing each other at all? This shit didn't make sense to me. I couldn't believe he could be this stubborn and this insensitive. I guess I never really knew him after all.

I looked up and fixed my eyes on the pictures of Alton and me on the walls, and I wondered how in the world I missed those in my rampage a few days ago. I stared. He looked so beautiful. *Damn, Alton. Was what I wanted all that bad? I was only trying to make sure we stayed together forever.* I jerked myself back and forth a couple of times to shake off the dark clouds that were approaching overhead.

"Van, open up."

The door sighed as I pulled it out of the reach of Synda's hammering fist. She glared at me, sprung her neck back, and pasted a thick frown on her face. "Lord, I never thought I'd see the day. Girl, you look like an ol' battered, malnourished crack addict." She fanned herself with her hand as she walked inside. Her ponytail swished as she brushed past me and proceeded to crack open the windows in each room. "It's so stuffy in here."

"I'm not up for it, Synda," I said. I pulled up my floppy socks. "Not now."

"No, you need to just pull them thangs off and go take a shower. You stink." She turned up her nose and went to the bathroom off my bedroom. The faucet screeched and an army of water droplets crashed to the ceramic shower floor. "Lord, and what is all this crap on the floor in here?" She fussed as she came back through the bedroom. "This place is a pigsty."

Had Alton showered? I wondered. Had he eaten? Was his house in shambles? Had he been to work in the past three days? I made it to the door of the bedroom before my legs gave out on me again. In slow motion, I slid down the doorway and collapsed on the cream carpet.

"Oh, no you don't," Synda said as she charged at me before the cement of misery set around me. She propped her hands under my armpits and hoisted me up. "Humph. This is like picking up sticks." She chuckled alone at her attempt to lighten me up.

I stood up with her, embraced her, and allowed my tears to rain upon her shoulder. I heaved and ached as tears gushed from my eyes onto her red turtleneck sweater. She stood there and hugged me tightly, patting and rubbing my back and head. "It'll be all right. Sshhh. It'll be all right."

She had traded places with me and was in the spot that I had been in so many times with other girlfriends. Now, it was my turn to be the one resuscitated and brought back to life.

I sobbed, "I can't believe he's gone. I can't believe he walked out on me. He left me. I don't understand how he could be so cruel." Howls mixed with my babbling as I tried to get it all out.

"I know, I know, but, sweetie, I can't understand a word you're saying," she sassed. She guided me to the bathroom. "I'm not sure I want to just yet either." She fetched my toothbrush, slathered it with toothpaste and handed it to me. "Try this first." She smiled. I smiled back weakly as I took the toothbrush and began brushing my teeth.

Synda retreated and said, "I'm going to put on a pot of coffee and make us some breakfast. You could use a couple of meals. We can talk if you want to. If you don't, we won't. I'll try to start cleaning up for you a bit, and then we're going to have to do something with that bush on top of your head. I almost cut myself. Ooh. Can I have this?" She picked up Alton's Indians jersey, looked at me, and grinned. She paused, then spoke softly. "You gonna be okay?"

I nodded.

"Whew. I'm just glad it's not my fault this time," Synda said.

She dropped the jersey and walked out the bedroom door toward the kitchen.

"You didn't have these pictures up the last time I came here. Is this Alton?" She paused. "Damn, he *is* fine."

It was my first Sunday without Alton. Days passed without a word from him. I knew he was aware by then that I had called. I dialed his number several times over the past few days, and he still hadn't called me back. He let the answering machine pick up, but I'd bet anything he was home. God, did he hate me now? I refused to leave a message so I kept calling back, but he would never answer—not even at two in the morning.

I jumped at the sound of the phone ringing. I ran to pick up the handset and looked at the caller ID. I did this all the time now, hoping that it would be Alton calling me back.

"Hi, Mom. What's up?" I asked after reading the number and picking up the phone.

"Hey, Van. Just calling to check up on you. How are you doing?"

"Doing fine."

"Any word from Alton yet?"

"No."

"Well, just give him a little time. He'll call and I know you all will work things out."

"Yeah," I said, but I didn't believe it. "What's going on over there?"

"Well, that's why I'm calling."

I released a weary sigh.

"Your father threw Kizaar out of the house and locked him out. He even had a locksmith come over and change the locks while your brother was job hunting. He accused Kizaar of trying to hide his walking cane. He found it a little while later right where he last left it. He didn't admit it or apologize, of course. He did let Kizaar come back, but not before calling him a sissy again for the cooking thing and yelling at me for giving birth to a sissy, and well . . . things are a mess here. The tension is so thick you can cut it with a knife."

"How's Kizaar holding up?"

"I'm worried about him. Despite all of that, and the other little things your father manages to find to throw a fit over, he's still trying to gain Jesse's approval. I can't talk him into just going out there and living his own life." She paused. "But you know, sometimes he listens to you. Anyway, I was thinking that this might be a good time for you to take some time off and come home for a little bit. You need some time to get away from things yourself, and your brother and sister haven't seen you in months. I'm sure they'd love to see you."

I cleared my empty throat.

"Something's going on with Babysista, too, by the way," she added. "I just haven't been able to get to what it is. She's been acting a little strange over the last few weeks. I wish she'd stop buying expensive gifts for these nappy-headed little boys around here. They sure aren't men. She just bought Cyrus a five-hundred-dollar watch the other day."

I sighed again. Apparently, her little stint in jail and court appearances hadn't taught her anything.

"I can't get away now, Mom, but I'm going to schedule a little time off in the near future. Okay?"

"Okay, but make it soon. Things always ease up a little bit when you're around, and it stays that way after you leave. At least for a little while."

I heard a knock at my front door. "I will. Hey, I gotta go, but I'll talk to you soon. Love you, Mom."

"All right. I love you too, Van."

As I walked to the front door, my heartbeat quickened. Maybe it was Alton coming by to check up on me. Maybe he wanted to talk over the Browns game. I flung the door open.

"Hey girl. How you been?" Synda asked as she walked in, panting. Her eyes were shifty and her thoughts seemed undecided.

"You okay?" I asked.

"I should be asking you that. It was just a few days ago that I came over here and had to scrape you up off the floor. Give me a hug." She leaned into me and gave me a tight squeeze. "Look at you. Hair combed, a little eyeliner and a little lipstick. Breath ain't kickin'."

"Shut up," I said, and we both laughed. I closed the door and followed Synda to the couch in the living room. I sat down on the opposite end from her. "I'm doing okay. Trying to make it." I stared at my hands in my lap. "You know, he won't return any of my calls. He won't even pick up the phone."

Synda fidgeted and squirmed a couple of times on the couch as if to find a more comfortable position. "Well, you trampled all over his heart. He probably needs time to pick his face up off the floor. He'll call. Men are used to women chasing them down and trying to trap them into marriage. You cut down his ego, girl. He's probably at home regrouping now." She crossed, uncrossed, then crossed her legs again.

"I don't think it's a crushed ego with Alton. Alton's an old-fashioned kind of guy and—"

"Even TC was worried about you." She cut me off.

"TC?" I asked in amazement, partly because he'd asked about me, and partly because Synda talked about it like it was nothing.

"Yeah. Let me call him now to let him know you're okay." She leaned to the left and pulled her cell phone out of her pocket. She started to dial, then stopped. "Um . . . my battery is low. Can I use your phone?"

Cold air skimmed my tongue as my mouth hung open. I felt like I should have been looking around for the candid camera somewhere. Was she trying to set me up or something?

"Yeah, but I don't think it's necessary to call—"

Before I could finish, Synda had set her phone on the coffee table, got up, and grabbed my phone out of the cradle in the kitchen and had Tucker on the line. "Hey, T, what's up? I'm at Vanella's house. Checking on my girl. So, I'm going to be here for a little while. You know, girl stuff. Huh? Yeah. Okay, well, hey, wait a minute . . ." She held the handset in the air and said to me, "Say hi to TC."

I looked at her with widened eyes and a raised right eyebrow. What was her problem? What had gotten into her? I just stared.

"Say hi," she said in a forceful whisper.

"Hi, Tucker," I said aloud.

She turned her back to me and brought the phone back to her ear. "Did you hear her? Okay, I'll tell her."

I leaned over and glanced at the face of her cell phone on the coffee table. The battery display read full.

"Well, I'll see you a little later this evening. Bye." She clicked the phone off and came back to reclaim her seat on the couch.

"What's up with that? You're acting a little strange." I leaned back.

"Strange? What are you talking about? Well, anyway," she continued before I could answer, "like I was saying. Men just don't know how to handle women like you. A woman who's not chasing down a man and a proposal." She got up. "I gotta use the bathroom."

Synda clutched her purse and stalked off to the bathroom in a hurry. I heard the bathroom door shut firmly. I sat still for a minute and reviewed Synda's behavior and the completely charged cell phone. I picked up the cell phone and hit the scroll button to see calls placed: Cedric . . . Cedric . . . Cedric . . . I looked at calls received: Cedric . . . Cedric . . . Cedric. My blood warmed.

The bathroom door sprung open and a freshly powdered and fragranced Synda reappeared. She fastened the clasp on her purse as she came back into the living room. "Well, girl, I'm going to get out of here. I got some errands to run before I go back home, but you're looking good." She picked up her cell phone, buttoned her coat, and headed to the door. Didn't give me a chance to ask her to stay like she told her husband she was going to do. "You call me if you need to talk, okay?"

"Okay, I will." I eyed her as she hugged me again and left.

Fourteen

SOONER OR LATER IT looked like I was going to have to make good on my promise to beat Synda's ass if she messed around on Tucker. But then again, why did I care? Regardless, it would have to wait until later because I had my own crap to deal with.

After I got off the phone with Mom, I seriously considered going home to St. Louis for a little while. She was right. Maybe I did need to get away and spend a little time with the family, even if they were a dysfunctional mess. But what family wasn't? God knows I had enough vacation time saved up. Even with all the trips that Alton and I had taken over the years, my time off had never equaled the time I had coming. Since vacation days rolled over every year, I had managed to rack up a sizable amount of time off. My three weeks per year plus the additional vacation days that I purchased gave me two months of time. And I could get old Ms. Millie next door to get the mail, watch the condo, and water the plants. She was a nature lover anyway and I noticed that I always came home to healthier plants when she watered them when I took business trips. She said you just have to talk to them.

It was still just a fleeting thought until Mom called a couple of months later with more nonsense from home. That's when I started thinking that I might as well be there since I was getting reports on all the family drama anyway, which had become more frequent since Thanksgiving and Christmas. Maybe Alton would change his tune if he found out I was going to be away from Cleveland for a good amount of time. Never mind that my lonely holidays or the past two months did nothing to alter his unresponsiveness.

Mom called the last time because her car broke down and Dad refused to co-sign for her to get a new one, even after she had gotten a job to pay for it. It wasn't like Mom to go out and get a job. I had never known her to work a day in her life. But, apparently, they had agreed on her paying for the car and she had gotten a job at Wal-Mart as a cashier. Dad got up on the right side of the bed one day and took Mom and Kizaar out to breakfast before they all went out to the car dealership and they picked out a nice little Corolla for Mom. It wasn't exactly Mom's style, but since the transmission fell out of her twelve-year-old Caddy and with winter fast approaching, she was up for anything.

Mom said they looked it over, test drove the car, and even haggled the salesman down to the price they wanted. They waited an hour for the salesman to prepare the paperwork, in which time Dad's mood gradually went from cheerful to hateful. By the time the salesman asked for Dad's signature as co-signer, Dad had changed his mind, gotten up, and limped out.

So Mom had been car-less for two months but hadn't bothered to tell me. She only told me now because she needed a co-signer. Mom was at the bus stop in minus twenty—degree weather when a St. Louis snowstorm hit and the buses stopped running. When Dad refused to stop watching TV to go pick her up, she got a frostbite scare after walking home two and a half hours wearing three-inch pumps through twelve-inch-high snow. Dad was there to tell her how much of an idiot she was for walking home in those shoes, and then he drove off in the blizzard to see if his favorite restaurant was open so that he could pick up a tripe sandwich.

I plopped myself down in front of my computer to make plans for an extended stay in St. Louis. Somebody had to put Dad in his place. I was getting sick of being called about the misadventures of the crippled evil one. I grumbled as I began making my own travel plans and searching for the best flight time with the cheapest rate, a rental car, and a good place to stay. I thought about Alton. God knows if he planned my trip I'd have the least expensive, most comfortable place to lay my head and one less headache. I was sure of it. I gave up and decided to drive. I could use the time to think. I'd call into work tomorrow and put in for all my vacation time effective immediately. Family emergency.

I eyed the cordless sitting next to the computer. It had been a while since I had tried to call Alton. According to my caller ID, he had never attempted to call me after he broke it off last November. To keep myself from spending the next hour debating whether to call or not, I just grabbed the damned phone and dialed.

It rang once, twice, then . . . "Hello."

My arms went numb at the sound of his voice. It was as if he stood right next to me, as if he was leaning in my ear and talking to me. I smiled uncontrollably. I closed my eyes and a wave of calmness came over me. I pressed the phone deeper into my ear and listened to him . . .

". . . this is Alton Goode. I'm not available to take your call right now. But if you leave a message after the beep, I will return your call as soon as possible." Beeeeep.

I did something that I hadn't done in months. I left a message.

"Hi, Alton. Um . . . it's me, Vanella. Hey, I was just calling to let you know that I'm going out of town for a couple of months. I'm going home to St. Louis. Something's come up with the family and I really need to be there. Um . . . I don't know why I'm calling you. There's nothing I'm looking for you to do. Just wanted to call to let you know. Bye."

My head felt hot, but my hands were cold and clammy as I put the phone back down. It was like the first time that I called to talk to him after I discovered I was in love with him. I was giddy then and had spent hours doing stupid little things until he called me back. But this time, I didn't think he would call back.

I got up and pulled out my suitcases to begin packing. I was two hours into doing laundry and folding fresh clothes when the phone rang. I jumped. Could it be him? I got excited, then got mad at myself for getting excited. I briskly walked to the kitchen and grabbed the phone before the answering machine picked up.

"Hello?"

"Hey, Van."

It sounded like sweet music on the other end. Alton's voice serenaded me through the phone with a song that I hadn't heard in months.

"Alton?"

"Yeah. Hey, I got your message. I just wanted to call to make sure everything's okay. I mean, nobody's hurt, are they? Moms? Pops?"

This was the Alton I knew. Concerned. Considerate. Loving.

My hand trembled as I held the phone up to my ear. My

palms were cold and clammy all over again and I felt my back break out in a sweat along my spine. I shifted the phone from the right side to the left.

"Oh, no, nothing like that. Well, there are some issues going on with Mom and Dad. The usual, but it's picking up a little. So, I thought I'd use those couple of months of vacation time I have to go home and see if I could ease the tension a little. Plus, I could use the time away. The last few months haven't been the greatest, you know." I laughed in staccato. Began to pace between the living room and the bedroom.

"But everybody's fine? What about Kizaar and Baby-Jae?"

I stopped and sat down on the floor between the bedroom and the living room. I tried to find some leverage to keep my body from shivering and to remove the tremble from my voice. I couldn't believe it. I was talking to Alton. I missed him.

"Well, no one's been shot or anything. At least not yet." I released another nervous laugh. "I didn't mean to alarm you. I just wanted to call to let you know that I was going to St. Louis to be with the family for a while. You had always been concerned about my family in the past."

"I'm still concerned. If you ever need me for anything, if there's ever anything I can help you and your family with, just give me a call. I'll do what I can to help."

He was back. He was himself. He was no longer mad at me and was probably just waiting on me to place one more phone call to him. "You always did. My family always appreciated you for that."

"Well, I'm glad to hear that everything's—"

"I miss you, Alton," I blurted.

The line grew quiet a second. Alton's voice was low. "I miss you, too, Van. I'm sorry for not returning your calls in the past. I just couldn't take it, back then. I couldn't stand to hear your voice. To talk to you and know that you would never be mine."

I leaned my head to the side and smiled into the phone. I wanted to kiss it. "No need to apologize. I understand. That was just a bad period in our lives."

"You don't know how much that hurt me. I have never felt like that before in my life, and I never want to feel like that ever again."

"I know, I know," I whispered. "I'm sorry. I'm sorry for making you feel that way, for causing this bad spot between us. I'm sorry."

"Nothing to be sorry about. You were speaking what you felt. You were just being you. It's funny, but that was always what I admired about you. You were never one to just tell me what I wanted to hear. You were always honest and spoke what you felt."

My stretched-out legs rocked wildly on the floor. "Look, I'm not leaving until tomorrow afternoon. Why don't we have breakfast?"

Silence.

"I just called to make sure everything was okay with your family. But now that I know everything's okay, I'm going to go on with my life, and I think you should go on with yours."

I felt like a fireball formed, exploded in my stomach, and fried my insides. I struggled to stay composed because I didn't want to break down like a blubbering idiot with Alton on the phone. I had my dignity . . . or at least I tried to act like I had some.

I cleared my throat before speaking. "Oh, I'm not talking about resuming our relationship." The hell I wasn't. "I just want to see you. I thought that we could get together and just talk. You know, catch up on old times."

"I just don't think that would be a good idea." He hesitated. "Vanella, I still love you. I still have feelings for you. I don't think you realize how much our breakup hurt me once I realized we didn't want the same things. I don't know. Maybe in the future when we're both dating other people and are in love, I can see you again and we can be friends. But not now."

My jaw stiffened. My dignity was losing grip. "We should talk this out, Alton. I just want us to be friends. That's all. Why don't you come by tonight? I'm not expecting anything. Just to talk."

He paused again before answering. "I can't. I . . . I'm going out. I have a date."

His words stung me and knocked the speech right out of my mouth. Slapped me tasteless. I gasped to find the breath that had escaped me.

"A date? With a woman?"

"Uh . . . yeah. I was hurt, not turned out."

"Anyone I know?" I knew it was a stupid question. What did it matter? Even my costume dignity had taken a leap out the window and left me defenseless.

"Van . . ."

I surprised myself. Before my brain could reason a thought, the words jumped right out of my mouth. "I'll marry you, Alton. Yes, I will marry you." I spoke loudly into the phone. With much confidence. I screamed it. I spit the words out so fast that I showered myself with saliva.

"Don't do this, Van. Don't do this. I was just calling to make sure everything was okay."

I began to pant. I had him on the line and I didn't want to lose him again. I said it again. Louder. "I'll marry you, Alton! Yes! I will marry you!"

The air buzzed before Alton spoke. "You know, two months ago that was all I wanted to hear. But now you're only saying that because I left. That's not what you really want. You're only saying that now to get back what we had. That's not good. I don't want you to feel like you were manipulated into marrying me. Then it would be true that five years from now, you'll want a divorce. All because you didn't get married for the right reasons."

"I do want to marry you. It's what I want." I was crying fully now. "Yes, I was afraid of marriage. I still am a little. That's why I had an idea about just living together, because I thought we'd have a better chance at being together forever."

"Van."

"Oprah never married Stedman and they've been together for so long. They'll never break up. I was just trying to do what Oprah was doing so that we could last longer. It works for Oprah." I panted harder and my head started to float.

Alton blew into the phone. "Van." He paused. "You're not Oprah." He repeated, slowly, "You're *not* Oprah."

And then the only sound was the sound of my sniffles.

"I gotta go. I wish nothing but the best for you. Take care." With that, my connection to Alton was severed. Again.

I packed up the RX300 a few hours after our most recent painful separation. The next day I started out on my ten-hour drive to St. Louis. I left Cleveland, and on that drive decided that I had to let go of Alton. Forever.

Fifteen

THE "ES-TEE-EL."

I cruised into my city westbound on Highway 70. After a ten-hour drive from Cleveland and crossing the Mississippi on the M. L. King Bridge from Illinois, seeing the St. Louis Arch always brought on feelings of nostalgia. Caused me to have a resurgence of all types of memories. Usually, the good ones came first.

Like how good I felt about being from St. Louis long before Nelly and the St. Lunatics supposedly put my city on the map. To me, it had always been there. After all, St. Louis was where entrepreneur and social activist Madame C. J. Walker set up shop; where Josephine Baker grew up and first shook her der-riere; where Dred and Harriet Scott fought eleven years for emancipation; where Chuck Berry and Miles Davis seared our souls with rock and roll and jazz; where native writers John Keene and Jacqueline Powell set their novels; the birthplace of Maya Angelou and John Elroy Sanford, better known to the world as Redd Foxx or Fred G. Sanford of *Sanford and Son*; where St. Louisans could enjoy a home-brewed Budweiser while watching Ozzie Smith open each home game with a running backward flip onto the field; where Lou Brock helped the Cardinals win the World Series in '64—yes, the team that has won more World Series Championships than any other National League team; and where Cedric the Entertainer and Joe Torry first kept us in stitches.

Across the river in East Boogie—East St. Louis, Illinois—where Anna Mae Bullock began rolling down the river as Tina Turner; and where Jackie Joyner-Kersee trained her legs to win Olympic gold medals. My city was where Marshall Faulk could rush a football from New Orleans to San Diego to the Edward Jones Dome and still have the wind to rush a few more yards. St. Louis was *my* city, and would always be my home.

I ramped off the highway on Broadway and headed downtown. Picked up Market Street and drove past Kiener Plaza, which was usually stocked with musicians and brown baggers lunching outside the office—for some of them, a forty-five minute break away from the chaos. Most were seeking solace and a welcomed chew to a groove. But it was cold out, and the only people in Kiener Plaza were the ones hurrying on to a warm spot.

I looked to the left and the glazed smile on my face dropped when I noticed the driver of a rebuilt sky-blue deuce and a quarter staring at me from the next lane. I turned away and then glanced at him again. He was still staring. In one smooth motion, his eyelids hung low as he jerked his head back to gesture a hello. He spread his thick lips and displayed a heart-shaped, gold-capped tooth while a toothpick dangled from the corner of his mouth. He winked. The light turned green and his whitewall tires screeched as he peeled off.

I chuckled. Yep, I'm home.

I headed up Eleventh Street, turned right onto Washington Avenue, and parked in front of my temporary home: the Merchandise Mart. It looked as beautiful as it did in the brochure I requested a month ago when I'd first begun contemplating an extended visit. The Romanesque design fluttered with a bold medley of polished rose granite, terra cotta, and sandstone materials. The second story was framed by sturdy arches, and the huge warehouse windows mirrored the sky. Hard to believe that this building had been vacant for the last few years and was slated for demolition until a real estate development company renovated it last year. Dad talked about how he wished it were his company. I stepped into the office, completed the required paperwork, and obtained the keys to the furnished loft I would be renting for the next couple of months.

I took my suitcases up to my loft on the sixth floor. The door opened to a trendy living room with maple floors and exposed brick walls. They hadn't skimped on the furnishings, which included an oatmeal sectional, two tan leather chairs, a maple dining set, and an assortment of decorative vases. This was going to be a comfortable stay. Alton would have been proud. No, I needed to stop thinking about him.

I dropped everything on the living room floor when I spotted a telephone book on the black granite kitchen counter. I flipped the pages until I found it: Imo's Pizza. Wrapping my lips around Imo's Pizza was always the first thing I did when I came to St. Louis. Imo's was about the only thing in which I could drown myself and come up asking, "Alton who?" I picked up the phone and ordered a large sausage and mushroom pizza, a large salad with that tangy Imo's dressing, and a two-liter bottle of Diet Coke.

Then I called Synda. I needed to get to the bottom of my sus-
picions, but apparently I would have to do that a little later. I left
her a voice mail that I was in St. Louis and needed her to call me
back as soon as possible. I didn't know what I was going to say,
but I would be damned if I was going to let her cheat on my first
love. If she risked our friendship and tore me up just to be with
him, then, dammit, she was going to be with him for life without
cheating on him. So help me, she would.

Tucker made a mistake, but what person hasn't? Especially in
youth and in college? He was still a good man. It occurred to me
that maybe this was why I'd kept her within reach—not that I
wanted him back or was waiting for them to break up or anything, because that's not my style. I just wanted to make sure that
she didn't back out of the vows she made to Tucker—the vows *I*
should have made to him.

I inhaled the large pizza before I headed to Mom and Dad's
house on Lindell Boulevard across the street from Forest Park. A
tension headache took over my face and became more intense
with each tenth of a mile I drove. I pulled up in Mom and Dad's
long driveway, then dug in my purse and waded through re-
ceipts, makeup, and pens for my savior bottle of Excedrin.
Since working at Kawamichi, I'd learned to keep a bottle of
pain reliever close by at all times. Never stepped foot out the
door without it. I took two pills, washed them down with the
bottled water that I kept in my ride, and prepared my senses for
the unexpected.

The gold-colored three-story mini-mansion looked drab as I
stepped out of my SUV. The drapes were drawn and all the windows in the house looked dark. The stained glass windows that
lined the front side of the house seemed darker than I remem-

bered. I walked up to the front door, rang the doorbell, and waited several minutes before Kizaar finally pulled open the heavy wooden door.

"Hey, what's up, sis?" He pulled me into the dim foyer and gave me a bear hug. Darkness filled the hallway beyond the foyer and spilled from the living room on our right to the kitchen at the end of the hall.

Kizaar closed the door, took my leather coat, and hung it in the foyer closet. He asked about my drive as he turned on lights and led the way into the open living room. Kizaar hopped into the oversized chair and put his slippered feet on the ottoman.

I slowly walked around the living room and reacquainted myself with the reminders of my childhood. I recognized the light fruity scent from the air fresheners that Mom plugged in around the room to mask the melancholy. She still tried to do that. Always had a different scent for each room.

"Mom and Dad aren't home?"

"No. Don't you hear how peaceful it is?" He chuckled. "They should be home any minute now. You're catching Dad on the upswing of a good mood. He just walked up to me and handed me fifty bucks for no reason yesterday. Said it was just to put a little change in my pocket and that I didn't have to pay him back. And he's actually picking up Mom from work today."

"Without having a heart attack first? So what'd he do? Take a Midol?"

Kizaar hunched his shoulders and bent the tips of a few of his soft locks. "I think he found out about you coming all the way here to co-sign for a car for her and he got a little embarrassed."

He should've, I thought. "Humph," was all I said aloud. "So, what's up?" I asked, changing the subject. "Is my little brother going to be a chef or not?" I leaned back against the side of the fire-place and folded my arms.

He clasped his hands and extended them forward to stretch his back. "Naahhh, I've decided to join Dad in the business." He popped his neck by leaning his head from shoulder to shoulder. The cracking resonated in my ears and caused me to shudder.

"But you don't even like the real estate business."

"I've never really given it a fair chance. I think I may have acted in haste by dropping it the first time. Besides, I know that my working closer to him is actually what he really wants—to have his son take over the business when he retires. I think things will change a little bit once we're working closer together."

I uncrossed my arms and slowly walked over to the front window. I parted the heavy emerald drapes and leaned on the window-sill. Night was falling and traffic on the busy boulevard in front of the house was easing up. The streetlights flicked on and covered the street with that midwest neighborhood appeal—a quiet and nonobtrusive, picture-perfect scene. Several coat-clad children did an about-face in the midst of double Dutch and headed like walking zombies to their homes. I kept my back to Kizaar.

"So what makes you think it will get better when you don't even know what's wrong?"

He hopped out of the chair. His eyes danced as if he were the sole possessor of the answer for peace in the Middle East. "I'm putting improvement plans together. Hold on." Kizaar did a light sprint from the living room and up the stairs to his room on the third floor, then he flew back down with a notebook secured be-neath his armpit. Dark strands of hair stood up on his arms against his golden skin.

"I'm using updated business techniques to develop continuous improvement plans for Dad's business. You know, Kaizen." He smiled at my expression of surprise at his knowledge of the Japanese term for continuous improvement.

"I take a couple of months off from work and drive ten hours to St. Louis to hear Japanese terms?" I joked.

His dreads shook as he flipped through the pages of his notebook. "Take a look. I've been going over Dad's current day-to-day operations and eliminating waste. Right now, I'm still documenting and evaluating all of his processes, then I'll calculate the cost savings that can be generated from implementing improvements. When I'm done, I'm going to present it to Dad. It shouldn't take more than a few weeks."

I took the notebook from him and flipped through flowcharts of current processes, improvement plans, and projected benefits. I closed it and gave it back to him. "This is good, but this is not you. This might even be me, but it's definitely not you."

Kizaar huffed, tossed the notebook on the wood and glass coffee table, and plopped back down in the oversized chair. "You know, I really don't understand this family. I'm always the one trying to find a way to make things better, but all I get from you, Mom, and Babysista is that I shouldn't. That I should let things be and just leave this house." He leaned forward and flung his hand over his head. "Am I the only one who wants our family to be closer? We need some love up in here."

I circled the coffee table and took a seat on the couch across from Kizaar. "That's the point, Zar. *You're* the only one who's always trying. Tell me, has anything you've done in your life ever improved your relationship with Dad? Better yet, what have you done to deserve half the crap he's dished out to you? When we were growing up, Dad would throw birthday parties for me and Babysista—never you. We always got more gifts, better gifts, and more expensive gifts than you for Christmas. When you were sixteen, Dad made you get a job, but he increased our allowances. He always came to our recitals, powder puff games, and gymnastics competitions, but he made you work in the yard in lieu of sports. I mean, really, what's it going to take for you?"

The chair burped as he sank deeper into it. "He gave me gifts." He paused. "Just less often than with you and Babysista. And maybe not as extravagant. Anyway, I'm not going to sit up here and blame my life as an adult on the fact that my dad didn't give me G.I. Joes for Christmas. At least I had a dad and he was just trying to make a man out of me. To teach me responsibility."

"Oh? So calling you a sissy makes a man out of you? Exactly what type of responsibility does that teach?"

Kizaar's nostrils flared and he mumbled something I couldn't understand. He opened his mouth and then hesitated at the sound of a key entering the lock. The front door opened and Mom and Dad walked in. Kizaar closed his mouth and rolled his eyes at me.

"Nelli-Nell!" Dad exclaimed. He always called me that when he hadn't seen me for a long time. It had tickled me as a little girl. We met at the room's entrance and he grabbed me in an elated embrace. Couldn't figure out how I felt just yet. I was always happy to see both my parents, but at the same time I was feeling pissed off at my dad for how he treated Mom and Kizaar.

I returned the hug. A dry hug.

"Hey, Dad. How are you?" I patted indifference into his back.

Dad had thickened since the last time I saw him, and his already receding hairline was deepening further. He took off his hat and displayed a desiccated forehead. His face was starting to droop, and permanent worry lines seemed to be carved into his forehead and across the bridge of his nose between his eyes. He balanced on his cane when he pulled away.

Mom tiptoed over with wide-stretched arms. She hugged and kissed me on my cheek after Dad let go. She smelled of a new full-bodied fragrance, and I felt her rich lipstick being smudged on my face. She had cut her silky, shoulder-length hair into a chin-length bob, another chic, new look. Even with her coat still buttoned, I could tell that she had not gained an ounce on her small, curvy frame.

She looked at me, then at Dad. "What time did you get in?" She had worry in her eyes and voice. She knew me.

"A few hours ago. Got a place downtown at the Merchandise Mart. I've only been here for a few, and Kizaar and I were just talking about his job interests. Do you know his real job interests, Dad?" I went right for the jugular.

"Van," Kizaar said with a stern voice. His eyes burned a hole in me.

"The Merchandise Mart? I hear that place is nice since they renovated it," Dad said. He ignored my question.

"Ooooh, yes. It's really nice," Mom chimed in. She unbuttoned her coat.

Dad cut sharp eyes at Mom. In a flash, he transformed from the meek old man who greeted me at the door to an evil little troll. "What do you know about the Merchandise Mart? You don't know anything. I don't even know why you open your mouth sometimes 'cause nothing good ever comes out." The creases on his forehead deepened as he continued to fuss. A vein popped out of the side of his neck.

Mom pressed her lips together and silently cast her eyes downward.

This was the crap that I was tired of, and one reason I didn't believe in long, happy marriages.

Out of the blue and for no reason at all, Dad went off like he usually did. Well, I wasn't having this anymore. "What was that all about?" I asked Dad. I dropped my smile and put my hand on my hip. Out of the corner of my eye, I saw Mom look up at me. "You know one of the reasons I wanted to come was to—"

Mom shifted her eyes from me to Dad. "Look, let's not get into anything too heavy now. You just got here." She placed a hand on my shoulder and nudged me backward. Dad cut his eyes at Mom while he shed his coat and tossed it on her shoulder.

She nudged me again to face her. The bottom half of her face said joy, while the top half said fear.

"I'll go warm up the food that Gloria prepared yesterday." Mom wasn't much of a cook anymore, and Gloria was hired help who came in twice a week to make and freeze meals. "Then we can all sit down and catch up." Mom smiled and rubbed my shoulder. She raised her charcoal-penciled eyebrows and pleaded with me with her eyes to let things be.

"Humph. Can't even get a fresh home-cooked meal around here except from sissy-boy over there. Good for nothing," Dad said to Mom. He snatched his coat off her shoulder and grumbled as he hobbled over to the foyer, hung it up in the closet, and limped away.

I turned to Kizaar. "I thought you said Dad was on the up-swing of a good mood."

"He was, but a whole day and a half has passed." Kizaar walked upstairs, shaking his head.

I walked around the living room alone while Mom went to heat up dinner. Mom still had a display of pictures of each of us at various points in our lives: me at my nursery school graduation, Kizaar playing with my racing car track at Christmas, all of our high school graduation pictures, me and Jaelene at gymnastics tournaments, Kizaar riding my bike.

The killer to me was the family portrait that hung high over the fireplace. We looked so poised, so happy, like nothing could be wrong. Mom and Dad sat together with Dad's hand cozily placed over Mom's hands, which were crossed in her lap. Kizaar stood next to Mom with his hand on her shoulder. His dreads looked like buds compared to the length they are now. I stood on the opposite end next to Dad. Jaelene stood between Kizaar and me. The three of us had smiles plastered on our faces. I stared at the strange family. That could have been me, Alton, and the three kids that he really wanted—although he joked about wanting six—looking like heaven on a picture, but living life in hell.

I stepped back from the portrait and moved over to the couch. I stared at it, too. I could see the couch in the old house with Dad stretched out on it. Sometimes he'd be watching TV, sometimes listening to gospel music, sometimes sleeping. If Mom or Kizaar walked across his path, then the rampage was on for any reason he could find: Kizaar disrespected him by bringing gangster-rap music in his house; Mom didn't starch his clothes just right; Kizaar disrespected him by bringing home a pet gerbil; Mom said something stupid—which was all the time with Dad; Kizaar didn't separate trash correctly for disposal. Dad was heavily into environmental conservation, and even joked that sending Styrofoam or plastic to a landfill would get you shot. We all thought that was what was going to happen once when Dad found a joint in Kizaar's room, and a gun another time. We all had gotten used to the routine of Dad's storming off in a rage and ripping Kizaar's room apart looking for the object of Kizaar's disrespect. Kizaar developed a fascination for guns just as Dad developed an aversion to them. It probably made Dad a little nervous when Kizaar got into guns and started going to the shooting range.

Dad had always showered Jaelene and me with love, toys, candy, money—you name it. For Kizaar, these things were few and far between. I would have thought that Kizaar would resent us for that, but he never did. Instead, he spent so much time trying to shine in Dad's eyes that we were just an afterthought. Kizaar always bought Dad the biggest and best Father's Day and Christmas presents, which Dad always found a clever way to demean or devalue. He wounded Kizaar countless times, but like a little warrior, Kizaar would pick his face out of the gutter and plan another route to get into Dad's good graces.

Kizaar tried getting good grades in school and taking leadership roles in church activities—all to no avail. Dad never acknowledged Kizaar's efforts except for those occasions when he may have felt guilty about being too mean. Then there would be a day or two when he would shower Mom and Kizaar with all the love in the world. Inevitably, his kindness would slowly diminish, and he'd revert to his old, evil-assed self.

The living room's scent of tropical flowers merged into candy orange as I made my way through the hallway to the kitchen. Mom and I dined together at the kitchen table. Even on my first day back in town, she was pressed to get the family to sit down at the table together for dinner. Hell, we hadn't done that when we were growing up, but Mom still made the effort during every one of my visits.

She sat across from me and carried on about what she was learning in the financial class, joining the working world, the plans she had for redecorating the house, and anything else she could think of to keep the conversation on safe topics for as long as possible. She talked as if nothing had happened earlier, and kept all visible signs of unhappiness covered up. I could see lines beginning to extend from the outer edges of her eyes, even with the concealer she'd smudged on, but the rest of her caramel face was still as smooth as pudding. As a child, I remembered being fascinated by my mother's beauty, and jealous of it when I was a teenager. Her looks had rubbed off on Jaelene, but not me. I couldn't do anything about my skin color, which was the darkest of the family. My complexion took my white maternal grand-mother by surprise. I had heard that my black grandfather had left her for an older, dark-skinned black woman. She took that unsolved trivia question to the grave with her, but her living heart had hardened to black men and dark-skinned black women. The grapevine had it that when she was allowed to name me, my parents' first child, she named me Vanella to "make up for the difference."

I insisted on cleaning up after dinner and let Mom retreat to the shower, then relax in her bedroom—the one that Dad did not share with her. That's what she needed: someone to make things easy for her, fuss over her, and love her—someone who treated her like the upstanding, God-fearing, straitlaced woman that she was. Dad needed to appreciate the woman that he had. Not many women would put up with the mental abuse for so many years. I rinsed the dishes and loaded the dishwasher, then went upstairs to tell Mom I was leaving for the night.

The scent of wildflowers greeted me as I climbed the car-peted stairs to the first floor. The stairway opened to a hallway, and directly in front was the bathroom. The door was slightly ajar, but the lights were off. I figured Mom must have finished her shower and gone into her bedroom, which was adjacent to the bathroom. A soft light seeped through the slit beneath Mom's bedroom door, so I knew she was still awake. I opened the door slightly and peered in to see if she was up and clothed.

Mom's slender frame stood in front of her dresser before an open jewelry box. I could see her image in the mirror, which allowed me to see what was in her hand. Her face was emotionless, at first. She stared down at the inside of the black velvet jewelry box before she reached in to pick up a tarnished chain-link necklace. The necklace supported a locket shaped like half of a heart. A tear rolled down her right cheek. She held the locket in the palm of her right hand, then closed her fingers around it. Sadness swept over me as she brought it to her chest and began to weep.

Mom opened the locket and stared at the picture inside. Her lips quivered as she shook her head from side to side. After staring for a while, she placed the necklace back inside the jewelry box and carefully closed the lid, then dabbed at the tears on her face with a tissue and headed for the door. I quickly tiptoed over to the bathroom and turned on the water.

"Van, is that you?"

"Yes, Mom. I'll be out in a minute."

"I'm going to run downstairs and get a glass of water. Do you want a glass?"

"No, that's okay. Thanks."

She sniffed and descended the stairs. I turned off the faucet and went directly to the jewelry box in her bedroom to retrieve the necklace. It was an old, cheap necklace, like the kind you get at parking lot carnivals to exchange with your teenaged sweetheart. I opened the locket to look at the picture inside. It was a picture of her and Dad as a young couple, maybe a few years younger than Alton and I were now. It couldn't have been taken long after they were married.

I always knew that Mom had to be hurting more than she let on, but until then I hadn't realized just how much she obviously missed the man she originally married.

I closed the locket and replaced it in the jewelry box. Strangely, I felt both angry and relieved. I was angry that Dad could make Mom feel this way. She didn't deserve this. There was no reason for him to constantly treat her like dirt. The few moments when he treated her like a queen could never erase the evilness. I knew Mom wouldn't want it, but I vowed to put an end to it, and soon. You have only one life to live, and no woman should be made to feel like crap at the hands of any man.

No doubt, I had done the right thing about sticking to the O Theory. I was certain that Dad wouldn't have treated her as he did if she had opted to live together instead of getting married. Men tend to be nicer to a good woman when there is a chance that she could leave at any moment and set up shop with another brother.

The couple in the locket was me and Alton. I could see that. I viewed my parents as what we would have evolved into. Yes, I knew I had done the right thing.

Sixteen

EVERY TIME I CAME home, it was always tough to decide which charitable organization to get involved in. Ever since high school, when community service was actually a graduation requirement for Jaelene—and Mom thought it was a good idea for the rest of us to do—I vowed to always contribute in some way, shape, or form. Monetary donations were always good, but time *and* money were even better.

Since I was going to be here for a couple of months, I wanted to work with some type of community service during my stay. Preferably something that benefited inner-city kids. I remembered being eight and spending the night at a friend's house in the Darst-Webbe housing projects years before they were slated for so-called renovations. Yeah, renovations that made them a gigantic eyesore. I remembered thinking how cool it was at the time—spending the night in the projects. It wasn't until I grew up that I realized the social disparity that took place there and the hopeless situation of some of my friends. I had even come back a few years ago to cheer with the crowd as a demolition company finally took a wrecking ball to it. It didn't go out in im-

ploding fashion like the infamous Pruitt-Igoe monstrosities of
the seventies, but it was a victory to bring down a huge housing
failure, nonetheless.

I sat at the kitchen counter sipping a cup of coffee and sifting
through the information I had brought with me on three local
organizations. Previously I'd donated time to the Matthews-
Dickey Boys Club, the Annie Malone Children's Home, and to
Joe Torry's Give Back the Love Foundation. This time I wanted
to see what others I could get involved in. I read brochures for
the Marshall Faulk Foundation, 4Sho4Kids, and the Cedric the
Entertainer Charitable Foundation. I decided on the Marshall
Faulk Foundation, and called the number on the brochure to get
volunteer information.

With that decision made, I decided to go out and kill some
time around downtown before meeting Jaelene in Laclede's
Landing. Although I loved seeing what was different whenever I
came home, I mostly wanted to get out of the apartment to keep
the quiet from muscling thoughts of Alton into my head.

I stopped at Union Station and watched employees of the
Fudgery belt out songs while whisking around a marble table
turning runaway fudge until it stiffened. Alton always got a kick
out of that little show, even though he hates fudge. He'd back off
when they began passing out samples with a sales pitch. We
would hang in the background until the next show. *Alton.* Perhaps
the Fudgery was not the best place to be at that time.

I desperately shook my head to try to push out the thoughts
of Alton as I returned to my SUV and drove to the Landing. My
mind slipped into memories of when I first brought Alton to Laclede's Landing. He loved the atmosphere. We walked hand in
hand down the cobblestone streets with the hot St. Louis summer sun beating down our backs. He loved to sit on the street

benches and gaze at the antique street lamps and buildings and the occasional Clydesdale pulling a carriage with rose-toting lovers. We'd hang out here for the Memorial Day weekend jazz festival, Fair St. Louis, and the Big Muddy Blues Festival. I passed by the various places we had hung out on Second Street: the Wax Museum, Bar St. Louis, Fat Tuesday's, and Jake's Steaks. My stomach grumbled as my nose inhaled a whiff of the different restaurants that we had sampled. The Landing would close off First and Second Street at lunchtime, and Alton would always have more than his fair share of St. Louis ribs at the Trainwreck.

A soft wind licked the side of my face. I smiled to myself as I glanced up at the Arch.

I had taken him to the Arch grounds, too. He loved my childhood stories of the river creeping up the river banks and the steps leading up to the Arch. His ears would perk up as I showed him the points where the river would rise up to swallow the sidewalk. The street would be closed to traffic, and we would come down and walk on the arcing ledges alongside the rising water. Strangely enough, the riverfront flooding was always a beautiful thing—an attraction of sorts except for the business owners. People would come out just to see the flooded grounds and take pictures.

My hair tickled my neck as I stared up at the tiny Arch windows. I remembered taking Alton on the long, rough cable elevator ride to the top of the Arch. I laughed to myself as I remembered how Alton stiffened and got wide-eyed every time the cable car made loud screeches as it shifted backward to straighten out on its angled move up. If you didn't grow up with it, it was enough to make anyone petrified of a cable failure and a plunge to the bottom of the Arch.

I remembered the depth of his concern when we reached the top and peered through the tiny windows on each side. On the west side, the view was of a vibrant city: football stadium, baseball stadium, high-rise apartment complexes, and business offices. Then he moved three feet to the other side and peered through the window at the Illinois side. East St. Louis looked barren, almost like a ghost town. Alton never understood how that could happen. Two cities separated by only a river. One resembled a vibrant city, and the other looked like Ethiopia. He didn't understand it; having grown up there, I did.

Alton. Getting out of the apartment to stop thinking about him wasn't working so well.

I strolled down First Street past the Wax Museum and the restaurant, and went back to the Trainwreck, where I was supposed to meet Jaelene. I didn't see her anywhere, so I took a seat at the bar, ordered a Pinot Grigio, and watched the door. I dug into my purse to retrieve my cell phone: eight calls from Kawamichi—Dexter, no doubt—no calls from Synda. By now I had left three messages, and she had not even attempted to call me back. I had no desire to call the house and take a chance on Tucker's answering the phone. I still wanted to avoid him, especially since I hadn't yet figured out those weird vibes that seemed to be floating between us. If I didn't hear from her soon, I was going to have to call the house to see what was up.

I was about halfway into my drink when Jaelene came prancing through the door with a big, burly, black-as-night man attached to her hand. *Damn. Can't I even meet the girl without her being joined at the hip with some man?* And from her previous descriptions of him on the phone, I knew it was Cyrus. She spoke to the hostess, then spotted me at the bar and tugged him along.

"Hey, sis! It's good to see you." Her long, thick hair swept my ear as she latched onto me and hugged me as if she hadn't seen me in years—rather than three months ago when I bailed her out of jail. I gathered that she hadn't told Cyrus.

"Hey, Babysista. It's so good to see you, too." I pulled away and looked at her face. Her makeup was thick and her face was heavily dusted. "Hello, Cyrus." I tried hard not to sound too indifferent. "Nice to finally meet you in person. Babysista . . . uh . . . Jaelene talks about you a lot."

He smiled and shook my hand.

"I told the waitress that there were three of us. She's getting us a table," Jaelene said. She beamed up at the towering Cyrus, then unbuttoned his leather jacket—compliments of Jaelene, no doubt. "I hope you don't mind Cyrus coming along."

"Why would I?" My voice was dry, I knew, but it wasn't like she was listening to me anyway.

A waitress holding three menus gestured for us to follow her to a table in the middle of the room. "So whurr y'all from?" she asked as we opened our menus to the drinks list. Mostly tourists came to the Landing.

"We're from here," I said, "but I live in Cleveland now. Just came back to visit family."

"Oh, you from herre? What high school did you go to?"

"Sumner bulldogs, baby." I smiled as if displaying an ace in the place.

"Vashon's in the house over herre." She trumped my ace as she raised her palms to the ceiling and laughed. She looked over at Cyrus and Jaelene.

"Soldan," Cyrus said. "Y'all know what's up." He cheesed and nodded like he was king.

Jaelene displayed a big grin and proudly stated, "Metro High."

Everybody's smiles deflated.

"Metro?" The waitress drew her head back and twisted her lip as she spoke.

"Yeah, Metro," Jaelene defended her school. Cyrus and I smirked. Jaelene looked around at the three of us, hunched her shoulders, and bugged her eyes like, "What?" But she knew. Metro was a small college preparatory high school for eggheads that got no respect when it came to the battle of the high schools. The entire school population of around 250 didn't even make up the entire freshman class of most other schools, and drew as much interest as a bunch of engineers throwing a summer jam. Like I said, it got no respect.

"Y'all just jealous." She flipped her menu up and pouted.

"Yeah, okay," the waitress said as she raised an eyebrow. She looked at Cyrus and me as we also suppressed our laughter. We ordered drinks and appetizers before she rushed off.

Jaelene slid the flatware off the napkin in front of Cyrus, snapped it open, and spread it across his lap. She smoothed it out as she playfully wrinkled her nose at him. I wanted to puke; the girl was making me nauseous.

"Well, Cyrus is almost finished with premed. He's trying to decide whether to continue at SLU or Wash U. My baby got accepted to Wash U., and got scholarships to both." Jaelene bounced Cyrus's hand on the table as she spoke. I looked at Cyrus, whose wide, shifty eyes found the table. Only peeing in his pants would have made him look slightly more uncomfortable.

"That's great, Cyrus," I said as flatly as I could. The last thing I really wanted to talk about was how some man was successfully furthering himself while taking advantage of my sister's idiotic generosity. "Headed for the big bucks, huh? Well, I certainly hope you'll remember all the little people when you make it, and those whose backs you climbed on top of in order to get there." I tried to stare discomfort into him.

Cyrus stroked his chin. "A lot of people been helping me out. Some more than others." My dumb-acting sister flashed a full grill and squeezed his hand, undoubtedly thinking he was referring to her. "I will never forget the people who have helped me out. Not many people that would give a nigga from the projects a chance."

I cringed at his use of that word. It made no sense for a man to refer to himself that way. It said a little something about him to me.

"Well, for one, if we think of ourselves that way, we're fulfilling a prophecy, aren't we?" I stared at him intently.

"Um, anyway, Va-a-a-an," Jaelene said. She tried to break the tension I was trying hard to set. "So I heard about your visit to the house. Dad's a trip, isn't he?"

"Same as always. Seen one, seen 'em all." I kept my eyes on Cyrus.

"Naw, but this time, I don't know. He seems to be getting worse in his old age."

"He's always been like that. The perfect husband and father for a day and a half, then Lucifer himself for the next six months."

"Mmm." Jaelene took a swallow of soda. A drop of soda popped up on her nose and blended with her makeup when she pulled back from the straw. "I'on know. Sumthin's up." She dabbed her nose with a napkin, then pulled out a small makeup case to recake.

Cyrus cleared his throat yet another time. "Excuse me, ladies. This sounds like the perfect time for me to make a run." He flashed a timid smile at me, pushed back his chair, and headed to the back of the restaurant.

Jaelene waited until he was out of earshot before speaking. "Really, Van. Do you have to act so snooty around him? Or any man I'm with? You act like nobody's good enough for me."

"Don't flatter yourself, girl. This has nothing to do with being good enough for you."

"He's done nothing to you, and he hasn't done anything bad to me, either."

"Except take advantage of you by allowing you to be his Sugar Mama. It's mighty convenient for a man living in the Blumeyers to have such a generous girlfriend as you."

She huffed. "Well, thanks a lot. Why don't you tell me what you really think of me? You're saying a man will stay with me only because I'm paying him?"

I couldn't believe she had the nerve to even ask the question. Sometimes I'd swear that underneath that scalp, she had a USE ME sign hanging on her brain. "Why don't you give it a chance to find out? As soon as you meet a man, from day one you're buying him designer clothes, TVs, jewelry. Who wouldn't stay around for that?"

Jaelene displayed a scowl under her ton of makeup. She rolled her dark brown eyes under her long, mascara-heavy eyelashes and puckered her plum-colored lips. "Sometimes I just get so tired of you being Miss Uppity Negro."

"Now, I'm going to ignore that because you know that I have always been far from uppity. You've never seen me sporting any designer's name on my back or driving what I think is a bland-

on-the-inside BMW just to say I have a Beamer. I drive what I
drive because I like it, not because of what people will think
about me or to fit an image."

She raked her fingers through her hair. "No, I'm not saying
that. But you do have a way of looking down on others when
their status is beneath yours."

"I don't look down on Cyrus. What gets me is men like him
who accept everything under the sun from a woman, knowing
full well that he's not in love with her."

"Oh? So, now Cyrus doesn't love me? You know everything,
right?" She turned her lips inward and sucked.

"Has he told you that he loves you?"

She huffed aloud.

"But I bet you've told him that you love him, right?"

"Men have a hard time saying those words, even when it's
what they feel. We have an understanding."

"An understanding?" I scoffed.

"Yeah," she said, setting down her soda and folding her arms on
the edge of the table. "Something that you *didn't* have with Alton."

Her words bit me in the ass. I picked up my glass of ice water,
swirled it around, then placed it back on the table without taking
a sip. I decided to move on.

"I think you should see a therapist."

"A what?" She cleared the laugh out of her throat. "Oh, I don't
believe this shit." She leaned to the left as she crossed her legs
under the table, then straightened. "Now I'm crazy?" she asked.
Her voice rose an octave.

"I'm hardly calling you crazy. But I do think that you have
some issues that you need to talk to someone about. If not me,
your sister, then a professional." I nodded toward her. "Bouncing
checks for men, low self-esteem as evidenced by the heavy

makeup that you needlessly pile on to cover up those cute little moles you have. But it's not your fault. Babysista, you're an incredibly beautiful girl," I said. "You know, if we'd had a better upbringing, you wouldn't be in the shape you're in. It's Dad's fault, really."

"Un-fuckin'-believable." Her jaw dropped. "Here you are, turning down the proposal of the man that you love because of," she made air quotation marks, "'the O Theory,' and you're probably still hanging around that back-bitin', good-for-nothing Synda in Cleveland, aren't you? And you think that *I'm* the one who needs to see a therapist? You gotta be out of your damn mind." She cocked one side of her face into a half-smile.

I looked around and stared back at a couple of nosy women looking our way. My stare-down worked, except on one thick, gold-grilled, dark, dusty, blond-streaked, bouffant hair–wearing sistah a couple of tables over who looked about ready to give me a beat-down if I stared one second longer. I shuddered and brought my eyes back to the suddenly pleasant sight of my sister. St. Louis sistahs don't play.

"No need to get indignant, Jaelene."

"I guess not. Not if you're not the one who needs to be admitted to Malcolm Bliss."

"There is no Malcolm Bliss anymore."

"You know what I mean. You act like I need to go to some psychiatric ward somewhere."

Cyrus came back to the table. As he sat down, Jaelene purposefully flipped out his napkin and placed it in his lap again. She leaned over and pressed a peck on his lips, then carefully wiped the corners of his mouth.

I saw the corner of his right eye tighten before he grabbed her wrists and pulled them down beneath the table. He looked at her as if to say "stop it." Jaelene smiled that dumbfounded smile of hers.

We ordered and ate while talking about the changes in St. Louis since I'd been gone, and the surfacing talk about the home of the Cardinals moving from Busch Stadium to somewhere in East St. Louis. The waitress brought our check, and I reached for my purse.

"How much is our share?" Jaelene asked.

"I got it. Don't worry about it," I said.

"No, I got mine and Cyrus's."

Cyrus sighed. "No, I'll get it."

"No, that's okay, honey. I'll get it. You're in school."

"No, Jae!" Cyrus leaned over and pulled out his wallet. Before he had a chance to open it, Jaelene had slapped two twenties on top of mine, snatched up the check, and was carrying it to the front counter. Cyrus seethed.

"Must be nice being a full-time student and having a girl like Jaelene, huh?" I asked.

"Look, Vanella. I know what you're referring to. I'm not like that. I'm not taking advantage of your sister. It's just that she keeps throwing things at me."

"I don't see you saying no and refusing gifts, especially when it's a plasma TV."

He leaned against the table. "That's your sister's doing. I told her not to buy me that. That's all I need is to have somebody in my neighborhood seeing a flat-screen TV being taken into my place. But no. She insisted. She insists on paying for everything. I don't get a chance. You see how she was with the check. That's the way she is all the time." He was losing the battle at keeping the frustration out of his voice.

He blew out an exasperated breath and leaned back as if he had just given birth to a twelve-pound baby. I looked into his eyes and at the flare of his nostrils, and suddenly I could see that he was as sick of her ways as I was.

The armed guard in my mind stood at ease. I could see his manhood taking a backseat on a ride with a woman driver at the wheel, much to his dismay. "I'm sorry. I didn't know."

"It's bad enough having the start that I had. I'm trying to make something of myself. I'm trying to be a man. Then I have your sister, Jaelene, belittling me every time I turn around. Buying me expensive gifts that I can't afford, or even need. Reaching for the bill every time we go out. Buying me clothes, shoes, watches . . . I ain't a gigolo." Cyrus's face displayed a heavy frown and his forehead tightened. I was speechless.

Jaelene returned to the table and looked at me. "You can leave the tip." She smiled and rubbed Cyrus's shoulders. "Are we ready to go?"

"Yeah," he said. He jerked out of her reach and headed to the door.

"What did you say to him?" She looked crossly at me. Her arm hung in the space Cyrus had vacated.

We headed to Hadley's Lounge on Olive, and by the time we got there Jaelene had buttered Cyrus up so well that he had started to curdle. She didn't let up on him. And Cyrus seemed to have given up—at least for the night—on trying to get her to stop fussing over him. By the time the live band finished jamming old-school jams and jazz, and after only one drink from the Hadley bartender—because only one drink from the Hadley bartender was usually all we could handle—Jaelene knew she would have the brother singing high notes and cooking her breakfast in the morning—or so she probably thought.

I dropped them off downtown at Jaelene's car, and drove back to Mom and Dad's. After I rang the doorbell, I heard Dad's voice sassing as he approached the door. My stomach recoiled.

"Just shut up," he said. "I don't want to hear your mouth right now."

He opened the door with a deep scowl carved into his face. His grayed, receding hairline looked dull, as if it had been drained of life. It took him a minute to even attempt to change his expression to something close to upbeat. I wouldn't say that he fully succeeded either.

"What's going on?" I asked, knowing full well that it was probably nothing, just something that Dad was blowing out of proportion for no reason.

"Your mother's being stupid. Acting all crazy like she normally does."

"'Stupid' is a strong word, Dad." The liquor in my stomach was starting to heat me up. I heard Mom's feet scuttling over the carpet.

"Van, is that you?"

"Yeah. What's going on over here? What are you fighting about this time?" I demanded.

Dad closed the door behind me and hobbled around with his cane. "Your momma defending that son of hers . . . that sissy. Making plans to take over my business. She's probably trying to help him. They must be scheming. Probably why she took that money class, so they could get their paws on my money."

I squinted and drew up my nose as I looked over at Mom. She looked weary. Her large eyes drooped and her mouth hung open a little. Looked like she was searching for new words that she hadn't already said to Dad at least one time or another.

"He found a notebook of Kizaar's on the coffee table in the living room. It had some pages labeled Improvement Plans for Dad's Business." She spoke low and slowly.

"Oh, that's nothing," I said to Dad, thinking that I had the situation cleared up. "Dad, that's Kizaar's plan to make you happy. I don't know why he keeps trying to impress you since it's obviously a waste of time. He's putting improvement plans together for your business to save you money." I emphasized "you" to try to trigger the guilt that I knew had to be there somewhere.

"No, that's what they want you to believe. That's him and his momma over there, trying to take over my business." He lifted his cane off the floor and pointed it at Mom.

"Jesse, that's far from true. I took that class because—"

"Because you're crazy." He pounded his cane into the carpet. "Crazy. Just like your dead daddy." A vein bulged on the side of his neck as his eyes sizzled with anger. He lifted his hand and briefly massaged his chest over his heart. The diamond cross on his chest swayed before stopping against a button on his shirt.

His words hit the target square on the mark. They grazed me, too. Mom looked dazed, as if she had just been hit by a tranquilizer dart. She stood frozen, and her eyes watered. From her open mouth, she expelled a wounded breath. She hugged herself around the waist with one arm and covered her mouth with the other hand. Her calf-length skirt flew around as she spun on the balls of her feet and rushed out of the room.

Only mentally did I make a swift move and sweep the cane away from my father. I wanted to see him fall to the floor. Wanted to hurt him the way he had just hurt my mother. I wanted him to have a heart attack, a stroke, or something. I was so sick of this—of him.

"What the hell was that, Dad? Why are you always doing this shit?" the alcohol in me dared to ask. I had never cursed at Dad before. "This has got to stop. It's got to stop now." I stood with one hand on my hip and the other held a finger two centimeters from my father's nose. My eyes were tight. I felt the heat rising from the back of my neck.

"That was the most despicable thing I have ever heard you say. Granddad suffered from mental illness years before he died, and you say some shit like that?"

Dad stood there leaning on his cane. Looked directly into my eyes. His eyes offered no apologies, no sadness, and no regret.

My jaws tightened and my teeth clenched together. My breathing quickened and my chest heaved as my heart went into overdrive pumping blood through my body. I lowered my voice and spoke through my teeth. "You're my father and I've never disrespected you. But, I swear to God, if you ever hurt my momma like that again, I'll . . ." I moved in closer to his face. "I'll . . ." My chest burned.

Dad just stood there staring. Stared through me with empty, emotionless eyes. Unmoved. He twitched his cheeks, looked down at his feet, adjusted his cane, and said, "You're doing the right thing not to get married. Doing the right thing."

Then he hobbled off to his bedroom.

Seventeen

"WHAT DO YOU MEAN you think you're separating? Are you about to get a divorce?" I asked her.

I had stayed overnight with Mom and slept in the guestroom across the hall from her. After talking to her to make sure she was all right—or as all right as she could be—I made hourly trips to her room and peeked through the crack of her door to check on her. At times I saw her lying in bed with her eyes fixed on the ceiling, sometimes crying over that damn picture of Dad in the locket, sometimes sleeping.

It must have been during one of those trips that I missed hearing my cell phone ring when Medena called from Cleveland. I got her message that morning and called her back.

"I'm only thinking about it right now. I need more time to think. That's why I'm calling to ask if I can stay at your place since you're going to be out of town for a while," Medena said.

"Yes, of course you can, girl. I'll just tell Ms. Millie that you'll pick up the key and will stay at my place for a while. But the last time we talked, you were so excited about learning football for

Aneaus, cooking for him, being with him. Now you're talking divorce? What happened?"

She spoke slowly, "Well, that's it. I've been doing that for going on three years now. I'm tired. I take care of Aneaus, the baby, the house, and the dog, and I just don't know if I can keep this up forever."

"But I thought you loved doing all that married-life stuff."

"I love Aneaus. That hasn't changed. But I feel like I'm giving up so much of myself. My life. My dreams." She exhaled. "And Aneaus is happy. He doesn't see what the problem is. I feel empty, like I don't exist anymore."

"Damn. Not you and Aneaus," I accidentally said aloud. My heart plummeted in my chest while we talked. Medena and Aneaus were the last of my friends I'd had faith in and thought would make it. I admit that I thought she went a little overboard by trying to be everything to everybody, but the last thing I expected was for her to just drop out of the race completely. Medena was my last thread of hope that there was a possibility of having a happy marriage. I paced the room as I listened.

"I haven't made up my mind, but I need some space to think. Aneaus and I aren't seeing eye to eye on things right now. I told him I was going to Florida to stay with my mother, but I don't feel like going there and being hassled about my marriage every day."

We talked a little more before we hung up. Damn. If Medena and Aneaus couldn't make it, then what hope did Alton and I have? I hated to think it, but I was beginning to agree with the statement that Dad had made. Even if the statement had come from pure wickedness, it seemed to have some truth to it. I did think that I'd made the right decision. It was better to get over it and move on now rather than five years after the wedding.

Dad remained in exile while I took Mom out for a day of

shopping. I wanted to get her out of the house and get her mind off things. Open her up a little bit. For her, shopping always seemed to do the trick. Since last night, she hadn't uttered a word about the incident, and seemed to have awakened with a brand new head, as if last night had happened with somebody else's family. But I knew she was pretending to be okay when she really wasn't. Seeing her cry alone in her bedroom told a different story, and that's the one I believed.

A light wind blew under the cloudless sky. It was one of those unusually warm February days. Across the street in Forest Park, mothers pushed strollers full of well-swaddled infants, and mammoth dogs on leashes pulled joggers along.

We hopped into the RX300 and took Kingshighway to I-40 to I-64. Mom didn't care to go to Northwest Plaza anymore—not since it had been converted from an actual plaza into a huge mega-mall and become overrun with teenagers cruising the parking lots for chicks and thugs. So I took Lindbergh to Plaza Frontenac, where Mom felt more comfortable. I tagged along behind her as Nieman Marcus and Saks worked their magic on her.

She glowed as she talked about outfit after outfit. We left Plaza Frontenac with bag upon bag of Mom's hidden grief, hopped back on I-64, and took the Brentwood exit to the St. Louis Galleria. I sat on mall benches and store chairs as Mom went from rack to rack, picking out separates and holding them flush against her body.

Flashes from the diamonds in her ears, around her neck, on her wrist and fingers glinted in my eyes every time I looked up at her. Her bright red lipstick coordinated well with her red silk blouse and red leather pumps. Her shortened hair swooshed as she went through size eight clothing and matched skirt to blouse and blouse to slacks. Football's not her sport, but she racked up a lot of yardage shopping.

We hit nearly the majority of the one hundred plus stores in the Galleria. I joined her for shopping at Victoria's Secret, Nine West, and Enzo Angiolini only. I'm not much of a shopper, with the exception of lingerie and shoes. Even there I was no match for Mom. When I need clothes, I go from store to store to see what the mannequins are wearing that day. If there is nothing to my liking, or if I haven't found anything in more than an hour and a half, then I'd leave empty-handed until the next quarterly shopping trip.

"You haven't said anything about last night," I said finally as we walked out of Nine West. It was obvious that we were going to spend the entire day out there, and she was going to avoid talking about it.

"About last night?" Mom narrowed her brow as if wracking her memory for an incident gone wrong in the midst of a drunken stupor. She switched the shopping bags from her left hand to her right and used one bright red fingernail to scratch the tip of her nose.

"With Dad. What he said," I reminded her, although I couldn't believe that I had to.

"Oh, that," was all she said. She pointed to an empty mall bench and motioned for us to sit down. As soon as we sat, she slid her feet halfway out of her pumps.

"You gotta do something about Dad. You can't just let him verbally abuse you like that all the time."

"Oh, I never pay him any mind. I forgot to tell you that he's planning a trip to Africa. Me, him, and Kizaar. He doesn't mean it when he talks like that."

"You always say that."

"He feels emptiness and anger at the loss of—"

"Mom, for as long as we live, I don't want to hear that excuse ever again."

Her silky brown hair leaned toward the floor as she bent down to rearrange items in her shopping bag. Three older women power-walked past. One pointed at an object behind a store window as the other two furiously pumped their arms to an unheard cadence.

"Van, it's not as big a deal as you always make it out to be. He doesn't hit me. All he does is talk. I can take that."

"But why should you have to take that? Since when is it okay for one human being to belittle another? What gives him the right?"

Her voice turned flat. "That's the problem with your generation. You all can't handle the little problems that come along with marriage. If a man even looks at you wrong nowadays, you all are ready to divorce and take half. My generation is more devoted and more willing to do whatever it takes to keep the family together. We stand by our men."

I rolled my head slowly around to face her. "You're right. Women of my generation are not willing to put up with abuse of any kind to keep a family together. No man will ever talk to me the way Dad talks to you."

Mom reached down and slipped a finger inside each of her shoes to help slide her foot back in. "Mm-hmm. Too independent. Just like that Zandra friend of yours," she said with assurance. "And your generation has a problem honoring the sanctity of marriage. Love, honor, and—"

"Stop right there. I can't believe I'm hearing this." I waved my hand while I looked away.

"I know you don't want to hear it, but it's true. And that's probably also why a lot of your men are running to white women. You all mouth off to them and run your mouths about any- and everything. Some things you just have to keep quiet on and let go."

I hung my head and stared at my jeans as I absorbed the words that had just come from her lips. I leaned toward my knees and drew my palm down my face. Was this woman for real? Was this how she thought about marriage, about women's roles in marriage? I cringed and shuddered.

A couple pushing a stroller greeted and passed another couple about the same age. One of the women was with child, and she rubbed her rounded belly as her husband admired the sleeping baby. They talked for a moment, then moved on. Two seconds later, the woman pushing the stroller turned and hungrily studied the well-stocked backside of the other man as her husband readjusted their baby's blanket.

"Why don't we head on over to Babysista's, okay?" I asked. I felt a lump forming in my throat. I didn't want to continue to have this conversation with my mother. Here I had been trying to salvage my mother's dignity, trying to fight for her, and trying to save her from Dad. I had been giving myself ulcers and tension headaches on her behalf, and here she was saying that her situation was fine and not to bother.

Well, I was done. From here on out, I was done.

Mom nodded. I gathered her bags and she walked on aching feet to exit for the parking lot. Mom was silent on the ride. I drove back up Kingshighway Boulevard, past the Central West End. We crossed over Page Avenue, MLK, Natural Bridge, and the White Castle parking lot where, as teenagers, Synda and I would hang out till the wee hours of the morning after skating at Skate King. We took Bircher to Riverview and continued north until we were right across from Calvary Cemetery. I turned on North Pointe and drove up Park Lane to my childhood home.

I pulled into a parking space a few feet from the house. Jaelene's place was easy to spot because it was the only two-story brick house fully lit under the darkened St. Louis sky. The front door was wide open with the bright lights from the living room illuminating a pathway up to the porch. I straightened the steering wheel as I peered through the living room window. Mom looked, too.

Two figures were visible: a tall, bald male and a shorter female. As I pulled the key out of the ignition, the small shadow thrust two palms into the larger shadow's midsection. He moved back a fraction of an inch, then rebounded. Her arm wound up and, in windmill fashion, began furiously flogging his chest. He caught her arms and held them as she began to flounce and lash about.

"Come on, Mom!" I yelled as I hopped out of the SUV. I ran up the lawn and to the front door, glanced behind for Mom, but she hadn't made it yet.

I opened the screen door and stepped inside the living room. Cyrus's back was to me. He was still holding Jaelene's arms when I ran up behind him and flung a forearm across his bald head. "What the hell do you think you're doing to my sister?" My forearm caught him across his ear and the right side of his head.

Cyrus dropped Jaelene's arms and whipped his body around to face me. His eyes looked straight ahead at first, then dropped downward a few inches and landed on me. His mouth drew into a pucker and his cheeks puffed in and out. His fists were closed.

"Oh, I wish you would so we can call the police and have you in jail for assault." I stood firm and still.

Cyrus unclenched his fists. Jaelene ran up behind him,

hopped on his back, and tried to wrap her legs around his waist. She fell off, but locked onto his neck and shoulders and managed to make him stumble. Cyrus wobbled backward, then fell over on top of Jaelene, who was still clinging to him, beating him in the face.

I stepped forward. His back angled toward me. My foot shot out and plunged into his back. I hopped and swept more kicks onto his back. Cyrus grimaced as he tried to catch Jaelene's hand with his free arm and roll over on his back to get out of the way of my kicks. He began swinging his legs wildly.

That's when I saw Mom with a red pump in her hand, pounding Cyrus in the calves with the heel of her shoe. She had the hardest scowl she could muster on her soft face. She mouthed something with each randomly placed hit. "Don't . . . you . . . mess . . . with . . . my . . . babies!"

I stopped and watched my mother for a minute. She was going at it so fast and furious that a giggle bellowed up from my gut at the uncharacteristic sight. I hadn't even seen her come in. In the midst of all the commotion, I couldn't help but stare in amazement as Mom frantically attacked Cyrus's legs. I didn't know she had it in her.

Cyrus let out a scream, "Stoooppp!"

That's when I suddenly realized that I had no idea why Mom was beating this man to a pulp, why Jaelene was clocking him in the face something awful, or why I was trying my best to slip a disc in his spine.

"What's going on here?" I asked.

"Oh, *now* you ask?" Cyrus bellowed. His eyes bulged. Mom and Jaelene held off on the beating—for the moment.

"Shoot first, ask questions later," I responded as I straightened my clothes and smoothed my hair back into place.

Jaelene kicked her legs and pushed Cyrus off her. Her eyes spewed black tears and her beige top wore half of her makeup. "He's cheating on me." She popped him in the face once more for good measure. Mom mistook that as a signal to commence the beatings, and began having at him with the heel of her red pump again.

"Hold on, Mom," I said. She wouldn't stand up for herself against her husband, no, but you mess with Momma's babies and your ass was toast.

Mom had a death grip on her pump. She stood with her left foot flat on the floor and her right knee bent above three inches of heel.

Cyrus got up on all fours, moved across the sparsely furnished living room to safer ground, then stood up. He huffed as he straightened his clothes. "Y'all crazy."

"What's going on?" I asked him again.

"I came over here to call it off with your sister. It's not working out." He rubbed the side of his battered face and stared at Jaelene. "I told her that I didn't have the same feelings for her as she does for me. I was trying to be honest."

"You've been cheating." Jaelene grabbed a pillow from the couch and threw it at Cyrus, hitting him in the chest.

"No." He alternated pleading looks between me and Mom. "Van, Mrs. Morris . . . Jaelene asked and yes, I told her that I was interested in another woman. A woman in one of my classes."

"A student?" I asked. "A student with no money?"

He held his hands up in a surrender position, like he was in the presence of the Cincinnati PD. "Yes, but we're not intimate. We haven't even gone out yet. But I want to . . . go out, that is. I thought the best thing to do was to end it with Jaelene before I asked Carmeleta out." Cyrus's words ran together as he spoke.

"Carmeleta? You've been cheating on me with some bitch named Carmeleta?" Jaelene picked up a magazine from the coffee table and flung it at him. It flapped open as it flew and fell at his feet. "What about everything I've done for you? All the money I've given you for school? What about the TV? The clothes? The jewelry?"

"I kept telling you not to buy me all that stuff. I never asked you for any of that, and you can have it all back. Everything." His eyes darted between the three of us, as if making sure we didn't make a move toward him.

"Damn right," I said.

"Well, if she's a full-time student, she won't be able to give you any of that. You know that!" Jaelene picked up a glass vase from the coffee table and cocked her arm back. Cyrus scrunched his body in anticipation of the blow as I ran over and pried the vase from her hand. She kept her eyes on Cyrus.

"I don't need . . . no, I don't *want* a woman to buy me all that stuff. I kept telling you that. I want to be the one showering my woman with gifts. I'm not a gigolo, Jae. It's like you're trying to buy me, and I just don't have feelings for you."

"And I don't have feelings for you anymore either. Get out of here!" Jaelene shouted. "Now! Move it!"

I put my arm around Jaelene and tried to pull her away. Mom gripped her shoe tighter.

"I never meant to hurt your daughter, Mrs. Morris. I'm sorry." He looked over at Jaelene. "I'm sorry, Jae."

Jaelene leaned into my shoulder and cried. She let out a high-pitched, wounded moan.

Cyrus retrieved a blue denim jacket from the floor in the corner and eased past Mom. He walked slowly at first, then he bolted through the front door. I think I heard a "Y'all crazy . . . all y'all."

The sound of Cyrus's hooptie faded as Jaelene's body went limp in my arms. I guided us onto the floor, where her body heaved as she coughed and choked on tears. Mom slipped her shoe back on her foot and sat on the floor next to us. She rubbed the back of her neck. Beating a man's ass was a brand-new experience, and had apparently gotten the best of her.

We consoled Jaelene for a while, then Mom led her to her bedroom, helped her out of her clothes, and put her in the bed. I retreated to the den off the kitchen, but kept going over to peek in as Mom talked to her. After a while, Jaelene stopped crying, but she didn't say much. I stayed out to let Mom handle it. I didn't think that Jaelene would want to hear what I had to say about the whole matter. I was wishing Cyrus well.

I sat back on the couch, pulled my cell phone out of my purse, and scrolled through the call list. Kawamichi, Kawamichi, Kawamichi. No calls from Synda. I figured that now was as good a time as any to place my dreaded call to the house. Why not keep the drama going?

On the third ring, Tucker picked up the phone. "Hello?"

"Hello, Tucker. It's me, Van." There was no response, so I continued. "I haven't heard from Synda in a while, so I was calling to see if she was home."

"You haven't heard from her?"

"No."

"When was the last time you talked to her?"

"Tucker, is something wrong? Is Synda all right?"

"I don't know."

"What do you mean, you don't know?"

"I mean I haven't seen her in a while either."

"What? Is she missing?"

"Well, yes and no."

I was getting impatient. "Tucker, will you tell me what the hell is going on?"

"Van, Synda left a couple of weeks ago. After . . ."

"Left? After what?"

"After I told her I wanted a divorce."

Tucker paused as if to get his thoughts together. Finally he said, "I've been trying to get up the nerve to call you, and hoping you would call here at the same time. This has all been one long nightmare." His voice grew shaky. "A seven- almost eight-year nightmare. I never stopped loving you."

I pulled the phone away from my ear and peered at the receiver. *What? Did I just hear what I thought I heard?* I put the phone back up to my ear. "What?"

I could see him running his tongue under the gap between his two front teeth like he used to do when he was nervous about something. He would do that and periodically pound his fist into the palm of the other hand. "There's so much you don't know, so much that I never got to tell you after I found out. You didn't want to listen—although . . ." He was rambling. "But I can't blame you for that. After a while, I just left it alone. I gave up the fight, and that was my fault."

"Tucker, I have no idea what you're talking about."

"Hmm . . . where do I begin?" He blew out a long breath. "Okay. I'll start with now. Synda was seeing someone else."

I scooted over and leaned my back into the center of the couch. "Yeah, I figured that. I was trying to track her down to get to the bottom of it."

"So you knew?"

"Yeah, about Cedric. She didn't tell me. I kinda snooped and found out on my own."

"Cedric?"

"Yeah, the guy she was seeing."

"I don't know anything about any Cedric."

I gasped.

"Synda got caught up with some Nolan guy," he said. "She claimed she fell in love with him. If she did, she apparently fell in love with the wrong guy. Turned out he was trying to be some sort of pimp or something. He was a pretty boy, and used the fact that she wanted him as a way to get money out of her. From what I understand, they were never intimate because he was using that to string her along. He made a plan for her to steal money from our account to set them up with a fresh start. Then the plan was to divorce me, take an additional half of my assets and be on their merry way. Only he took the money she put in their joint account and ran."

"That doesn't sound like Synda."

"Yes it does." He hesitated. "It would sound like Synda to you if you knew that this was her third affair. I found out, we went to marriage counseling, but it didn't help because she kept seeing him right through the sessions. It would sound like Synda if you knew she faked a pregnancy to break us up in college, and if you knew that she planned to seduce me that night when you went to St. Louis for the weekend. Now, I'm not saying that I played no part in it. After all, I was intimate with her."

"Yes, you were." I was stunned.

"I was young. I was stupid. I was drunk. But I never stopped loving you. I never loved Synda, and she knew that."

I felt dizzy. I glazed over as Tucker told me all about Synda's confessions, the fake pregnancy and miscarriage, more details of her trysts with other men—three that he knew of—and now possibly Cedric, and how he found out when she placed a call to Nolan from the house while she thought he was working out in the basement. Tucker said he then did some digging, had a buddy follow her, got a lawyer, and set her up. Now Synda was on the run. He suspected she was here in St. Louis with her parents somewhere.

After briefing me, he said, "I can't help but believe this is fate."

"What do you mean, fate?"

"Synda told me about you and Alton, and now with me and Synda . . . here we both are . . . single . . . or I'm about to be single."

"Tucker, I know you're not suggesting anything between us. First of all, this is too much information too fast. You don't know what kind of day I've had today. But even with all that about Synda, that doesn't change the fact that you slept with her. She didn't force you to do that."

"You're right, and that's one thing I've regretted to this day. But it wasn't like I made a habit of sleeping around with a lot of women."

"No, just my best friend."

"Was she, or is she *really*, your best friend? Time means nothing. The length of time you've known her means nothing."

"That's beside the point."

"I know I messed up back then. I wish I could take it back, but I can't. I just have to say that I loved you then and I still do. I thought I was losing you for good when Synda announced that you were getting married, but you're not."

Surprise clamped my mouth closed. He continued, "But if you still can't forgive me for that one mistake, if you don't have any feelings at all for me, then tell me and I will back off."

Synda and our college days ran through my mind, then Tucker and how we met, became best friends, and fell in love during freshman year. My memory flashed with trips to my home in St. Louis and to his home in Columbus, Ohio; to Six Flags, Cedar Point, and Kings Island in search of the tallest and scariest rollercoaster; and to friends' homes where we all piled our broke behinds in somebody's car—anybody's car that rolled—and traveled from state to state, bumming off family and friends and sleeping on floors. I had memories of our blanket-on-the-fifty-yard-line talks about our dreams, what we wanted to do, and where we wanted to live after graduating college. His dream was New York. Mine was L.A. We compromised on Atlanta. Silence controlled the line for a bit.

"Well, hey, you're pretty quiet, so I take that to mean that I have my answer then. I won't bother you. I wish you nothing but love, Vanella." He paused, then whispered, "Take care."

I felt yet another lifeline being viciously severed. Being horrendously carved out and permanently detached.

"Wait!" I yelled into the receiver.

Eighteen

MY TRIP HOME WAS a little more than I had bargained for. I knew the family had issues, but this was getting to be a little over the top. Dad seemed more bitter than usual, and he bit off and spit out Mom's and Kizaar's heads any chance he got. Kizaar had gone into hiding since he had heard about Dad's blowup over his improvement plans for the business. Mom was vacationing in the dark ages, and shedding tears every night over a picture of the man she *used* to be married to.

I winced from pain as I sat with Jaelene, who had sunk so low during the last three weeks that I didn't know who she was anymore. She lay on her face in bed while I did her laundry.

Tucker's revelation about Synda and his feelings for me was a whole 'nother thing. It confused the hell out of me. Stirred up a lot of memories from the past, and brought once-settled issues floating back up to the top again, creating perplexity. Even though I felt he had done the unthinkable, for some reason I didn't feel so closed off about his feelings for me. That grudge was disappearing. After all, it was years ago. People make mistakes, and people change.

The night of our conversation a few weeks ago, I didn't know what I felt. All I knew was that when he was about to end our connection, when he was about to sever our rekindling bond, my skin began to burn. My heart hammered in my chest—why, I didn't know—but it made me yell "Wait!" at the top of my lungs. My heart pumped, my hands were damp and trembling. I was sitting still, but I felt deathly out of breath.

I didn't know what to tell him because, hell, I didn't know what to tell myself. I just knew right then that I didn't want him to go. Not for good. But I needed time. Time to digest. Time to take it all in. Time to think. Tucker understood that. His soothing voice flowed through the phone, wrapped around me and held me as he went through everything again slowly. He stayed on the line as long as I needed him to. He didn't rush me when the line fell silent as I absorbed what he had already taken in. He waited patiently and let me digest it all, then he let me recuperate. We slowly became reacquainted over the phone for the next few weeks, and he became the old Tucker I used to know. The one before Synda came into our picture.

I was jarred out of my thoughts as Jaelene rolled over and stared at the bare wall.

"Babysista, why don't you get up? Get something to eat or walk around," I said as I folded her laundry. Since Cyrus had called it off, she hadn't done anything around her house or elsewhere in weeks. She got up, went to work, and then went straight home to bed. I didn't see how she could manage to count hops and barley at work and not depress all her coworkers. Hell, she was depressing me. I hardly ever saw her eat anything except junk food. She was doing the same thing she'd done when she was sixteen and didn't have a boyfriend, while all of her girlfriends did. Jaelene blamed the tiny moles on her face for driving the boys away, and wouldn't leave her room for months. We finally got her to see a therapist after she began to pass out from not eating. She was making herself sick.

Jaelene didn't respond to me. Her hair was mashed on both sides and rose high above her crown, nearly stroking the headboard. Her skin seemed to flow without the constriction of the heavy makeup she usually wore. Depression made her too lazy to worry about her face, and she actually became prettier than when she was upbeat. The small dark moles that she usually hid added a unique and beautiful charm to her cool maple brown face. Even now, with her crusty eyes and pasty mouth, she had a natural beauty going on that I couldn't match.

"That's it." I slapped a T-shirt against a chair. "You're going to get up and out, if I have to drag you by your hair."

I moved toward her and reached for the royal blue comforter that covered her. She pulled it over her head and rolled up in it so that it tightened around her legs and sides.

"Leave me alone, Van. I'm not playing." Her voice was agitated but weak.

"I don't care how mad you get." I yanked at the comforter, determined to rip all the sheets off her and roll her onto the floor. "I'm not going to stand here and watch you get into another deep depression that you can't pull yourself out of. Get up, girl."

I yanked. She held tight. I yanked again. She held tighter. I tugged and pulled until, finally, the covers slipped from her fists. Face to mattress, she reached over her head, grabbed a pillow, and swiped at me with it.

"Oh? You wanna get jiggy with it, huh?" I picked up the other pillow and lightly swung it at her head and began hitting parts of her still body. "Okay, take that . . . and that . . . and that. Had enough?"

Jaelene sat up, raised her arms to block my shots, and swung back when she found an opening. "Leave me alone," she said. A reluctant smile developed on her naked face. I felt like I had swallowed a rainbow.

"Gotcha now, baby! Get up, Jae."

Jaelene sat up in the middle of the bed. She stopped swinging and clutched the pillow between her crossed legs. She sat still for a moment and the smile drained from her face as her eyes locked on a spot on the bed, then she fell back and her eyes flooded like an overflowing creek in a raging thunderstorm.

"Why can't I get anyone to love me?" she wailed. "Why won't anybody stay with me? Am I that ugly? What's wrong with me?" She wailed harder. Her face was etched with the pain that seemed to have clustered in her gut and dripped out in each teardrop. Every drop reached over to where I stood, lodged in my throat, and choked me.

I picked up the comforter and draped it over us as I slid into the bed beside her. I rubbed her back as she cried into the pillow.

"Babysista, that's what I've been trying to tell you, girl." Her pain was hurting me. "You are such a knockout. I think you're the prettiest of all of us, to tell you the truth, and you won't ever hear me admit that again. But here you are slathering on pound after pound of makeup to cover up what you think are flaws and what to me and the rest of the world are your beauty marks. No one else has them like you. They're different. They're beautiful. You need to flaunt what you have instead of trying to cover it up and be like everybody else."

She continued to cry. I felt her tremble as I stroked her back. "Just be yourself, Jae. Keep your money to yourself. It's okay to reciprocate a dinner or a night out, but you gotta stop trying to impress men by buying gifts just because you can. Well, you really can't because you owe me four thousand dollars, but that's beside the point." She sniffed. "Most men aren't looking for a Sugar Mama, and you don't want to deal with the ones who are. Real men enjoy taking care of the women they love. Men still want to play the role of breadwinner and provider, even if you do make more money. Don't try to take his role."

Her trembling stopped, except for an occasional shudder from her gasps for air.

"Come on. Get up, get out, and go do something." I pulled her up like a rag doll and turned her around to face me. Her eyes were red and getting puffy. Her long eyelashes were clumped with tears. I grabbed her chin and squeezed her face gently. "And I'm not going to let you stay depressed."

Her eyes widened and a tear dripped onto the back of my hand. I grabbed the sides of her knotty head, pulled her snotty-nosed face toward me, and hugged her. I tried to squeeze her as tightly as I could to let her know that I loved her and would always be there for her.

"Now," I said, pushing her away. She tried to step into another smile. "I really would like for you to see a therapist again. You can go back to the same one, or I'm sure we can help you find a new one. Just a couple of visits to get you back on the right track again. There's nothing wrong with that, Babysista. You're not crazy, okay?"

She sniffed, nodded, and wiped her face and nose with her hands. "I'll think about it, Van. That's all I can say right now."

"Fair enough." I squeezed her again. "And I want you to get up and get out of here. Now. Go do something. If you want me to go with you, I will. Go visit Mom. God knows that woman needs to see a therapist, too." I chuckled.

Jaelene chuckled a little as she got up and threw the covers onto the floor. She stood and stretched, arching her back as the hem of her gown fell to her knees, then she looked at me.

"Thanks, Van. You're always there . . ." She stopped as if she were at a loss for words.

"Hey, that's what big sisters are for." I picked up a pillow from the foot of the bed and tossed it at her.

She caught the pillow and smiled heaven.

I got her to get up to take a shower and put on clothes. She didn't go anywhere but to the den, where she turned on the radio and began flipping through magazines. It was a start. I finished folding her clothes and took a seat beside her on the floor, where I snatched up a few magazines, too, until Tucker called. I got excited as I picked up the phone to talk to him.

"I'd like to come to St. Louis to see you next weekend, if that's okay," he said.

Over the past few weeks, his voice began to sing to me again. Just like the old days. The pre-Synda days.

"I don't know if I'm ready for that yet, Tucker. There's still a lot we need to talk about, and I'd still like to talk to Synda."

"That's something I never understood, how you could be friends with someone like her. The two of you are so different. Synda is the most conniving, deceitful, it's-all-about-me person that I have ever met. You're just the opposite."

"Yeah, my girlfriends say the same thing," I said as I thought about Sherron in particular. "And my sister. Well, I guess I just thought that everyone makes mistakes. Hell, I'm not perfect. Everyone deserves a second chance."

"There's a difference between a mistake and something that's ingrained in you. That girl is just evil. Syn is just pure sin."

"Once a ho, always a ho?" I asked softly, mainly just repeating what Sherron had said before.

"Huh?" Tucker asked.

"Nothing. Let's talk about a visit another time. Is that okay?"

"Well, I'm dying to see you now. It would be fun to see St. Louis again. I haven't been there since going with you, and wouldn't want to go there with anyone else but you."

We talked a little more, and by the time we hung up the phone, I was feeling Tucker slide further into that place in my heart that Alton had left empty. Jaelene and I sat listening to music and flipping through magazines until we both fell asleep on the floor.

"Get here quick!" Jaelene shouted into the earpiece of my cell phone.

I was driving in the University City Loop. I'd decided to hang out in U-City and treat myself to a nice lunch when Jaelene rang my phone.

"I'm at Mom and Dad's." Her voice was frantic and wavered. "It's Dad and Kizaar . . . they're going to kill each other." Fear permeated her voice.

"What's going on?" I asked as I swung the RX300 around and headed for Mom and Dad's.

"Mom said Dad found another small bullet casing in the basement and went ballistic. He started mumbling to himself until he worked himself into a frenzy. That's when I got here. I came over to see Mom. Dad was already in a rage worse than I've ever seen him before. Then he charged upstairs to Kizaar's room and said he was going to find that gun, and how dare he disrespect him again."

"What gun?" I asked, trying to keep her on the line as I

weaved through traffic. "I thought he got rid of it the first time
Dad got upset about it."

"I thought so, too."

"Does Kizaar have a gun in the house?"

"He used to, but I thought he got rid of it. Maybe it's an old
bullet." We were so frantic that we didn't realize we were talking
in circles. "That's what Dad's mumbling about. About Kizaar's
disrespecting his house by bringing a gun in there."

I breathed heavily through my nose as I maneuvered in traffic. My family was driving me absolutely insane. What I wouldn't
do to be one of Ozzy Osbourne's kids right about now.

Jaelene held the line, and I heard Dad on a rampage in the background. Doors and drawers were being opened and slammed
closed, Dad ranting all the while. I heard Mom speaking to him
in an effort to get him to calm down.

"Hurry, get here quick, Van. This is the worst I've ever seen
him. He's up here tearing Kizaar's room apart."

"Where's Kizaar?" I asked.

"He's here, too. He's trying to reason with Dad and talk some
sense into him. Dad keeps poking him back with his cane. His
face—oh, his face, Van. I've just never seen him this mad before.
You gotta get here quick. Are you almost here?"

"Yeah, I'm almost there," I said.

I rounded the corner and pulled up behind Jaelene's beige
Camry. I jiggled the seat belt buckle loose and went for the door
handle. It popped back in my hand and broke one of my nails to
the bed. I didn't have time to think about the pain. I grabbed the
door handle again, pulled it, and yanked the door open. I left it
open and ran across the lawn to the front door. It was locked. I
looked around for my keys. *My keys. What the hell did I do with the*

keys? I looked back at my SUV and remembered. I ran back and grabbed the keys out of the ignition, then raced back to the house and let myself in.

Dad's voice carried down the steps from upstairs and hovered over the rooms below. "Where is it, boy? You're not going to be disrespecting me by having a gun in here. Where is it?"

"Jesse, please," I heard Mom plead.

"Move outta my way! It's all your fault anyway. Bringing up this sissy."

I ran through the living room to the hallway and reached the base of the stairs.

"Dad, please. Let's just talk about this, man." That was Kizaar's voice.

"Dad, stop it. Stop it, Dad. You're going to hurt yourself." That was Jaelene.

I charged up the stairs two by two. I rounded the first landing and headed up the second.

"Here it is," I heard Dad say after a loud rustle.

Then Mom and Jaelene screamed. I heard nothing from Dad or Kizaar, then I heard a clank as something hit the floor. I thought it was Dad's cane. Then I heard nothing but a lot of bumping and tussling.

"Stop it, stop it!" Mom and Jaelene screamed.

My heart raced up the stairs faster than my legs. Adrenaline pumped through me as I reached the top landing that led to Kizaar's room. The door was wide open.

Kizaar and Dad were intertwined. Dad's teeth gleamed and were clenched tightly. His brows puckered around streams of sweat and fury raged in his beady eyes. His hairline seemed to recede even further. He struggled to gain possession of the gun.

The whites of Kizaar's eyes stood out as he tried to wrestle the gun away from Dad. His jaw was tight. His eyes were fixed on the gun between their chests. His lips puckered.

Mom and Jaelene danced around them like they were playing Ring Around the Rosie, Mom alternated reaching in and pulling back, as if unsure of what to do.

Jaelene watched the position of the gun between them. She looked as if she were waiting for the perfect opportunity to jump in and steal the gun away from both of them.

As I reached the door, I heard a loud pop.

Mom and Jaelene screamed. "No!" Mom held her face. Her hands slid down, dragging her cheeks toward her neck.

Dad and Kizaar embraced each other. They held each other tighter. Tighter than either of them had ever held the other before. They'd never been closer than at that moment, and they looked into each other's surprised eyes. Kizaar's arm was wrapped around Dad's waist and they danced around a ragged circle with slow, stiff steps. Dad's hand braced Kizaar's shoulder as his eyes left Kizaar's and inched toward the ceiling. The gun dropped and spun on the floor.

Their dance slowed as they dipped lower and lower toward the floor. They held each other closer as they drifted downward like a winding staircase. Then, they fell, Dad on one side, Kizaar on the other, blood on both, the gun between them.

Nineteen

TWO AMBULANCES PULLED UP in front of the house. The paramedics examined Dad and Kizaar and whisked them down the street to Barnes-Jewish Hospital. Mom was shaken as the paramedics helped her into the ambulance with Dad. She cried, clutched his hand, and talked to him as his eyes remained affixed on something directly above him. He didn't look at her. His breathing was shallow under the mask the paramedics had placed over his nose and mouth. His chest barely rose and fell.

Jaelene rode in the other ambulance with Kizaar. Before the paramedic closed the door, I saw Babysista rubbing Kizaar's arm. She rubbed his arm as if she were trying to rub away the agony and pain. He just moaned with his eyes closed.

I locked up the house, hopped in my ride, and drove to the hospital. I was dazed, unable to believe this shit was actually happening.

The moment I walked through the emergency room entrance, I saw Mom and Jaelene sitting in the waiting room with blank faces. Jaelene rested her head on Mom's shoulder. Mom's arm was wrapped around Jaelene. She alternated pats and strokes while she studied the face of every nurse that came through the emergency room doors. I sat down beside them silently. Sat down. No eye contact. No discussion. We sat and listened to one another breathe.

Finally, a nurse called out for Mom. She was too exhausted to get up, so she waved a frail arm and signaled to her. Nurse Clay hustled over to where we were slumped and explained Kizaar's flesh wound to the shoulder and Dad's heart attack.

With his stubby finger wrapped around the gun, Dad's hands had tightened and squeezed the trigger when the veins in his chest constricted. After grazing and snatching a good part of Kizaar's shoulder, the bullet careened through the wall.

I still didn't know what to feel. Relief? Worry? Anger? Compassion? What was I supposed to feel? Something was drastically wrong here, and once again, we weren't talking about it. We were moving around it. No one talked about what had just happened or why or how to change things for the better. In a few weeks, we would all walk out of the hospital and back to the same old mess. The same old drama.

I wasn't going to let that happen.

"Can you leave the message for him at his desk?" I asked Dexter.

My vacation time was just about up, but I was in no way prepared to return home. I called Kawamichi Finishes and initiated the necessary paperwork for a leave of absence. Policy was that we could take up to three months. I didn't know how much time I needed, but I had to tidy up everything at work so I'd have a job to go back to when this mess was over—if it ever ended.

I knew that my boss needed to be notified immediately so

that he could make long-term arrangements for the handling of my projects. With my luck, the administrative assistant was out sick, and all of upper management were in the weekly managers' meeting. Consequently, I regretfully felt that Dexter was the best person to call, both to forward a message to my boss and to give him background info on the projects that I knew he would be dying to take off my hands and show the head honchos that he could do them better than I could.

"Certainly. Anything going on that we need to know about?" he fished.

"No, I just need some extra time off to deal with a few personal issues."

"Personal issues? Hmmm. Yes, I can see how that would be a problem for you. This job can take a lot out of a person. Nothing to be embarrassed about. Sometimes even I have to take a step back from things myself. Take a breather. Not everyone is cut out for this job." He punctuated his remarks with a sinister chuckle.

"Can you make sure he gets the message as soon as he gets out of the meeting?" I ignored his comments. Dexter was probably salivating more than a *real* black man at home watching the Super Bowl in front of a big-screen TV and being served a soul food dinner by none other than a half-naked Tyra Banks in the flesh.

"No problem. Oh, and since I've already taken over the Toyota account with absolutely no problems at all, I'll just help myself to your other projects—the most urgent ones, of course."

What he meant was "the ones with the highest profiles that will make me even more visible than I try to make myself in this company."

"Whatever, Dexter." I hung up the phone without bothering to say good-bye.

A couple of days later, Kizaar was released from the hospital. Jae-lene, Mom, and I visited Dad together and alternated shifts one by one. When I visited him, his diminishing body lay in the bed despondent. That was the first time I noticed how he now looked. He looked so small and helpless. His face seemed to have aged a little more since the shooting. The skin around his eyes and on his cheeks drooped. His lips developed a slight arch in the direction of a frown. He looked tired, as if he were ready to give up whatever battle he was fighting.

He didn't have much to say. It could have been due to the tubes and all the medication, but I didn't think he would have said much without them, either. On visits with Mom, he didn't say a word to her the whole time. Never even looked at her once. I had had enough. It was time to put an end to this for good. Things had gone too far; it was time for somebody to step in and help Kizaar at least try to make us a family.

"This has got to stop, Dad," I said as he lay captive to the oxygen mask and miles of tubing. I felt guilty for trying to talk about this now with him lying on a hospital bed looking pitiful, but, then again, no time would be a good time. At least I knew there wouldn't be a cane swinging my way.

He fixed a gaze on me first, then the window. The bright April sun spotlighted a section of the floor.

I walked to the edge of his bed and pulled the adjacent chair around to face him. I really wasn't sure if the little bumps on my arms were from the freezing-cold hospital room, or from what I was about to get into with a man trying to recover from a heart attack.

"I don't want to get you excited, but we've got to do something. We've got to talk, Dad. You've got to change. Our family is falling apart. We have no family anymore." I leaned toward the bed and rested my forearms on my thighs. I shook my head and stared at the metal bed guards as I added, "Because no one can stand to be around you. You've become so evil. Just evil for no reason."

His slow breathing was starting to get loud. Sounded like the last bit of water being sucked up through a straw one breath at a time. I had to admit that he didn't look so evil now. He looked meek. Even his gray hairs looked tired, like they had been to the mountaintop and back.

I tread carefully. "We're not a family. You bring Mom down any chance you get, and you nearly killed Kizaar."

He shifted his head and studied the striped wallpaper.

"What has Mom done to deserve all of this? Nothing." I got up from the chair and paced back and forth at the foot of the bed. The heels of my shoes clicked loudly against the floor. My stomach began to turn.

"I remember, Dad, when you left her—left us—for no reason with two small babies and one on the way. Was it an affair?" I didn't wait for or expect an answer. I already knew it would never come. "I remember when you tried to crawl back. You begged her. She did nothing for you to leave but bear your children in the first place. Then she forgave you, allowed you back, and you treated her like crap for the next two decades. And now you nearly kill your son. For what? I don't understand.

"Mom swears by her loyalty to you. I can't understand that either. She's been loyal, and this is her payback? You talking down to her, making her feel worthless, like nothing?"

Dad's suctioning sound picked up the pace. I had excited him. Didn't want to. After all, he did need to recover. But this was still the same man who nearly killed my brother.

"Mom doesn't deserve to be with a man like you. She deserves better." My own breathing quickened as the load on my chest got lighter and lighter.

Dad slowly moved his left arm. The stiff white sheet puckered, lifted, and fell as he slid his arm beneath it. He exposed a tightly clenched fist.

I looked down at him curiously.

His fist rested on top of the white sheet, and, one by one, he lifted a finger and opened his hand. Opened it until it exposed a locket like Mom's.

"That's Mom's locket," I stated with surprise. "She keeps that in her jewelry box. Looks at it every night." I stopped and stared at it. It wasn't exactly the same. It was the other half to the broken heart.

I stared and realized what this meant. He had the same thoughts as Mom, the same dream. It seemed like they both wanted to get back to what they had had in that picture, to go back to where it all started. "See, I knew you and Mom still loved each other. You're both holding on to the past and yearning to get it back. I knew you still loved her."

He shook his head no and held out the locket. I moved in closer and looked at it. A tear escaped the corner of his eye, rolled down the side of his face, and hit the pillow.

I took the locket from his hand, opened it, and saw the same picture of a young couple happily in love a long time ago.

"It's not too late, Dad. You can get this back. You and Mom can get back to this place. It's not too late."

Dad shook his head no.

"It won't be easy, Dad, but it can be done," I tried to assure him.

He shook his head no. His lips were parched. They clung to each other as he pried them apart to speak. "James," he said.

"What?"

He cleared his throat. "James. Not me. James." He stared at the locket in my hand. "My brother . . . James."

My heart nearly stopped. I looked down at the happy couple again. I choked. "Tell me you're not saying that this is not you." I swallowed so I could speak again. "Are you saying that this is Uncle James?"

Dad didn't shake his head no.

I opened my mouth and hesitated as all my thoughts fell in line like soldiers. "Are you saying that Mom had an affair with Uncle James?"

Dad said yes with a hardened stare. He continued to stare at the locket in my hand. His temples bulged.

"Not my son," he said with watery eyes. "Kizaar's not my son. He's James's son."

Twenty

THE ROOM BEGAN to spin. My head felt light and dizzy as if it were teetering from one side of the room to the other. Faces flashed in my mind: expressions from Kizaar, expressions from Mom, beaming smiles, frowns of pain and disappointment, raised eyebrows of surprise and disbelief. Their faces swarmed all around me. The faces that I'd known all my life were now different. I sat down, leaned back in the chair, and gripped the armrests tightly with numb fingers for the rest of the ride.

Dad plunged me right into the details of how he had found out, and it wasn't from Mom. The news came from Uncle James on his deathbed. He told me how Uncle James lay in the bed, bandaged and bruised, fully aware that doctors could not stop his internal bleeding. How he spoke with pain—from the accident—not from what he had done to his brother.

Uncle James told Dad that he and Mom had gotten friendlier while Dad spent time building the business. Dad was the brains behind the real estate operation, while carefree Uncle James did the grunt work. Uncle James said that Mom felt neglected and he had just tried to keep her company. At first.

While Dad sought out business loans, Uncle James and Mom grew closer during midday lunches, motorcycle rides, and, eventually, afternoon trysts. Uncle James had confessed that the child his three-months'-pregnant sister-in-law was carrying was probably his. Dad said that this was right around the time that Mom suddenly became more affectionate with him. He then put two and two together and figured out that it was a cover-up so that he would not suspect that there was a chance that he couldn't be the father. He didn't believe his brother until he figured out and later confirmed with the doctor that Kizaar had not been born six weeks early, as Mom had once claimed. He knew, but said nothing.

I listened as Dad told me how that sickened him so much that he had to leave Mom and us without a word. He was hurt and confused, and felt he had lost the woman he loved and was building a family with—the woman he had worked hard for. And to his brother, no less. His best friend. His twin. He roamed for five months as he felt everything coming to an end. His world wouldn't turn anymore.

"So why'd you come back?" I asked. I stared at my thumbs.

Dad told me about his resolve. "During those five months, I thought about you and Babysista and the life you would have without me there. I even thought about Kizaar and how this wasn't his fault. His father was dead and somebody needed to teach him how to be a man. A real man. I couldn't give up on my girls and let them grow up fatherless. I couldn't let my nephew grow up feeling like an outcast. Only, I know I failed at that anyway. Maybe I should've just stayed gone."

I grabbed his hand and held on to it. We were quiet for a while before I asked, "Mom didn't know?"

"Not sure. I never mentioned that I knew. I wasn't going to be the first to bring it up. It hurt too much to think about it, let alone bring it out in the open and talk about it. And have her say it to my face. And have blood tests and papers in my face showing me and the world that my wife had an affair with my brother and had a child. I couldn't open up that can. It would have hurt worse than it already did."

So he came back to us. He put his pain aside to raise Babysista and me. Tried to accept Kizaar as his own. Tried to forgive Mom in his heart. Dad choked on his voice as he talked about his failure to bury the pain, and his resentment, and the constant renewal of his resolve to do right by Kizaar and Mom. Year after year he tried. He would suddenly buy gifts, take them out to dinner, and try to be part of a normal, happy family. He told me about how it would last a day or two, until the thoughts of his brother's confession crept back into the recesses of his mind and rose with much hell and fury. That hell and fury came barreling out of his gut and cloaked Mom and Kizaar like fire on a bone-dry forest.

"I tried to let it go, to accept it, but it kept building up. I'd look at her and in my mind I'd see her with him. See them touching each other. Hugging and kissing. I'd see them in bed together. I'd picture the three of them together: her, him, and the baby. I'd start to get angry and angrier. I'd drive myself crazy until I just wanted to hurt . . ." His fist was clenched. "But I didn't. Well, at least not physically. I know I hurt her. Deep down, I think I wanted her to pay. I wanted her to feel the way I felt inside. I wanted her to feel just as torn up as I did. I guess I wanted her to suffer, but I didn't want to admit it to myself. I kept telling myself I was doing the right thing. The right thing for the family. But I hurt him, didn't I? I hurt him bad. I didn't want to do that."

He looked up at me with such sorrow in his eyes. Sorrow that I had never seen before. "I should have just stayed gone."

Dad drained the words out of his heart and suspended his thoughts somewhere between the fading sun through the blinds and yesteryear. I let go of his hand when he drifted off into sleep. I allowed him that temporary escape from his misery and tipped out of the room. I kept that secret for him for two weeks—until I figured out what to do with it.

"Whoa! Ain't that some shit?" was all Tucker could say as he sipped his coffee at the kitchen counter across from me.

The next time Tucker called from Cleveland and asked to come see me, I gave him the green light and told him to get here quickly. I needed somebody. I had to get this off my chest and out of my head. And he happily obliged. He wrapped up projects with some of his clients and brought his laptop with him to finish up a few more. He said that that was the thing he loved about being his own boss. He could pick up at anytime, go anywhere, and work from wherever.

"Yeah, that's what I thought. I still can't believe everything he told me."

"What are you going to do with it? All that info?"

"I don't know. If our family was broken apart before, now there's a big boulder in it separating everybody even further."

"That's the last thing I would have suspected from your mother though," Tucker said as he looked away over the edge of his cup.

"You have no idea. Alton had always said that something was

up with—" I stopped my words dead in their tracks, not knowing if Alton's name was something I could say or not. I stood up and walked behind Tucker, heading for the open windows. Tucker didn't flinch. He followed me and sat on the edge of the couch. Picked up his *Cyberforce* comic book off the coffee table, rolled it up, and repeatedly slapped it against his knee.

I stared out the window at the downtowners heading for somewhere important as I told him about the "loyalty" conversation I'd had with Mom when we were shopping.

"All this time I was pissed at Dad for being evil to Mom and Kizaar for no reason, when I should have been pissed at her."

"Well, you didn't know."

I walked away from the window and sat next to him on the couch. Tucker scooted over, so I leaned back and lay my head on his shoulder. His fresh, soapy scent played in my nose. He placed the comic book on the couch, reached up, and ran his fingers through my hair.

"I know. I'm so angry with her. I defended her because she never would stand up to him. She never wanted any of us to say anything to him."

"Could have been from guilt. Or fear that the truth would come out."

"Definitely wasn't because she was a victim like I thought. I have to see her."

"You're going to confront her?"

"I have to."

"What about Kizaar?"

"That's what I'm dreading the most. It's going to kill him that this man isn't even his father. After spending his life trying to gain his approval? He's going to blow."

"Who knows? Things usually change after lies are revealed.

Maybe this could be that step in the right direction to finally make things better for your dad and Kizaar. After all, your father gets to let go of a secret that he's been carrying around for years. Kizaar will at least be able to see what's been up with Dad. Might even share his pain."

"Maybe you're right."

I closed my eyes as we fell silent. I tried to clear my mind and just concentrate on Tucker's touch. I needed him to take me out of that place in my mind and away for a while to a land of peace. I reached up and placed my hand on his chest. Felt his heart pump against my hand. I sighed deeply and slowly.

"What?" he asked.

"Hmm? Nothing."

I raised my head and looked up at those familiar brown eyes looking back at me. His smile was soft and inviting. I was happy to have my old friend back, my once before lover. He moved closer to my face. I froze. I felt his breath on my nose, then my lips. It brushed across my face and warmed my soul. His lips lightly touched mine. Once. Twice. I kissed him passionately but briefly, pulled back, smiled, and lay my head back on his shoulder. His heart beat much faster underneath my palm.

Just for a moment, the family drama lifted from my body and suspended itself overhead. The sun settled as we sat there reminiscing about the good old times. Tucker massaged my mind with funny thoughts from our trips together, past discussions of our dreams and our goals, and our love for each other and how it had never left. Everything. I lay my head in Tucker's lap as he stroked the worry from my head. It felt good, even if it was only temporary.

"I had Synda served," he said after a long silence.

I said nothing aloud, but I wondered what that meant for us. I thought that he must have been wondering the same thing, but neither of us said it.

My jaw began to hurt as I watched Mom dust furniture in the floral-scented living room. The back of her head jerked as she ran a cloth up and down the cherrywood curio. Her backside waggled as she moved from the curio to the blinds, the coffee table, and back to the curio. She seemed intent on removing each dust speck, each fiber, and each grain of dirt from the almost spotless furniture, as if that was most important. She dusted the ledge in front of the stained glass window.

She turned to focus her attention on the baby-grand piano and caught a glimpse of me from the corner of her eye. A tiny hiccup escaped her when she jumped. She brought the dust cloth to her chest. "Woo! You scared me, Van. What are you doing standing there?"

"What are you doing?"

She gave me a puzzled look that asked if I was blind. "Dusting." She proceeded to dust the dustless piano.

"Why?"

She raised both eyebrows before answering. "Just preparing the house for your father. For when he comes home."

"He has a release date?"

"No, not yet, but he's getting stronger."

"Have you talked to him?"

Her dusting slowed, then picked back up. "No. He really hasn't felt much like talking, and I don't try to force him. I just want him to get his strength back up so that he can come home."

She turned the cloth over and began attacking the pictures on the wall.

I walked closer to her. I wanted to examine her face. "How do you feel?"

"Well, I'm just happy that he's getting better—"

"No, Mom. How . . . do . . . you . . . feel?"

She finally stopped. She brought the dust cloth down to her side and turned to me. Her face was twisted. "I'm feeling fine, Van. But what's wrong with you?"

"Feeling fine? Not feeling guilty?"

"Guilty about what?" She hesitated. "Van, if you're suggesting that all this was my fault, then—"

"Isn't it really?"

"Oh, I see. Now you're going to jump on the 'blame Mom bandwagon' with your father. I'm stupid. I'm dumb, right?"

"No, actually, I would beg to differ. You're not dumb at all. Quite clever, in fact. I mean, a dumb person wouldn't think of changing their child's conception date and saying he came early, now would they?"

Her jaw dropped. "Wh— wh—" I could see her brain scrambling for another cover-up. Her eyes shifted from corner to corner as her jaw bounced up and down.

I decided to show her mercy in the lion's den. "I know, Mom. Most important, Dad knows. He's known for years. He's known since he came back to us years ago."

"He knows what?" She was obviously too smart to confess until she was 100 percent sure of what it was I knew.

I stood with all my weight on one leg and my foot patted a beat on the floor in double time. The pocket of air around me was thick, and getting thicker. "He's always known, Mom. About Uncle James. About Kizaar."

Her eyes dropped to the floor. She staggered backward. Her hands searched behind her for the piano bench. She braced herself and slowly backed down, still almost tumbling over. "How? How?"

"Uncle James. Deathbed confession. Gave Dad the half of the locket that belonged to him. The half that matches yours."

She looked up at me. Her mouth still hung open. "He suspects?" she asked, as if we hadn't been talking for the past two minutes. Her eyebrows lifted.

"No. He doesn't suspect, Mom. He knows. I guess that answers my question as to whether it's true or not," I stated flatly.

She spoke soft words. Words that weren't meant for me. "He never said anything. I had a feeling he suspected, but he never said anything." She shook her head and looked down at my shoes. "I didn't want him to say it. I thought if I didn't argue with him, there would be no chance of it coming out, if he knew."

"So it's true? Kizaar's father is Uncle James and not Dad?"

Her eyes slowly lifted from my shoes, to my midsection, and to my eyes. "I don't know. I never knew for sure."

I didn't like her anymore. She was my mother, but I didn't like her. Thunder settled in my stomach at the sight of her now. Her once beautiful and slender body, her gracious nails, her mild frame—they all looked disgusting to me now. Mrs. High and Mighty took a nasty fall from grace that exposed hideous scars.

"That was a long time ago," she finally said as if she had to say something, and those words seemed like they would do for the moment. Then her hands began to tremble as the truth settled in the small of her back. Apparently she realized suddenly that she was exposed. Naked. "Oh, God. Oh, my God!" She shook her head back and forth as she studied my shoes again.

She wrapped a hand around the diamond bracelet on her

wrist and stroked it, then her hand went up to her diamond neck-lace. She stroked it back and forth with the tips of her fingers. Her face said that her mind was moving a mile a minute. "Would I be able to get a settlement?"

I sucked my teeth at the revolting question. "There really are no words that I can think of to tell you what I think about you right now."

She looked at my face. "Does he want a divorce? What is he going to do?"

"What's he going to do? You're not interested in explaining? Clearing things up? What about Kizaar? Do you see how you've ruined his life?"

"Is he going to leave me?" Her eyes glazed over and looked through me, searching for her own answers instead of supplying me with mine. "How am I going to live?" She had erased me from the room. I couldn't believe this woman. Who was she?

"Don't know," I said. I walked out of the living room and out of the house. "Don't care."

I drove. Drove to Ted Drews for frozen custard before going back to the Merchandise Mart. Then I headed straight for the phone in my apartment, ordered a large mushroom and sausage Imo's pizza, and waited for it to be delivered.

Dad had actually been the one tormented over the years. It had screwed me to think that Dad had been evil to Mom and Kizaar for no reason. He had really been fighting a battle within himself. While I thought that Mom was a defenseless, frail, righ-teous, never-did-a-damn-thing-wrong Glinda the Good Witch, in actuality she had cheated on my dad with his twin brother, and hidden my brother's true paternity to boot.

Imo's and guilt slid down my throat and numbed my stomach. I had believed that the love in their marriage died for no reason. I thought it just went sour because of Dad. Thought it was because men just fell out of love over time. I thought it would just happen if you married the man you loved. That was the O Theory. Damn, what now?

Twenty-One

KIZAAR LOOKED AS IF he had been shot all over again. Since Mom had checked into a hotel and shut herself off from everyone, I had to tell him and Jaelene the whole story.

His face was long as he tried to digest what I had just told them. They sat at my dining room table nursing Tahitian Treats, looking like they were ready at any moment to get up and take a flying leap out of the sixth-floor windows.

"Let me get this right," Jaelene said, her face perplexed. "Mom cheated on Dad, and with Uncle James? And that's why he left us back then?" Her face lifted and her mouth remained open after she spoke. Rigid hills and valleys developed in her forehead as she tried to comprehend. "And Kizaar is . . ." She looked over at Kizaar and stopped short. She shuddered. "No. I can't believe that she would put him through that." She closed her eyes and rubbed her forehead with her hand.

"Believe it," I said.

Kizaar's usually dancing dreads were stiff and lifeless. He gently placed his hand over his bandaged shoulder as if the wound had a whole new meaning now. It seemed that the news had caused the pain to well up again. He brought his hand down, slumped in the chair, and draped both hands around his glass.

"Can't be," Kizaar said. In that moment, his expressions ran the gamut of surprise to disbelief to anger. His eyes caught fire and blood drained from his fingertips as he tightened his grip around the glass. "I don't believe that. Uncle James is not my father. Dad is."

Jaelene kept quiet and stared down at the table, unsure of what to say or do. We both watched Kizaar's temperament rise from low to high.

"Kizaar, Mom all but admitted it," I said.

His breathing got harder. "All but? So she didn't admit it? She didn't say that Uncle James was definitely my father?"

Jaelene reached around to hug Kizaar. His face tightened. He jerked away from her and out of the chair. Jaelene looked at me apologetically and I signaled her not to worry about it.

Kizaar began to wear a path on the floor behind the table. His baggy jeans made tiny, abrupt swishes with each step. "He *is* my father." Veins popped up on his forearm and the side of his neck. "There's no way he's not my father. I can feel him." He tried his best to will it into the truth.

"I know it's hard to believe, Kizaar, but that's why he's been so mean to you and Mom." I stood and moved behind my chair. Jaelene remained seated, staring down at the table. She went back to rubbing understanding into her forehead.

"He wasn't mean. He was tough. He was trying to make a man out of me. I just want to show him that I am a man and that I'm not a failure. I want him to be proud of me as his son." His dreads now shook with fury as he paced.

"Why else would Mom move out and into a hotel if it wasn't true?" Jaelene asked, almost in a whisper.

"Kizaar, why don't you sit down," I said. "This is a lot of information to—"

Kizaar stopped dead in his tracks as if he'd slammed into an invisible wall. "I want a paternity test," he stated with clear conviction. He was all but yelling now. His voice was deep, strong, and determined.

That was the last thing our family needed and the last thing Dad wanted: some Ricki Lake paternity sideshow. I needed to talk him out of this. "Zar, Mom confessed to the affair with Uncle James. Dad said that Uncle James told him about it right before he died. And, well . . . I just don't want to see you put yourself through all that and make it more painful than it already is. Dad doesn't want it either. That's one of the reasons he never said anything. He accepts you as his son anyway. Believe me. I'm pretty sure things are going to be different between the two of you now. He knows he hurt you and he didn't want to do that. I can tell he's sorry. You don't need to put him and yourself through a paternity test. He's your father in every sense of the word."

"No one's calling into question your parentage. If someone is going to say that the man that I've called 'Dad' for the past twenty-five years is not my father, then I want to see the proof. I want a paternity test."

Kizaar took up pacing again and lengthened his path until he reached the brick wall. He stood before it and impatiently rocked from one leg to the other, swaying from side to side. The air whistled as he sucked it in and out of his mouth through gritted teeth. He lashed out and slammed the side of the fist of his uninjured arm into the brick wall. Following a quick pause, he threw his fist into the brick wall three more times. His shoulders fell. He then pressed his forearm against the wall, leaned in, and rested his forehead on it.

I walked to my baby brother after he seemed to have exhausted his frustration. Jaelene got up and followed me. We got on either side of him. Leaned into him. Hugged him. Wished we could do more for him.

"I'll see what I can do to get the tests going," I told Kizaar, against my better judgment. Jaelene grabbed his hand. He let her hold it.

Kizaar pulled himself together after a while. He went to the bathroom and rinsed his face before he headed home. Before he left, I got the name of his doctor so I could get things started for him. I told him that I would take care of it for him, although I wished he would just leave it alone. Seeing it on paper would be even more devastating, not only for Kizaar, but for Dad, too. He had been through enough. He didn't need to be upset more and risk the possibility of another heart attack. That's what worried me the most about this paternity test thing.

Jaelene stayed after Kizaar left, and we talked a little more about the situation. She suddenly looked at her watch and tapped the face with her fingertip. "Oh, I gotta get out of here."

"I was hoping you would have time to hang out for a late lunch. I'm meeting Synda in a little bit."

Jaelene wrinkled her narrow nose and frowned. "She's here? No, thank you. I'd rather have a pap smear. Anyway, I'm on my way to my first appointment with my therapist." With a shy look, her eyes fluttered in my direction. I just smiled. I didn't want to make a big deal out of it, but I was happy for her.

Synda had been in town, as Tucker suspected. She finally called me on my cell phone last night and said she had some news to tell me. She was surprised to find that I was in town, too, then asked if we could meet for lunch—like old times, she said. I agreed. Didn't tell her that I already knew. Didn't tell her about me and Tucker. I wanted to save all that for later. For when I saw her.

"I would love for you to join us, but that's okay. Maybe next time," I said to Jaelene.

Jaelene ran like hell, but not before saying, "Not in a million years with that hoheffahbitch," or something to that effect.

After Jaelene left, I hopped on the Suzuki GXR600 that I was renting for the weekend. The warm weather was kicking in and reminding me of my bike. I love riding in weather like this, when winter is breaking and the fresh, clean spring breeze is moving in.

I took 64 West to 270 North and drove to West County to meet Synda at Ozzie's Restaurant in West Port Plaza. The heavy warm air tickled my nose as I took off my helmet. I could tell already that the months to come would bring another blazin' hot St. Louis summer. The humidity was already on the verge of a rise. I felt the weight of the air creeping up and pushing against my white knit pullover.

I walked into Ozzie's and told the hostess who I was looking for. She led me through the late lunch crowd to a table where Synda was seated, already sipping on a Long Island Iced Tea. I ordered a Pinot Grigio, and the waiter asked me for ID. I wanted to kiss him for that. I flipped out my Ohio driver's license—with much commotion so that people could see that I was getting carded—and flashed it in his face. He stared at the out-of-state license, looking for my birth date. He found it, looked at me, and nodded his head.

"Visiting our wonderful city, I see?" he asked.

"Not visiting. I grew up here. I just live in Cleveland now."

"Oh, you're from here? What high school did you go to?" he challenged me with a beam.

"Sumner, baby." I saw his beam and raised it by a bulldog.

"Roosevelt. Representing," he stated with pride as he nodded and displayed the imaginary "R" on his chest. He looked over at Synda.

"Northwest," she exclaimed and flipped her ponytail. We laughed and nodded. Each of us proclaimed our school to be the best high school in all of St. Louis. Didn't matter if or where you went to college or how many bachelor's, master's, or doctorate degrees you had, what mattered was what high school you went to. That could make or break you in this town.

After we got the customary St. Louis greeting out of the way, he rushed off and returned with my Pinot Grigio. I looked across the booth at Synda, who looked as polished as ever. Honey skin smoothed, hair slicked back and up into a ponytail, lips lightly glossed. Looking at her, no one would ever have been able to peg her as the type of person that Tucker, Sherron, Medena, and Zandra insisted she really was.

But my seeing her as a trustworthy friend had been wishful thinking and total denial on my part. I had pretty much created my own image of Synda since moving to Cleveland. She was the only person I knew when I got there—the only person I had known for most of my life—and I needed to have a girlfriend there in my corner, no matter what. So I had made Synda out to be what I wanted her to be, and didn't want to see her as she truly was. I realized now, though, that Synda was not the person I made her out to be. She wasn't my sista-friend, didn't have my back, no matter how many years we had behind us.

"I've got some things to tell you that are going to blow your mind," she said softly. She put her elbow on the table and began stroking the scar on her forehead.

"Tucker is here," I said nonchalantly, before she could get out the confession I was expecting. I sat back and watched her face.

Synda stopped midstroke on the scar and anxiety drew her face in. "Tucker is here? In St. Louis? What's he doing here? Is he looking for me?"

"For you? Hardly," I said in a flat tone. I took a sip of wine, rolled it across my tongue, then swallowed. I stared at the scar on her forehead. The one she said she got when she celebrated getting into Case by visiting an "old friend" in Vegas. She swore her innocence and that nothing was going on. That his wife was mistaken when she took a beer bottle to Synda's forehead.

She placed her hands together on the table and began examining her cuticles. She avoided looking at me. "He told you, didn't he?"

"Every single bit," I snapped back quickly.

She shifted her bottom. Her fingertips went back up to her forehead and again scanned the scar. "So, I guess you're about ready to beat my ass now, huh? You always said that."

"Yes. You're lucky that all his wife did was bust a bottle upside your head."

She dropped her hand to the table and began fiddling with her nails again.

"I'm not a bad person. It's not my fault. I think it's embedded in me. You know my dad . . . my father was a womanizer. Stepped out on my mom and had a slew of kids." She lowered her head while she spoke.

I growled. "I know you're not going to sit here and blame your father for your infidelities."

"Well, not totally. I think I got married too young, too. Before I really had a chance to experience life."

"I guess that's the way it goes when you seduce your best friend's man, lie about getting pregnant by him, then marry him under her nose because you know he's going to try to do the right thing, huh? You knew your best friend would eventually forgive you since you knew me inside out, right?" I asked sarcastically.

She let out a long, slow sigh that I recognized as the sigh that was supposed to mean she was sorry, the sigh that was supposed to make me want to forgive her. It was supposed to mean that she was requesting the empathy that she knew I would give, because that was the kind of person I was. It was supposed to mean "Let's argue this out, get mad, and get over it." That's what it was supposed to mean.

"Tucker and I have been filling in a lot of blank spaces, Synda. Catching up on old times. You might as well know."

Her eyes shot through me like a dart. I took another slow, confident sip of wine.

"What are you saying?" she asked.

"I'm saying we're getting reacquainted. Picking up where we left off before we were so *rudely* interrupted." I stared directly into her eyes as I spoke, daring her to challenge me.

Synda started to speak, then stopped. The words seemed to be jumbling around in her head, as if she was trying to come up with the right combination. Finally she asked, "Are you seeing TC?"

"What difference does it make to you?" I quickly snapped at her. "You have three other men, don't you? Or is it four? We can't keep count."

She looked around the room, then back to me. "I still love TC. I want him back. I know it sounds crazy, but I wanted to confess everything today and ask you to help me get him back."

I strained my eyes to glare at her as if I were peering over glasses. No she didn't even have the nerve, did she? Oh, but she did. Her eyes were hopeful. Her lips curled downward into a pout that almost fell into her lap.

"Oh, let me guess. Since Tucker served you with divorce papers, you suddenly realized what a good man you had and decided to drop all the others to win your good man back?"

She stuttered. "Uh . . . uh . . . well . . . kinda. Well, I haven't—"

I squinted and moved closer to her. She was coming across more clearly to me now. I could finally see who she really was. "You haven't stopped seeing the other men, have you?"

"Not yet. . . . It's just . . . well . . . you don't know what it's like. TC is a good man, I know, but it's going to take me a little time to—"

I'd had enough. I snatched the napkin off my lap and dabbed the corners of my mouth.

"If we were friends," she added, "you would do this for me. If we were real friends, you wouldn't get involved with him if I still wanted him. Real friends wouldn't do that to each other."

I balled up the napkin, threw it on the table, and grabbed my purse. "You're absolutely right, Synda. *Real* friends wouldn't." I scooted out of the booth as calmly as I could. I smoothed my pants as I stood and turned to walk out the front entrance, away from our twenty-year friendship, leaving her with the bill for the drinks.

As I took a couple of steps, I heard her say, "We still girls, right?"

I kept walking.

I called Tucker and took 70 West to the airport Marriott where he was staying. The door opened to a shirtless Tucker with bulging coffee brown muscles and an ice-cold six-pack. My tongue suddenly felt thick and parched as I strolled past him through the door. Tried to maintain a cool expression. I didn't want him to notice that I noticed him.

"Just got back from the Bally's around the way in St. Ann," he said. He closed the door and walked past me. "Make yourself comfortable. I'm going to jump in and take a quick shower."

"That's fine," I said.

I took a seat on the chair in his room and looked around. Much to my surprise, everything was pretty much in place. I had expected to see pieces of clothing tossed here and there, empty soda cans, and pizza boxes strewn around. That was the Tucker I remembered. But no clothes were in sight. Hardly anything was out of place.

I laughed to myself as I finally found the Tucker I knew. The television was tuned into the Cartoon Network and a familiar assortment of Spider-Man, Batman, and X-Men comic books were spread out on the bed.

I got up and grabbed one of the bottled waters from the mini-refrigerator and waited for him to finish his shower. I tried to get into X-Men on TV but it just wasn't working for me, so I turned to TLC, where some doctor was delving into the open chest of some unlucky heart patient. I twisted the cap off my water and snuggled into the chair.

Tucker emerged from the shower wearing a towel. The boy must have been playing on my weakness on purpose. Damn. I pretended to be unfazed, but oh, was I fazed.

"Just came from lunch with your wife," I said.

"Soon-to-be-ex wife," he chimed in quickly. "So she surfaced, huh? And you had lunch with her? You are an even bigger person than I thought."

"Well, we didn't actually get to have lunch. I walked out on her."

He gave a hearty laugh. "You have to tell me all about it."

"I'll tell you all about it, but first I was thinking that we could take your car and go over to the park. It's kinda nice out. I thought we could walk and talk."

"Sure. Sounds good to me," Tucker said.

Tucker got dressed and we took his rented Camry to Art Hill and sat down on the steep slope.

Tucker and I sat there and held hands as we playfully talked about the people walking by—something we always used to do for fun. Tucker maintained constant contact with me: a hand on the thigh, a finger on my arm, an arm around my waist. Making sure not to let me go. I loved it.

I told him about my lunch date with Synda and he chuckled humorlessly, as if to distract himself from thinking about the headache and the drama.

"I still don't understand why you married her in the first place. People don't get married just because the woman gets pregnant nowadays. That's so old-fashioned."

"I listened to my mother and father. They wanted me to marry her. They were going to cut me off if I didn't."

"Ouch. Didn't know that."

"Yep." He reached between his bended knees, pulled up a blade of grass and studied it. "They had a hissy fit when we figured out that she was never pregnant." He ripped the blade in two. "Mom wanted to kill her."

"How did you find out?"

"She confessed after my mother kept pressing her for details. Synda came here to St. Louis and supposedly miscarried. She said she was in the hospital, but she never called me until she got out and claimed to be recuperating at her parents' home. I took her word for it. But it didn't smell right to my mother. You know her."

I laughed. Yes, I did know Mrs. Scott. She grilled every woman that Tucker brought home—grilled me like I had stolen something—but then took me in like a daughter. "Yes, I know your mother. I'm surprised she let Synda get by her."

"She was, too."

I smiled and tried to change the subject. "Well, I see you still collect comic books."

"Yeah, still do, but I've changed a lot in other ways."

My smile changed into a smirk. "I'll bet. Like how?"

"Hold on for a sec," he said. Tucker got up and went to retrieve something from the car. He came back with a book.

"I want to read something to you." He ran his tongue under the gap in his teeth, then read me a poem.

"You're into poetry now?"

"Yeah, I guess you could say that." He half chuckled.

"Who wrote them?"

"Me." Tucker snapped the book closed and handed it to me.

I took it and looked at the cover. *Journey*. By Tucker Scott. I examined the cover and looked up at him, flipped to the back flap of the jacket with his picture, and looked at him again, then I looked at the table of contents, and back at him. I was speechless.

"I did it myself. Wasn't looking to make money or anything. Just wanted to put my thoughts in a book. I wanted to be able to give it to you someday. My inspiration."

"I'm surprised. I'm touched." I flipped through all his poems on love, losing it, and getting it back. I read the dedication to his first love that he foolishly lost—me.

He proceeded to read me a few more of his poems. Some were

short, some were a couple pages long. He put his soul into reading them to me. He held my hand and read them with conviction.

"I've changed, Vanella. I've changed a lot. I'm not that same irresponsible little boy you left in college. That was actually the start of my growing-up process. Until you left, I didn't know what love was." He took the book out of my hand, placed it on the grass, and held both my hands between his. "Now that I got you back, I'm never letting you go again. You hear me? Never."

He turned my face toward his. He pulled my face close and kissed me. Such a sweet kiss it was. I felt my shoulders relax and a tingle went through the small of my back. I was alive again.

I stared deeply into the pupils of his dark brown eyes. "Let's go."

He understood what I was saying. We got up and took a slow stroll arm in arm back to the car and drove to my place. I unlocked the door and we stepped inside. I pulled Tucker by the hand. I wrapped my arms around his neck, kicked the door closed with my foot, and kissed him. I gently sucked on his lips, licked them, and teased them. I took off my jacket without relinquishing his lips. He took off his jacket as well, then he picked me up and carried me to the bed.

And we became reacquainted again. Just like old times. It was as good as I remembered. No. Better.

The ceiling fan stirred a light breeze and cooled my backside as I stretched out over the rising heat of Tucker beneath me. His hard body was wet with a sweet sweat that found its way to my tongue. His sweetness lingered in the hollows of my throat before it evaporated and caramelized over my senses. He was doing it to me all over again.

I washed up and threw on my Rams jersey before cooking breakfast for us. I glided back into the room where Tucker sat watching *X-Men* on TV and flipping through a Spider-Man comic book. He saw me carrying a tray of bacon, eggs, and toast, and his eyes lit up like he hadn't eaten in three days. He tucked the sheets in around him and helped me to ease the tray onto his lap. I picked up my tray and took my place beside him on the king-size bed, and we ate breakfast between laughter and soft kisses. When we were done, Tucker carried our empty trays to the kitchen and loaded the dishes into the dishwasher. He then found an easy stride back through the bedroom door, hopped on the bed, and began a tickle-fest with me—just like he used to. And just like always, the tickle-fest worked its way into another love-fest.

I got up, went to the kitchen, and returned with two glasses of water and handed one to Tucker. We both drank it down as if our bodies had been drained of every drop and needed to be replenished.

"Ooh!" Tucker exclaimed when he finally looked me up and down. "You're going to catch cold in that thing, girl. You'd better put something on under that."

Or not.

I disregarded his comment and snuggled next to him on the bed. I picked up the remote and turned to the NFL Draft show.

Tucker moaned. "What are you doing?" He had the face of a dejected two-year-old.

"I almost forgot. The NFL Draft show is on. You almost made me miss it," I said as I playfully jabbed him in his side.

He didn't laugh. In fact, Tucker looked quite disturbed.

"*The X-Men* are still on." He looked at the remote in my hand as if this revelation demonstrated a great injustice that must be righted.

"Isn't it a marathon?" I asked, my grip firm on the remote.

"Yeah," he answered. My point appeared to have flown right over his head.

"Isn't it going to be on all day?"

"Not all day. Only until eight this evening."

I looked at the digital clock on the nightstand. "It's almost twelve-thirty now."

"Yeah?" He still seemed to be having a hard time connecting the dots. "Well, I can go in the other room to watch," he finally concluded. Tucker slipped from underneath my chest, retrieved a *Spawn* video from his overnight bag, and headed for the other room. I watched, flabbergasted.

"You're not serious, are you?"

"You know I don't care much for sports. I don't see the point of watching games on TV, or these shows where they talk about games, or pick new players for the next season." He gave a condescending chuckle before he left the room.

I had forgotten that about Tucker: he loved cartoons, video games, Foosball, and Froot Loops, but had never liked watching sports. Now I remembered. In college, Tucker would watch cartoons in one room while I watched sports in the other. It was I who would sometimes forgo Terry Bradshaw to spend a little time with Tucker and Superman, or Spider-Man, or whatever the superhero of the day was back then. Or I would be his miserable Max Payne opponent. Tucker had no mercy for anyone who dared challenge him on any of his PlayStation 2 games, not even me.

But I made it work back then, and I could do it again.

I got up and retrieved from the dresser the notebook I used to restart my business plan from scratch. New feelings from Tucker had given me the energy to think about leaving Kawamichi and starting my own business again. I got back in bed and turned up the volume on the remote as Houston picked David Carr as their first-round draft choice. I then placed the remote onto the soft, empty sheet beside me on that lonely football day.

Twenty-Two

KIZAAR'S GRIN STRETCHED FROM the Mississippi to the Ohio River as he brought Dad home from the hospital. He was so overjoyed that he insisted Jaelene and I wait at the house while he brought him home. His excuse was that we needed to make the house cozy, and he provided us with a list of homemaking duties. Even gave us a low-sodium, low-calorie, but amazingly high-flavor recipe to work on before they got home. We knew what Kizaar was doing, so we just went along with the program and let him have his day.

A couple of weeks before, Kizaar's doctor called with the results of the paternity test and tried to set up an appointment to go over them with him, but Kizaar insisted that he tell the family together. He insisted that the doctor meet us in Dad's hospital room and read the results to all of us. I have to admit, though, I was reluctant. I didn't want to see Dad slip into a coma and Kizaar lose his grip in the hospital, but my little brother insisted.

"There is a 99.9 percent chance that Jesse Morris is the father of Kizaar Morris," the doctor said with a grin.

Kizaar pumped the fist of his good arm. "Yes! Yes! I knew it! I knew it!" He stooped down, spread the fingers of his right hand on the floor between his legs, and dropped his head to his knees as if giving thanks to his creator.

Dad stared up at the ceiling with wet eyes, then closed his lids tightly. A single tear streaked down the left side of his face and died in his ear. It felt like a storm cloud had passed over my head and was replaced with heaven.

Kizaar stood and walked over to Dad, grabbed his hand, and looked into his face. They stared at each other like they were meeting for the first time, as if they were trying to figure out who the other was.

"I'll excuse myself now," the doctor said. He smiled and patted me on the shoulder as he opened the door. I tilted my chin toward the ceiling and signaled to Jaelene for us to give Dad and Kizaar some alone time. They needed it. Our family needed it.

That was a couple of weeks ago, and since then Kizaar had been fussing over Dad as if Dad had been declared *his* long lost son. Kizaar spent days and nights on end at the hospital. He made sure Dad was comfortable and eating right, and he flagged down nurses for Dad if he even thought that Dad needed attention. He'd even begun cooking him special meals and sneaking them into the hospital. The amazing thing was that Dad managed to be in good spirits for more than a couple of days. It had been two weeks, and he was still going strong.

Tucker flew back in for the weekend and joined us in welcoming Dad home. Although I could tell that everyone liked Alton a lot better than Tucker, they still accepted him. It was like they were supportive of anybody I was with. They seemed to trust my judgment.

Tucker walked out to the driveway when we heard Kizaar drive up and one car door open and shut. I peered out the side window as they both maneuvered our father into a wheelchair and wheeled him up to the house.

Dad looked even smaller. Being in the hospital for so long had caused him to drop weight. His shirt engulfed him, and his pants were being saved by the belt around his waist. The skin on his face drooped from long years of being tired, and the corners of his mouth sagged. His thin lips moved upward to a neutral position when he saw me and Jaelene. We both greeted him with a hug.

"Good to see you, Dad," I said.

"Good to be home," Dad said, almost in a whisper.

"Glad you're home, Dad," Jaelene babbled as she pulled back from Dad and brushed imaginary lint from his clothing. "We fixed up the house for you, made you something to eat for when you get hungry. You don't have to eat right now."

"Don't start fussing now," Kizaar told Dad. He tried to help Dad out of the wheelchair, but Dad wasn't having it.

Dad walked slowly from the hallway to the dining room, then to the living room. He examined everything. It was as if he had been on death row for twenty years and had just been released on parole. His eyes scanned everything from the baseboards to the ceiling. We were quiet as he studied each plant on the floor and those hanging from the ceiling; each figurine, dish, and souvenir in the curio; each framed picture over the fireplace and on the baby grand piano. He motioned for Kizaar to swing open the stained glass windows to allow the clear sky a presence in our living room.

Dad's eyes lingered for a moment on the empty spaces where Mom's pictures had once sat. Jaelene had removed pictures of Mom alone and posing with the family, and tucked them neatly away in the basement for storage until Dad was ready to have them around again. She didn't want to risk upsetting Dad as soon as he got home. Dad stared at the empty spaces and then his eyes drifted over to where we all stood bunched together. We weren't sure what his reaction was going to be or what to expect, so we stood waiting.

"Something smells good. Let's eat." Dad smiled hard at Kizaar.

Kizaar's teeth sparkled. He walked over and hooked his arm into Dad's and led him to the kitchen. Tucker got on the other side and helped.

Jaelene and I eyed each other across the table all evening as we watched Dad and Kizaar, who seemed to be trying to make up for lost time all in one evening. After dinner, Dad asked Kizaar to show him his improvement plans and they sat at the dining room table for hours. It was a great thing to see. The first time we'd had peace in the house. I knew this day would come one day. What I didn't know was that it would be with Dad and without Mom. Up until a couple of months ago, I was willing to bet my life that it would have been the opposite.

There were a lot of things that weren't exactly how I thought they were or how I'd seen them. My vision had been clouded. Jaelene and Tucker were cleaning up in the kitchen as I roamed around Mom's room. Looking for answers. Looking for clarity. Looking for understanding.

All these years, I thought that Dad was to blame for Mom and Dad's bitter marriage and for the breakdown of our family. Things were starting to look different now and I was taking it as a wake-up call. Maybe, just maybe, men weren't always responsible for failed marriages. Maybe I'd heard only one side of a three-sided story. Maybe I was only hearing what the injured party wanted me to hear and not the entire story.

"Earth to Vanella Morris. Come in, Vanella Morris."

Startled, I jerked as I looked up. Tucker stood in the doorway with his hands in front of his mouth in bullhorn position.

"Dang, babe. You really were on another planet. What were you thinking about?" He pushed the door open and walked in.

I knew I looked odd because I was standing in the middle of the room not doing anything. I searched for a save. "I was just going over everything in my mind. Mom, Dad, the whole Kizaar situation, Uncle James—"

"Yeah, I admit, that was some wild stuff." Tucker embraced me. My head relaxed comfortably on his chest as he wrapped his sturdy arms around me.

"The question is, where do we all go from here?" I asked. I wasn't really asking him; I just asked.

"Well, your dad's out there saying that he's thinking about permanently severing ties with your mom. He was asking your brother and sister how they felt about it. That's why I got up and left. I felt like that was family business."

I pulled away from Tucker and sat at the foot of Mom's bed. Wondered if Dad would be sleeping here in peace now. "Yeah, I expected that. I don't blame him. Now I admire him for staying with us."

Tucker sat beside me and I lay my head on his shoulder. He grabbed my hand and held it tight.

"Just think. He came back to us and lived all these years taking care of a child that he didn't even think was his. Not many men would put their wife's infidelity aside and try to raise the product of that infidelity as their own."

Tucker shook his head. "I've got to admit, your father got me on that one."

The room was dim and a mixture of Mom's fragrances swarmed around the room. Got into my head and brought visions of her to the forefront of my mind. I saw her small, innocent face. Pure. Sweet. Blemished. Scarred. Tarnished. "I've got to call her. Soon."

I shifted to one side and pulled Tucker closer to me. I was happy that he was there with me to help me through this. I felt safe and secure, but mostly I felt loved again.

Tucker pressed his lips into my cheek and moaned softly. I laughed and returned the smooch. "Thanks for being here," I said.

"I wouldn't have it any other way. I love you."

"I love you, too," I said.

I felt Tucker's intoxicating breath caress my face and turned toward it. He closed his eyes in anticipation and I supplied it freely as I tasted his lips over and over and over again.

Tucker pulled back and looked at me with drunken eyes. They swam someplace other than where we were.

"Will you marry me?" Tucker blurted out. Just as quickly as he had blurted it out, a surprised look bloomed across his face. I think Tucker amazed even himself with that one.

"Marry you?"

"Uh . . . well, yeah. I have to admit that I hadn't planned on that right now. I mean, I love you and I do want to marry you. I just didn't know I was going to ask you right now." His look of surprise suddenly turned to one of nervousness. His eyes shifted quickly from mine to the floor and back several times.

Well, what was I going to say now? Hell if I knew. I didn't know where I stood. I was just starting to get my thoughts together right before he came in.

I knew I loved Tucker and didn't want to lose him—not like I lost Alton. I felt as if God was giving me a second chance at love after I screwed up and lost love the first time around. Had to be God.

I felt a warm flush of excitement consume my body as I thought about the second chance at love I'd been given, and at the realization that the basis for my fear of commitment was ill-founded.

Tucker and I knew each other inside out. We had overcome a tremendous obstacle between us. I had forgiven him. After all, everyone makes mistakes, and I believed that Tucker had grown up and matured since our college days. I believed that he loved me and valued me enough not to make that mistake again.

Tucker tooted the *Twilight Zone* theme. "You left me again." His smile was nervous as he tried to read my face. "You still with me?"

"I'm here," I said. I looked into his eyes and felt ready to say yes. My first love had come back to me to spend the rest of his life with me.

"I hadn't planned on asking you like this. And I don't have a ring in hand right now, but"—he placed both hands on my shoulders, squared me in front of him, and stooped down so that we could look eye to eye—"I think it's right. I love you and I want to be with you forever. Will you marry me?"

Blood siphoned up from my toes and fingertips and filled my head. My heart pumped, and the adrenaline gave me a rush so high that I felt I could take off and keep running forever. I grinned as I gazed at his face to see his reaction to my yes.

My vocal cords braced to produce the softest tones he would ever hear, to provide him with a sweet song that would make him float on air. I moistened my lips for the kiss afterward—the long, sensual kiss that he was going to reward me with; that we would celebrate with. The letters "Y-E-S" eagerly got together in my gut and waited for the rocket ride to the top, through my throat and out of my mouth.

But the launcher wouldn't go off. Couldn't get the words out. My face was starting to hurt from the plastered-on smile. My jaw was stiff and tight and waiting for the yes so it could finally relax. I took in a deep breath to stir things up down there, pulled my stomach muscles tight, and blew out. I knew the word would flow right out after my calming breath. But it didn't. I couldn't summon the word up from the pit of my soul and out of my mouth.

Tucker focused anxiously on me. He waited to read yes from my quivering lips.

I felt pressure in the pit of my stomach, pushing up the words. Finally. My chest tightened as the words elevated upward, finally reached my throat, and propelled from the back of my tongue to the tip. "I need more time" is what came out. My shoulders drooped in exhaustion.

Tucker's eyes sank in disappointment. His back slumped. "Oh, um . . . yeah, I understand. I know this was kind of sudden and . . ."

I wanted to kick myself. Why couldn't I say yes? I wanted to say yes. I knew that I had no reason to have a fear of commitment.

"I love you, Tucker. Make no mistake about that. This is all just so overwhelming for me, and I just want to think about it and make sure I'm making the right decision for me. For us."

Tucker paused and looked at me with blank eyes that suddenly regained life. "Yeah. I don't know what I was thinking. Springing this on you like that. By all means. You take all the time you need. Just know that I love you. I want to spend the rest of my life with you. And if you have any fears that what happened in college would ever happen again, let me assure you that it won't. I would never hurt you ever again. I wanted to die when I lost you. It's a blessing that I got you back, and there's no woman alive who would make me turn my back on you. Not even for a minute."

"Not even Halle Berry?"

"Not even Halle Berry," he stated. He kissed me.

I pulled back from him and smiled. "Liar."

We laughed.

Twenty-Three

JAELENE PRIMPED IN the mirror while I transferred the contents of my black leather sack purse to my black leather clutch purse.

"So where's the hot spot in St. Louis? Where're we going tonight?" I asked.

Jaelene turned and helped herself to my shoe collection, searching for something to better match her outfit.

We decided that we had been through a lot over the past few months, and we needed to go out for drinks and shake our butts on somebody's dance floor, especially since she was the queen of her own mind now. Jaelene was sporting a natural look: Her foundation was light and allowed her speckles of beauty to finally have their day in the sun. Her eyelids were lightly dusted with a bronze shadow and smoked with a touch of cinnamon above her lengthened lashes. Her cheeks were natural and her ample lips were enhanced with soft spice.

"Depends on what you're up for. We can do St. Louis Nights or AJ's here downtown at the Adam's Mark Hotel."

"In the Adam's Mark? We're still going there?"

She nodded her head; I shook mine.

I said, "That's your generation."

She disagreed. "That's your generation. You know your generation won't let a discrimination lawsuit interfere with them getting their party on."

"What else?" I asked.

Jaelene was checking out a fifth pair of black shoes from my
closet. She slipped a strappy sandal on her left foot and compared it to the slingback on her right. She looked stunning, especially wearing my strappy heels.

"There's Hadley's on Olive on the west side if you're into live
music and strong drinks. Not really a good dance place, though."

"Yeah, Alton and I went to Hadley's when we were here to—"
I stopped. I didn't want to remind Jaelene about bailing her out
of jail.

"We can do JoJo's in Kirkwood or cross the river to East Boogie and see what's going on over there."

"I'm up for anything," I said.

"Well, why don't we just skip around? It's not like you're worn
out from working or anything."

"You just don't know. Volunteering with kids is work enough.
They're little darlings, but they know they can wear a woman
out."

"Yeah, an old woman," she joked.

"Mmm-hmm. Yeah, we'd better get going before you get
knocked out by an old woman."

"I'm not worried. You don't even have the strength. Oh, can I
wear these?" She stuck her foot out to show me my shoes.

"Do I really have a choice?" We collected our sweaters and
left my apartment. "Okay, where are we going first?"

"AJ's."

. . .

Tucker called early to make plans to spend the morning together. After watching the annual Annie Malone Parade downtown, Tucker and I went to the Arch grounds to hang out. Tucker spotted a vacant concrete bench along the steps that led from the street to the Arch grounds. He took my hand and gently tugged me behind, straddled the middle of the bench, then pulled me down in front of him. I leaned back on his chest. We had a view of the Mississippi in front of us. The bank was lined with boats: The restored *Admiral*, gambling boats, floating restaurants— McDonald's and Burger King—and gambling boats. Even East St. Louis was cashing in with a few boats on the Illinois side. Tucker stroked my hair as a tugboat went chugging down the river.

He was quiet, but it was one of those silences where it was obvious that he was waiting to hear something.

"I'm glad that we have this second chance, but I don't want to rush into anything right away," I said, as if he'd asked aloud.

"You think this is rushing? What else could we possibly learn by waiting?"

Hell if I knew. "We just need more time."

"Why?"

"What do you mean why?"

"Tell me why you think we need more time. To gain what?"

His hand dropped from my hair and landed on his jeaned thigh. I couldn't tell him why, but I still couldn't get the word "yes" out of my mouth, and I couldn't understand why either.

"I'm not going to be strung along, Van."

I looked up at the side of his face and gave him a "how dare you" glare.

He avoided my stare. "Syn used to talk about you and Alton

and your fear of commitment to him, even though you loved him. About some O Theory?"

He waited for an explanation that I didn't provide.

"Well, anyway, I want us to get married. I don't want to live together or wait around so that somebody else can try to take you away from me."

"Tucker—" I closed my mouth abruptly and let out a breath through my nose as a man passed a camera to a stranger to take his family's photo. They huddled together tightly and flashed hard smiles. "Just a little more time, Tucker."

"I don't want to go on for months or years, wondering if you're going to get over this fear that you have. I've wanted you since we broke up in college. I'm not going to lose you to someone else."

I loved him and wanted to be with him in almost the same way I had wanted to be with Alton—close enough—but fear still took up residence in my throat and prevented me from saying yes like I wanted to. I just didn't understand why anymore.

"I don't want to lose you either."

"Then marry me."

"I can't. Not now."

"Well then." Tucker ran both of his palms down the front of his jeans, lifted his left leg over the bench and stood slowly. I sat there like a stone.

"Where are you going?"

"Back to Cleveland." He stared off in the direction of the Eads Bridge.

"Your flight doesn't leave until tomorrow morning."

"Going to change it to tonight." He hesitated. "Marry me, Vanella."

I felt what was happening. Again. I wanted to stop it, but I didn't know what to do. I definitely wasn't going to make a scene out here in front of all these people and cry at Tucker's feet like I'd done with Alton. Damn sure wasn't going to bust my own lip again. I remained silent.

Tucker looked down at the ground and smiled. "Okay." He leaned toward me, brushed my hair off my forehead and briefly kissed it, then took slow steps backward without taking his eyes off mine. He waited for me to stop him. I wanted to, but I couldn't get myself to do it.

Tucker turned toward the Arch and never turned back around.

Bitchin' like a broke buster past midnight in a bar I was. I stretched my legs the length of the bench and faced the river. Pretended that everything was all right for the passersby as both my legs twitched frantically. When I felt enough time had passed to make it appear that Tucker hadn't left me, I got up and headed back to the Merchandise Mart. I stared straight ahead and avoided eye contact with the giddy tourists who were more than eager to smile just for smiling's sake. Well, I didn't want to smile, because I had nothing to smile about.

I walked through my living room door and dropped my keys and purse on the floor as I slammed the door shut. *What was wrong with me? Why was I being so stupid? So pitiful?* I clamped my waist with my left hand and slapped my forehead with my right. Briskly I paced back and forth. This situation was ridiculous. I was being ridiculous.

I reached the end of the kitchen counter and swung around to continue my rant. My elbow smacked into a glass of water, spilling the contents on the counter. I turned to pick up the glass from the puddle of water and ran into a bar stool, sending it crashing to the floor.

"Shit!"

Then all of my frustration came roaring out like an F5 tornado. I swiped the stack of newspapers from the edge of the counter and onto the floor. I flung my arms around as I stomped and kicked the paper across the carpet. I stomped the newspaper because it was one of the sources that told me I had little chance of having a successful marriage. I destroyed it because it was the one that told me how high the divorce rate was and gave me statistics on the chances of being happy in a marriage. It told me about Oprah's long-lasting relationship with Stedman, and how it didn't include a marriage. I whipped it because it pushed lawyers in my face. Lawyers who competed and advertised cheap rates for me to be able to buy my freedom back at the first sign of unhappiness—quick and easy and guaranteed. I beat the paper because I couldn't beat myself.

The phone rang.

I answered to hear a content-sounding Medena on the phone. I straightened up my face and smoothed my hair so that she couldn't sense my condition through the phone. She'd called to tell me she'd moved back home.

I steadied my voice. "So this means no divorce, right? I'm not going to have a scarred little godchild running around, committing crimes when he's forty, then blaming it on the traumatic breakup of his parents back when he was two, am I?"

"Girl, you are so silly. No, Aneaus and I are trying to work things out. Sad to say, but my moving out was what it took to get him to communicate with me."

"Or to see how valuable you were and how much he loved you. Didn't you leave Cornell with him?"

"Yeah, for the time being, I did," she chuckled. "I wasn't planning on leaving my baby, but I wanted to stabilize my situation before I had him moving all over the place. And yes, Aneaus had to do everything. Nearly drove him crazy. I think that made him realize how busy I was and how I didn't have time for myself. He's communicating with me more now and keeping Cornell for more than just a couple of hours, so I can have some alone time or take up a hobby or something."

"Yeah? Good for you. So what are you doing with all your free time, girl?"

"That's it. I have no idea what to do." We both laughed. "But at least I have some time to think about doing stuff. I've been working out and going to the day spa to gather my thoughts."

"Well, I'll tell you that this is good to hear. I was thinking that if Medena and Aneaus couldn't make a marriage work, how could I?"

"You need to get off of that. Quit looking at other folks and all these statistics. Stop trying to forecast the longevity of your marriage based on others."

"Oh, high five on that one," I said in response to Medena's attempt at getting technical and taking it to a level that I could understand.

"Yeah, that was pretty good, wasn't it?"

"Look at Sherron though."

"Honey, don't let Sherron fool you with her sob story about her divorce."

"I was there. I sat with her, nursed her."

"And you know why you did? Because I wouldn't. Sherron

brought that divorce on herself. Had a good man and tried to control him. She tried to put him in her back pocket and close him off from everybody else because she was scared that women were out to get him. She searched his pockets, called him or his secretary every hour, and monitored his calls. She wouldn't even let his sisters call the house for fear they were plotting to set him up with another woman. He gave her a divorce after six years when she gave him an ultimatum: his job or her. Frankly, I don't know what took him so long."

"But what about the woman he left her for? I saw her come over with Daylon to the house and pack up a few things."

"Orenthia? Yeah, that was his assistant. Nothing going on there. I had it checked out myself through a friend. Sherron knew, but just wanted somebody to blame and somebody to feel sorry for her. You know, whenever people get divorced, there's always three sides to the story."

Her words hit me like lead bullets.

"The only thing you need to look at is what you have to offer and what he has to give. Make sure you're compatible. Don't get married because you dreamed about some three-hundred-guest, half-million-dollar wedding in a fifty-thousand-dollar wedding gown."

"Oh, well, you know that's not me at all," I scoffed.

Medena sucked her teeth. "Yeah, you're right. It isn't. I'm way off base with that one. But you know what I mean—marry your best friend. You'll still have problems somewhere down the line, but if you marry for all the right reasons, you'll be able to get beyond those obstacles."

"Like you and Aneaus?"

"We're working on it." I could feel her smiling through the

phone and I knew they would make it. I knew they would work everything out.

I told Medena everything that had happened over the last months—about Mom, Dad, and Kizaar; about Synda and Tucker; about Tucker's proposal, but not about my refusal.

"Whew! I missed all that? Girl, you must be a mess."

"Well, things are on the upswing now."

"What does your mom have to say now?"

"She left. We haven't talked to her."

"Are you going to?"

"Not sure. Been thinking about it."

"Girl, haven't you learned anything yet?" She chuckled. "Talk to your mother. Get her side of the story. Maybe it'll make sense, maybe it won't. But regardless, she's still your mother."

"Yeah, I know you're right. She is my mother and I still love her. We can't shut her out forever, but it's painful. I'm just angry."

"Just talk to her. And I'm going to be honest. I'm not too crazy about this Tucker idea. I liked Alton better."

"You and everybody else."

"That should tell you something. However, we all made mistakes when we were younger. So, if you feel he's changed and you still love him, then go for it. But you keep planning for your divorce, well, then that's exactly what's going to happen. Just like you planned."

"I gotta get out of here."

"Okay, girl. But do stop trying to control every single thing in your life and everybody else's, because you can't." She paused. "Okay, we'll finish this conversation later, young lady," Medena mock-scolded me.

"Yes ma'am," I said. We said our good-byes and hung up.

I heard soft reggae playing and remembered that I had turned on the radio before I left. Something I had always done when leaving the condo to make people believe somebody was at home.

The sun had long since dropped behind West County. I closed the blinds and went to clean up the mess my frustration had tossed around. As I bent down, my thighs yelped and forewarned me that payback was going to be a mutha tomorrow. I gave them a quick massage before reaching over to gather up the *Post*. They weren't hearing it.

This was totally ridiculous. What was I doing to myself? I did love him, and wanted to be with him. In college, I'd hoped I could share my life with him. I'd even wondered what our kids would be like.

I now understood there was no guarantee on a lifetime marriage. The Census Bureau couldn't tell me whether Tucker and I could make it, nor could all the books I read. I couldn't use my friends' marriages as a standard, mainly because I wasn't sure exactly what went on behind closed doors. Wasn't even sure anymore that I was seeing anything other than an angry spouse's version of the truth. I couldn't even say that marriages fell apart because of men. Mom and Synda had proved me wrong there.

I got off my knees and sat on the couch. Bob Marley was singing "Waiting in Vain." I closed my eyes, and Tucker was singing to me and I was running.

I had to stop all this damned running. I had to learn how to let go and trust love. I had to trust what Tucker and I had together over some statistic; otherwise I would never allow myself the happiness of marriage.

I also had to go after my dreams. I had to let go of that job and go for what would make me happy: my bookstore. Since be-

ing with Tucker, I had rekindled my passion for starting a business and I had completed my business plan. I knew that was what
I had to do. I had to quit Kawamichi and go after my dream.

I wrote a letter of resignation to my manager, made a FOR SALE
sign, packed a bag, waited until morning, and tossed it in the
ride.

Twenty-Four

CHILDHOOD MEMORIES are a bitch. I drove north on I-71 in my fairly new Lexus—now with a FOR SALE sign in the rear driver's side window—thinking about the first thing I remembered in life. My first recollection of how relationships worked was definitely the start of my backward thinking. I'd spent the next fifteen years of my life watching a seemingly passive mother and crippled father live together in a loveless marriage. It appeared that Dad did whatever he could—outside of hitting her—to make her feel like shit, while Mom just struggled to keep the peace. I had trouble figuring out one good thing about marriage.

That was what I saw. Not clearly seeing things as they truly were, but only as I saw them—like counting raindrops through a stained glass window.

No wonder I was screwed up about love and marriage. I didn't have a fair chance from the start. Before I could even ignore the boys I liked on the playground; before the boys who liked me could pull my ponytail; before I could have my first boyfriend and my first kiss; before I could flirt and tease boys and think that

I was every man's dream; before I first dumped a guy; before my first heartbreak; before my all-men-are-dogs phase; before my first real love; and before I could fantasize about a large wedding, a long white gown, a house, kids, and a dog—I had already come to the conclusion that marriage and "happily ever after" was a sham.

As I got older, I nursed girlfriend after girlfriend through bad relationships, and later through knock-down, drag-out unforeseen divorces that appeared to drain their unsuspecting souls of all sensibility.

It's funny how you can look directly at something and not see a thing.

So here I was finally seeing the truth. It had taken me twenty-five years to even come close to erasing all that damage. But had I really? I wasn't 100 percent sure, but I guessed I'd find out by the end of the day. But first I needed to come up with a plan.

I pulled off Interstate 71 at Panera in Columbus, Ohio. I took the ring I bought along the way inside with me and ordered a cinnamon crunch bagel and a small coffee. Surprisingly, at least for a Saturday mid-morning, there weren't many people there. I took a table by the front window and stared at the little jeweler's box with the ring inside. How was I going to say it? Should I get down on one knee?

I felt lost because, unlike the usual case when I didn't know something, I couldn't run to the local library or bookstore and pick up a book about it. I was always able to find a lot of information on marriage failures and divorce rates. But where could I find a book on how a woman removes her foot from her mouth and proposes to a man after she turned down his original proposal and said she'd rather just shack up with him to make the inevitable separation process easier when—not if—they parted ways?

Now, I knew there were books on getting beyond the fear of commitment, but those are usually geared toward men. Or they're geared toward men or women who are just trying to play the field and don't want to settle for one person or those who feel that as soon as they tie the knot, something better is going to come along. I even knew where to find fiction on golddiggers or wannabe golddiggers.

None of those described me or my situation.

I sipped my coffee, then opened the box and pulled out the ring. I slipped it on my index finger and glided it around, feeling the power of commitment shoot through my finger, up my arm, and throughout my body. I slipped it off and examined its exquisite detail: a one-carat diamond set in a platinum band with diamonds running nine deep across the band. Far from second-rate, but not at all flashy or gaudy. He hardly wore jewelry anyway, so something that announced that he was coming from half a mile away would not be a good thing, in his opinion.

Earlier today, when I had decided I wanted to do this, I immediately went to the jeweler before I had a chance to think about it and apply a statistical analysis to the situation that would change my mind. I knew that no matter what, I had to walk out of that store with a ring in hand or else I would not go through with it at all.

I went into the jewelry store, and when a saleswoman came over after I'd been browsing the *expensive* men's rings for a good fifteen minutes, I explained my situation to her. Evidently, being part of such an amorous scheme brought out the romantic in her. Becky got giddy and went and grabbed Effie, and they put their two blond heads together and gleefully provided me with their assistance.

It took a couple of minutes to drag them out of the $99 section that they directed me to and back to the section I originally browsed. I knew I wasn't dressed the part, so maybe they were reading into my faded jeans, Cardinals baseball cap, and Air Force Ones. But I think they got the *subtle* hint when I point-blank told them that I had an executive management position with a Fortune 500 company, *and* how much money I made, *and* how much credit I had, *and* my low credit/debt ratio, *and* supplied them with my work ID and mother's maiden name. After that, all it took was a credit check, proof of registration and insurance, my license plate number, my driver's license, and a credit card to submit for verification while I shopped for them to lead me to the display case holding the elegant jewels. Well, maybe they didn't ask for all that, but their eyes scanned me from head to toe, then promptly and incorrectly summed up my worth.

Any other time I would have given them a few choice words and taken my money elsewhere, but there was already a little devil lounging on my left shoulder and whispering in my ear that this whole extra credit check rigmarole was a sign that I should just give it up and go home. If I had let it bother me, I knew I would have walked out of that store and not have gone anywhere else to buy a ring. I knew that if I didn't buy it then, my fear of commitment would have loomed up and slapped me in the face before Becky and Effie could ask me for a $5,000 deposit on one of their $2,000 rings—cash only, please. So instead, I persisted through all of their security checks and allowed Becky and Effie to assist me in choosing the perfect ring to win back my man.

Yeah, win him back—that is, if I could do it. That is, if he could forgive me. That is, if he still loved me.

I finished my coffee and wrapped up my bagel to go. As much as I love those bagels, I knew I couldn't keep it down anyway with all of the churning that my stomach was doing.

I got back inside my black RX300 for what would be one of the last times, set the jeweler's box on the passenger's seat, and sank into the plush leather seat. I had to do this. I wanted to do this. I put the key in the ignition and headed to Cleveland on a mission.

I tried to keep my eyes on the road, but I swore I heard the ring calling me from inside the box on the passenger seat. It taunted me: *You know you're not going to do it. You're too scared. Scaredest woman I ever met. Humph! And you're supposed to have it all together. Supposed to be a professional. A professional "what" is the question. You just like the rest of 'em. Men are right. Women don't know what the hell they want.*

I drove north on I-71 listening to the voice in the ring box trying to talk me out of this and get me to turn around and take my behind back home. I tuned it out. Kept driving. I wasn't sure what I was going to do, but I ignored the ring as I drove to Cleveland—up I-71, past Mansfield, past the Prime Outlets, and past the Akron/Medina exit to I-271.

My neck was stiff. I got closer and my hands began to slide over the steering wheel. I noticed how much they hurt, and I tried to loosen up the death grip I put on the wheel to keep my hands from sliding.

I took I-480 and drove. My body jittered all over, and I didn't think I could do it. I kept driving until I came up on 271 again—because my mind was acting like I didn't know Cleveland—and took the exit up on its offer. It took me up the street and to P.F. Chang's Chinese Bistro. Wasn't really hungry, but I needed to do something to calm my nerves so I could hurry up and get to where I was going before I turned around.

The waitress escorted me to a small table in the front, then led me to another table when I requested a seat toward the back for more privacy. As I sat down facing the entrance, a young woman brushed past me.

I needed a drink. The pain at my temples came alive. My forehead was knitted so tightly that I felt like I was about to give myself an aneurism.

"Something to drink for you?" the waitress asked.

I massaged my forehead with the tips of my fingers. "Apple martini."

A tall, sleek-haired man wearing shades flipped down his cell phone and headed to the men's room. Why was the waitress still standing there staring at me? Oh, my head. I pulled two pain relievers from the bottle in my purse and swallowed them dry.

"Are you all right, ma'am?"

"Be better if I had a drink," I said without looking at her.

"I'll get that right away for you." She scampered off and returned with my drink. As I felt the wind from yet another woman passing me, I finally realized that I was sitting near the restroom. I wanted to tell the waitress to move me to another table, but at the moment I wasn't that concerned about it. My nerves had grabbed hold of my insides and were having a ball whipping my ass all over the place.

I sipped my drink and let it swish around my mouth before gliding down and warmly coating my stomach like a muscle relaxer. After a refill, the tendons in my legs slowly succumbed and my arms were overcome with stillness. Finally I could focus. *Was I going to go through with this or drive my scared ass home?*

"You look like you could use some company," said a mellow voice. Before I bothered to look up, I tried to formulate the sharpest words the apple martini could muster to wound this man so deeply that he'd never want to hit on what appeared to be a lonely woman, just because she was sitting by herself in a restaurant, ever again.

I slowly lifted my eyes upward and they fell upon the most gorgeous smile I had seen in Cleveland in a while. A familiar smile. Damn. Where had I seen this smile?

His face was the color of light brown sugar. His lips were spread into a wide smile over a set of glistening white teeth. Perplexed eyes below raised eyebrows bore down on me as his hands pulled back the chair across from me.

I opened my mouth and gasped. "Jamel White?" I almost screamed his name.

He looked around and grinned before taking a seat. "That would be me."

"What are you doing here?" What are you doing at my table was what I was really thinking.

"Man's gotta eat." He laughed. "Just here picking up. Chinese is my favorite, but I didn't really feel like dining in. I was about to go wash my hands and I noticed you sitting here alone looking like you're about ready to go jump into the Cuyahoga."

"Not looking to get chemical burns."

He pointed a finger at me. "Ahhhh . . . good one. But you'd better not let a die-hard Clevelander hear you say that. They're sensitive about that, you know."

"I can joke. I'm a die-hard Clevelander myself."

I chuckled lightly as I shifted my gaze from the floor to his face and stared.

"What?" He playfully wiped his upper lip, then his face. "I got something on me?" His contagious smile continued to brighten my day.

"No, I'm just thinking about my best friend . . . excuse me . . . my ex–best friend. She would kill to be in my shoes right now."

"Hmmm . . . ex-friend. There's a story?"

"Yeah, but it's too trifling, long, and pitiful to get into."

"And what about you? What's your story? What's got such a fine woman in Cleveland looking like it's the end of the world on this bright, sunny . . . uh . . . overcast day?"

We both looked toward the window at the overhanging clouds and laughed breathy laughs.

"I love my Cleveland."

"Nice city, but I'm not crazy about the weather you all have here. Gets cold too early, stays cold too late, and too much snow."

"Well, coming from San Diego, I know you wouldn't be crazy about it. But it's gotta be better than South Dakota."

He was impressed. "Oh, somebody must be a football fan." He flashed those pearly whites at me again. Now I saw why Synda couldn't focus on his stats. Brother was making it pretty hard to do.

"Yes, I am. But I have to confess that I got that little tidbit from Synda. My ex–best friend. Me? I'm more of a Marshall Faulk fan myself. No offense."

"None taken. I'm a Marshall Faulk fan, too. I watch him on tape. Check out his running game." He sipped the water that the gawking waitress brought back to the table for us before joining the others behind the bar in a game of who-can-point-the-most-and-get-noticed. "So, are you all right, Ms.—"

"Vanella. Vanella Morris. And I'm not sure you'd really be interested in my story."

"Try me." He leaned his broad shoulders back and settled into his chair like he was about to detail a game play by play. His bald head caught a two-second ray from the peekaboo sun and shim-mered. He stared at me, waiting.

I wasn't one to discuss my business with strangers, but hell, I figured better Jamel than listening to a platinum diamond ring in a box.

I told him my story, expecting to see a smirk, laugh, or frown flit across his face or catch him looking at me like I was crazy or something, but he didn't. His steady gaze remained fixed on my face as I told him about the proposals that I'd had and turned down; about Synda and Sherron and how they single-handedly brought their marriages down but blamed it on their men; and about the nullification of my belief in men being 100 percent re-sponsible for bitter marriages—at which he did smile. He lis-tened as I rattled off marriage statistics and told him about Oprah, Stedman, and the O Theory. He listened much like I imagined Jaelene's therapist listened to her.

I emptied myself and sat back in my chair, released a long, dry sigh, and added a fresh coating of apple martini to my insides to prepare for what he was going to say and how crazy he was going to say I was acting.

"So what's the 'O' in the O Theory?"

I gave him a duh look. "Isn't it Obvious?"

Jamel's soft smile spread across his jovial face. I was willing to bet that he could be in an upset loss against the Detroit Lions and still beam like a buttered biscuit.

"So, what did Oprah say to you about her relationship with Stedman?"

"What do you mean what did she say to me?"

"You talked to her about it, right?"

I crossed my right leg over my left thigh and my arms across my breasts. "Okay, Jamel, you're cute and all, but don't make me reach across this table and smack you," I joked. He seemed like a baby brother. "You know good and well I haven't talked to Oprah."

"Hey, I don't know. I just met you ten minutes ago." He shrugged his shoulders. "Sounds to me like you know her inside out. So, what was her reason for not getting married again?"

"I don't know why Oprah does what she does. I guess she doesn't think it's necessary."

"Why would you say that?"

"Look, I don't know why she doesn't get married."

"And that's my point. You don't know what her reasons are for not getting married, yet you're using her lifestyle as a model to follow. Maybe she thinks like you, maybe she doesn't. Maybe she feels it's just not the right time for her. Maybe she's got it planned for the next five years. Maybe she wants to reach a goal of earning two hundred billion first, then she'll get married. Or maybe it's Stedman."

I widened my eyes on that one. Who wouldn't want to marry Oprah? Hell, *I'd* marry Oprah.

"Would you blindly follow Oprah's lifestyle if she wasn't Oprah? What if she was Wyshanta living in East Cleveland? You've got to do what works for you. You're not Oprah. You're not your mom or dad or your friends. It should be between you and him. Nobody else should matter."

I giggled like a little girl whose boo-boo had just been kissed and made better. "Yeah, I've heard some of that before."

"I've never been married myself, but if I could give advice, I'd tell you what I tell myself. Just make sure he's someone you trust. Someone you communicate well with. And he should probably be someone you can't live without. Someone who you breathe even when he's not around."

Someone who I breathe even when he's not around. I went over the sentence, word by word, syllable by syllable.

A slow smile crept across my face as the realization hit. I stared up into the lights hanging from the ceiling. "Yes. Yes, he most definitely is." I felt my head nodding.

"Then I guess you have your answer. Go on and do your thang, girl." He laughed.

I brought my eyes back down on the young, handsome football player. "How did you . . . where did you learn . . ."

"My undergrad was in psychology. Child psychology, but some principles are universal. So, I'm not just some dumb jock." He cracked a smile and flashed the pearlies again.

" 'Dumb jock' never crossed my mind in the first place. Hey, I hate to cut out after you've given me such good advice, but—"

"No problem."

I picked up my purse from the chair next to me and reached for my wallet.

"Hey, you get going. I got this one for ya."

I walked over and hugged him. What else could I do? "My girlfriend missed out," I said as I wrapped my arms around him and melted for a minute.

"Well, seeing that she's an ex-girlfriend of yours, my guess is that it's for the best."

"You got that right. Take care."

I left P.F. Chang's, hopped in the ride, and adjusted to my new bearings. I headed to his house with the ring box nestled between my thighs.

Twenty-Five

THE STREET WAS QUIET as usual. Mr. Coleman watered his lawn from his porch a few houses down and pretended he wasn't out strictly for the neighborhood watch. His plaid shirt was open and blowing in the wind, exposing his tight white T-shirt and peekaboo belly underneath. He waved at me and I half-waved back.

From the sidewalk, I looked up at the little bungalow that I had hung out in so many times before. This time the place stared at me like I was a stranger. Like, "What are you doing here?" I removed the ring and tossed the empty box through the window and onto the passenger seat.

The walk up to the porch seemed a hell of a lot longer than I remembered. I steadied myself on the hot metal railing on the left side of the steps because I felt wobbly, as if my legs were going to give way and I'd tumble backward. I was going to do this. I tightened my gut, willing strength into my legs to get my body up to the front door.

I looked back at Mr. Coleman as he got up to put away his hose and go into his house. I turned back to the house and wiped back the strands of hair that were stuck to my forehead. I felt sticky already. Wetness streamed down the groove of my back and between and under my breasts. I alternated holding the ring and wiping my palms down my thighs.

I rang the doorbell.

It had probably been only thirty seconds or so but it seemed like thirty days. My stomach felt like it was about to come up any minute and my mind flashed questions: "How do you stand? How are you going to say it? What if he says no? What if he slams the door in your face?"

My knees began to buckle and I started thinking that this wasn't a good idea. At the same time I convinced myself that it was the best thing to do. I was half a second away from turning tail and running when I heard the locks click open. The door opened to a crack, then widened until the man stood before me.

Everything grew quiet. I wanted to reach up and jiggle my ear, but I couldn't because my right hand was clenched into a fist so tight that my neck hurt and I just figured out that it was killing the hell out of me. I relaxed my fingers, but they had gotten numb.

I decided that was a good time to make my move. I needed to just propose to the man while his face was still wearing shock and awe and get it over with. Maybe he'd be too surprised to say anything and I could get through this whole thing before he lowered the gauntlet.

His lips were parted and his mouth hung open below wide eyes. His hand was spread against the glass door as he pushed it open.

I adjusted the ring with my left hand to a more comfortable position between my thumb and index finger, making sure to display the French manicure he used to love so much. I cleared the fear from my throat as my right knee dipped to the porch. The ring sparkled and my extended right arm lifted it toward his face like Mufasa presenting Simba.

"Alton, I know I've made mistakes—"

"Vanella—" Alton said with surprise.

I continued because I knew he was surprised that I was there on bended knee proposing to him and I didn't want him to distract me and make me lose the momentum it had taken me oh so long to build up.

I rolled.

". . . and I'm sorry. I realize now—"

"Vanella—"

I rolled.

". . . what I should have realized then. You and I are meant for each other. I believe that we're soul mates. You are the one that's always in my heart, even when you're not around."

"Van—"

I rolled.

"I'm ready to take that chance. Alton Goode, will you mar—"

The rest of the words lodged in my throat because my eyes nearly fell out of my head. The door behind Alton opened wider and a little brown woman ventured her tired little body out and leaned her head against Alton's arm. *My* Alton's arm.

"Honey, who's at the door?" She looked down at me as I perched on one knee, my arm extended like the Statue of Liberty toward both their faces.

I swore I heard the grass growing.

Alton stared into my eyes and so did she. Her thin lips nearly disappeared as her tiny chin left her mouth gaping open. Her eyes went from shock, to patronizing, to absolutely territorial. The little hussy slid her hand into the space between Alton's chest and bicep and wrapped her fingers around his arm.

My Alton's arm.

She positioned her finger to carefully display a V-style French manicure topped off with a diamond ring. Huge ring. I was damn near blinded by it. Her ring could out-glisten the one I held for Alton on any given day. Her lips drew upward into a smug smile.

"I got this, baby," Alton said to her.

He called her baby.

Baby didn't move. Instead, she had a death stare on me that she wouldn't take off. She removed her right hand from what was supposed to be her hip and traced a slow, upward path to the ring on her left hand, which she began to stroke lightly.

In a stern voice, Alton said again, "Robin, I got this."

Robin?

Robin's smug got smuggier as she blew a condescending breath through her nose.

"Hurry now. I'm almost finished with dinner," she said, keeping her eyes on me and my arm, which had long since dropped to my side. She leaned forward on her toes to kiss his cheek.

My Alton's cheek.

Alton leaned toward her a bit—just enough to receive a peck. The peck that told me: "Stay away from my man, bitch. You let him go; he's mine now." She gave me an extra *bitch* gaze for emphasis, just in case I didn't pick up on it the first time.

With Robin—or baby, or whatever the hell you want to call her—gone, Alton shifted his still-scrumptious-but-not-mine body from one leg to the other. His almond eyes searched the ground around me, awkwardly looking for the right words to say. He opened the screen door wider and stepped barefoot onto the porch. I stood and dusted off my knees without looking at him again. Alton stepped closer to me, bent over, and helped me dust my knees.

"Sorry about that. The last thing I expected was you stopping by to propose." He focused on my pants, intently brushing away my embarrassment.

"No . . . it's my fault," I stuttered. "I should have called first, like we always used to do. It's just that what I needed to do hit me all at once. I just hopped in the ride and wound up here." I tossed the ring from hand to hand.

"But it's good to see that somehow you've moved beyond the fear of marriage and you're now ready to take that step . . . with someone."

I looked up and down the street, mainly to see who was a witness to my act of stupidity. No one was around. Only me and Alton.

"Yep. That's me. Moved beyond. A day late and a dollar short, but I've moved on."

From the corner of my eye I caught the slightest movement of the curtains over the living room window.

Alton grabbed my hand and pulled me onto the porch steps, then guided me to sit down.

"I can tell you're sincere this time. I can feel that you've actually gotten beyond this thing and that you're not just proposing because it's what I wanted. What changed for you?"

I shrugged. "Lots happened that made me realize that I'd been trying to analyze everybody else's relationship and use it as a measuring stick for mine. The only problem with that is that you never really know what goes on in another person's relationship. You know only what they want you to know, which is probably going to be slanted in their favor."

"Mmm-hmm," Alton said.

"What matters is me and my relationship with my man. Us. Nobody else matters."

"Mmm-hmm."

"You and me. The love was there. We communicated about everything. As long as you have that, you can get through anything."

"Keep that. Don't lose that. Someday, you'll find the right—"

I snatched my hand from beneath his, stood, and faced him. "You're the right one."

"I wish you knew then what you know now."

Alton stood and moved so close to me that I could feel his breath against my cheek.

I wanted to tell him to still marry me—to just walk away from her. I didn't say that though. I knew Alton. He wouldn't do that to a person. Damn, I messed up bad.

"When's the wedding?" I asked. Like I cared.

"I just proposed a couple of days ago, so we haven't set a date yet."

I grunted. Just a couple of days ago? Damn!

"She's been throwing out dates here and there, but we haven't pinpointed anything yet."

I took a couple of steps back and Alton grabbed my hand again. He stared at it, holding it firmly as we stood in silence, then his eyes moved up to my lips and lingered there. I let them linger as I watched him swallow, then swallow again. He opened his mouth. "If only . . ."

The front door creaked open and the gremlin popped her

big-ass head out. "Baby, dinner's ready." I could feel it giving me the evil stare, but I refused to give the gremlin face time.

"I'll be right there," Alton said firmly. She stepped back and closed the door.

We stared silently at each other. Alton ran his hand from my shoulder to my wrist. He then brought the back of his hand to my face and stroked. He seemed to be looking past my eyes and deep inside me at where home used to be.

"You—" he began, pausing to clear his throat, "you take care of yourself now."

I nodded.

"And you take care of *him*. I know he's out there somewhere, and he's going to latch on to you quick. A lady like you will not stay single for long unless you want to."

The living room curtains swayed again as Alton hugged me for the last time. My soul veiled his for one last time. I couldn't let it.

I shook my head. "No. I can't do this, Alton. I came all this way. I got up all this courage." I pulled away and extended the ring to him again. "Will you marry me?"

Alton shook his head. "Van, it's not—"

"It is possible," I corrected, finishing his statement. "You can break your engagement."

I refused to take no for an answer. Refused to let him stand here and tell me no without giving it some thought.

"Van . . ."

"Just think about it." I backed away before he could say another word. "Think about it and call me in three days." I turned abruptly and climbed into the Lexus SUV. As I started the engine, I looked at Alton, who still stood in the same spot with his hand wrapped around the ring. I saw him staring at the FOR SALE sign in my back window as I drove off.

Twenty-Six

I WAITED THREE DAYS, plus one extra for good measure, but still no Alton. In a way, I wasn't surprised, but I hoped to hear from him anyway. I hoped he would come to the realization that he couldn't live without me; that I was his life as he was mine; and that we couldn't go on without each other. I was hoping that he would've come to the same conclusion that I had—the same one he'd come to a year ago.

I knew I messed up, but there was nothing I could do about it. After four days of sitting by the phone, bingeing on Strickland's butter pecan ice cream with hot fudge, I decided to pull myself together and get on with my life. What better way to start all over than a weekend trip to South Beach for closure?

I hadn't given up on love. This experience put me in another place that was a hell of a lot better than the one I was in before. I knew that there were no guarantees to marriage. I had learned what a lot of people learn after their first marriage, only I didn't have to go through the courts and a battle to find it out. I guess in a way, I could say that I had gotten what I wanted.

I'd be ready the next time around. It might not be with Alton, but I knew I'd have a successful marriage. It would be hard, it would take a lot of work. I knew I wouldn't be able to avoid that.

I tightened the sash of the hotel guest robe as I stepped over a pile of papers and released the latch on the sliding door that led to the balcony. I stepped out to see the sun waking up over the beach. Morning joggers worked to burn enough calories to work out last night's sins or the calories they expected to consume later that day. The fresh morning air mixed with the ocean and whisked a calming breeze against my face. My nostrils widened to take it in and the fresh air helped me to focus on my new life. My new beginning. My life without Synda. My life without Tucker. My life without Kawamichi.

My life without Alton.

I stepped back inside to the gurgling sound of the coffeemaker and headed to the kitchen of the one-bedroom suite to fix myself a cup of coffee. I added half an Equal and French vanilla creamer. As I sipped, reggae played on the radio, but I had come to grips with myself and I could leave it playing.

With coffee cup in hand, I picked up the stamped envelope that contained my letter of resignation off the counter. Yesterday, Dexter had called from Kawamichi again; that time I answered the phone. I had a new spirit and I wanted to spread it around. I let him go on for a minute. Let him talk about multitasking and handling my projects in my absence. I let him get out his snide remarks about my incompetence versus his superiority.

"It's people like you," I began.

"People like me what?"

"It's people like you who are a disgrace to our race."

He lowered his voice and it sounded like he cupped his hand

over his mouth and receiver. "People like you are the reason Affirmative Action should be eliminated."

"You're a real Clarence Thomas."

"Thank you for the compliment."

"Mmm-hmm. Just remember, Dexter. The women and minorities that you kick down now might be the same ones you'll look to later to pull you up."

"Ms. Morris, as usual, you're mistaken. Because once I get on top, I'll do whatever it takes to make sure that I'll always be on top. That's the difference between me and you."

"Thank God for that."

I made a mental note to be sure to FedEx the letter before I left, but first I danced with it to the reggae beat. I swayed and twirled with my coffee in my right hand and the resignation letter in my left hand. I tried my best to embrace my new life and put my mistakes behind me. Tried my best to begin to live for me and make myself a better person for me—and the next man. I would get it right next time.

I finished my coffee but I had to keep moving. I went over my business plans for the bookstore, filled out the forms to register my business name and limited liability corporation, planned my first board meeting, and reviewed my finances and personal savings before packing up the last of my suitcases to head back to Cleveland. Medena was happy to become a board member along with Kizaar, Dad, and Jaelene. She said it gave her something meaningful to do with her newfound time.

A call home told me that Babysista was doing fine. Even had a new man whom she allowed to take care of her while she took care of him. I thought she finally had that give-and-take thing figured out.

Dad and Kizaar were getting along sweet. So sweet that I believed they were going to give me a case of high sugar. Dad insisted that Kizaar find his own light instead of following him in his real estate business, so he was now helping Kizaar start his own soul food restaurant—where I would go as a nonpaying customer and not as a cooking relative. *Laugh.*

Dad filed for a divorce, and Mom got a place in Chesterfield. Babysista and I had talked to her briefly by phone, but Dad and Kizaar hadn't reached that point yet. At least Dad wasn't going to drag her through the mud and spread her dirty laundry all over the courtrooms. On top of that, he was giving her a healthy and undeserved settlement—even more than his lawyer recommended. I guess he hated court battles as much as I did.

I decided to call her. She was still my mother. She answered on the third ring. Her voice was somber. I asked, "Why?"

"I have no reason that's going to make you feel better or make things all right. I was selfish. I was only worried about myself. When you come right down to it, that's the God-honest truth. When I was with James, I wasn't thinking about Jesse. I was lonely. I never saw your father. I know that's not an excuse, but that's how I was feeling. And after James died, and even when Jesse came back, I couldn't bring up the question of Kizaar's paternity. I was ashamed and . . ."

"And you were worried about not having money if Dad divorced you."

She paused and blew a breath into the phone.

I continued, "And what about all that stuff you fed me about your generation being loyal and your generation standing be-hind their men? Huh?" My voice was increasing in treble and volume.

"I couldn't let it all come out. It would have destroyed our family."

"Correction. It did destroy our family. Then again, it actually brought the family together."

"Without me."

"What did you expect?"

Another hard breath. Then, "I couldn't expect anything dif-ferent. Look, I'm sorry. Not that sorry makes up for anything, but . . . what I did was wrong. Wrong for Jesse, wrong for Kizaar, and wrong for our entire family." She swallowed hard. "I do hope that one day you all will be able to forgive me."

I felt the sorrow in her voice. "That sure was a doozy, Mom." She mumbled something inaudible. "It could have turned out a lot worse, though, you know. Just give it time, Mom. They need time to heal. We all still love you. You gotta know that."

"You sure about that?"

"Sure. You gotta love a woman who can beat the hell out of a man with the heel of a red pump." I laughed. Tried to lighten up the tension. It was time to begin the healing. She gave an easy chuckle, too.

"Well, I know you're probably busy, so—"

"How about lunch and shopping next weekend?" I asked her.

I could feel her smile through the phone. "How about just lunch with my daughter?"

"Sounds good." I told her I loved her and we hung up the phone.

I called the bellboy to help me with my bags, but before I left I knew what I had to do. I had to stop avoiding the thought of

Alton. It would help me to get over him faster. So I closed my eyes, relaxed, and cleared my mind.

Alton walked into the hotel suite inside my mind like he had done so many times before. I remembered when Alton and I were in this hotel, christening each room, taking showers together, sipping wine on the balcony, listening to music in the living room, and ordering room service and eating together. I remembered it all.

I didn't cry this time—not to say that I wouldn't tomorrow—but I didn't today.

The bellboy knocked at the door and pushed Alton out of the room. I patted my face, and ran my fingers through my hair. I counted the three suitcases along the wall to make sure I hadn't forgotten any. I'd give the room a final once-over after the bellboy carried my bags to the front door. Alton had always said to give the room a once-over before leaving. Open drawers, even if they hadn't been used, and remove the sheets from the bed. We'd lost many panties, boxer shorts, and bras in those sheets. Some of my good bras, too.

I opened the door wide and stood aside for the bellboy.

"You can take these," I said as I gestured toward the bags like prizes on *The Price Is Right*. When there was no response I looked up at him and found myself staring at the hall wall. As my mind summed it up to be a stupid childish prank that somebody's badass kid needed to get a beat-down for, I caught sight of a body down low. I looked and saw a man on bended knee, huffing and puffing, with his arm extended and an eye-popping rock protruding from the end of it. His eyes were strong, determined. His arm was steady.

He said between breaths, "For . . . sure . . . no . . . doubt . . . lady."

I don't know what happened next. All I know is that I unexpectedly found myself sprawled on top of Alton in the middle of the hallway, wailing like a wounded cow. My tears streamed all over him. I threw my arms around his neck, pulled him close, and kissed his cheeks, his forehead, his lips, and everywhere I could reach.

The bellboy turned the corner with his luggage cart and stopped dead in his tracks. I had to convince him that I knew Alton and that this was not a mugging in progress.

Alton and I walked into the room. "You're not going to get me again," Alton said. "I want to hear you say it this time." Alton pulled me by the hips to the living room couch. He sat on the arm, squared me in front of him, and looked me in my eyes. "Will you marry me?"

"Yes, All Good. Yes, I will marry you."

Alton wrapped his muscular arms around my waist and pulled me to him. He kissed me softly at first, then deeper. I felt him all over again. He felt like heaven.

Alton slipped the ring on my finger and handed me his ring to slip on his. We sat wrapped around each other on the couch.

"How'd you know I was here?"

"Baby-Jae." He laughed. "Baby-Jae was all too happy to tell me where you were. She gave me your room number and flight information. I rushed all the way here. You gotta act surprised now, but I think she's going to have a pre-bachelorette party for you. I told her no strippers."

"You know, you could have waited until I got back to Cleveland."

"I know. But where's the drama in that?" He smiled as I pinched his arm.

My mind filled with questions. "What about Robin?"

Alton cleared his throat. "Of course she didn't take it too well. I wrestled with this for the longest. I didn't feel right about what I was doing—marrying her while thinking about you. I felt like I was playing with her heart."

I tilted my head to the side and smiled. "You were thinking about me?"

Alton dipped his head forward. "Yes, I was thinking about your crazy ass." His voice deepened. "I couldn't live my life without you. I just needed to know that you were in the same place. That you wanted to marry me as much as I want to marry you. And for the right reasons."

He hugged me again. "Mmm-mmph! You done picked up some weight, gulh. It looks good." He rubbed my hips.

I squealed and backed away. I hadn't been to the gym in months. With all that had happened with the family and Tucker and Alton, the last thing I had concerned myself with was my weight. I thought about all the Ted Drews custard and Imo's Pizza I had eaten since then, and immediately felt the urge to map out a diet plan of strawberry Slim-Fast and Metabolife.

"I got to get my butt back in the gym and on a diet when I get home."

"You do and I *will* divorce your butt." He laughed. "No, I will personally stuff your mouth full of cheeseburgers." Alton pulled me back to him. "You'd better not lose one pound. This is just the way I like you."

I ran my hands over my hips and down my outer thighs. What was it that I was trying to do, or who exactly was it that I was trying to look like? Exactly why was I living off diet shakes and pills when my man was happy with the way that I looked? It was time to stop ruining my body by trying to get it to do something that it wasn't programmed to do—be a size four.

"We'd better get going," I said. "My flight leaves in two and a half hours, and you know how security is. When are you leaving?"

"At the same time as you. Some of us have to work tomorrow, you know," Alton said as he grabbed two of my largest bags. "I'm sitting right next to you on the same flight. I got mad skills," he said with a wink, answering the question he knew I was about to ask.

"So how's the family?" Alton asked.

I laughed. "Oh, boy. Long story, and where do I begin?"

"I got time. Start from the beginning."

And I did. I told Alton on the ride to the airport and on the plane ride back to Cleveland. Even told him about the fall of the O Theory. He kissed his fingertips and lifted them to the sky. Then we talked about what marriage meant to us: communication, building a life together, encouraging each other to grow as individuals, and, most important to me, working to keep the love alive after the five- to seven-year mark. We talked about continuing this discussion with a premarital counselor.

The plane landed smoothly. Alton and I sat hand in hand with our rings sparkling as we waited for everyone to deplane before we followed.

The June air was warm and brisk. The blue sky hovered above, and hurried travelers shielded their eyes with sunglasses from the glaring sun.

It was a bright, clear, and beautiful day in Cleveland.

READING GROUP GUIDE

Wondering if this book would be a good selection for your book club? Here are a few discussion questions that are sure to keep your group members engaged after reading *Counting Raindrops*:

1. Do you believe there is any real-life rationale behind the "O-Theory"?

2. Vanella's friends had various opinions about the one-sidedness of marriage. Do you believe these issues are valid today? Do any of these issues contribute to the short-term marriages that are prevalent in today's society?

3. What is the root of the trouble in the Morris family? How did it play a role in the behaviors and lives of each family member?

4. Jaelene had her own issues with men. Do you believe the parents' relationship played a part in Jaelene's relationship issues?

5. Why did the father hold on to his knowledge of the family secret? Had the father brought to light the family secret, do you feel that things would have been different? If so, how? Were the father's actions ever justified?

6. Explain Vanella and Synda's relationship. Why has Synda never met Alton? Why did Vanella forgive her and keep her around? Would you have forgiven Synda?

7. Why do you think Vanella rekindled her love for her college beau? Was it true love, closure, a rebound, or something else? Was he deserving of forgiveness? Why or why not?

8. Vanella had issues with commitment in the form of marriage. Did she overcome them? What do you think will be the outcome of her final decision in the long run?

9. Veda raised some interesting points in a discussion with Vanella about the loyalty of women in her generation versus the loyalty of women in Vanella's generation. Does she make valid points? Are her words ever invalidated? If you were a child in the Morris family, how would you feel about Veda?

10. For whom did you feel the most sympathy?